EL PALACIO DE ELIANA

EL ENCANTO

ELIANA

VENOM & VOW

VENOM
&
VOW

ANNA-MARIE McLEMORE
ELLIOTT McLEMORE

FEIWEL AND FRIENDS
New York

A Feiwel and Friends Book
An imprint of Macmillan Publishing Group, LLC
120 Broadway, New York, NY 10271 • fiercereads.com

Our books may be purchased in bulk for promotional, educational, or business use.
Please contact your local bookseller or the Macmillan Corporate and Premium Sales
Department at (800) 221-7945 ext. 5442 or by email at
MacmillanSpecialMarkets@macmillan.com.

Library of Congress Cataloging-in-Publication Data is available.

First edition, 2023
Book design by L. Whitt
Map illustration by Virginia Allyn
Feiwel and Friends logo designed by Filomena Tuosto
Printed in the United States of America

ISBN 978-1-250-82223-9 (hardcover)
2 4 6 8 10 9 7 5 3 1

TO DAYNA MARIE BRYANT,
PRINCESA, REINA, AND THE BEST FRIEND
TWO BOYS AND A GIRL COULD ASK FOR
(AND TO THE PRINCE WHO PROVES WORTHY OF YOU)

CHAPTER ONE

VALENCIA

O f all the things my father taught me, this is the one most likely to keep me alive tonight: *Your hair, mija, can always hold more knives than you think.*

I give my hair another twist and shove in two more of the tiny blades I've spent half my life learning to throw. Tonight I'll be getting close enough to Adare's borders to taste the salt in the air. Whenever you get close to Adare, you can never have too many knives.

I learned that the hard way.

My father told me not to go out there that night. Just like he'd probably tell me to stay at el palacio right now.

But my father had to know I'd follow him. He had to know that the best way to get me to do something was to forbid me to do it. And besides, he needed me. I've always been my father's mano derecha, his right-hand boy or girl or whoever I am at the moment. Whoever I need to be to sneak around somewhere unnoticed or slip into a room I'm not supposed to be in. I can't count how many times I've showed up in disguise before he even knew he needed me to go get a look at some dignitary's correspondence or a visiting prince's books.

And that night, I dressed the part. I put on the most spectacular outfit I had. A deep green gown refined enough to make me look older. A velvet cape stitched with so many leaves of gold, red, and amber fabric that I looked like I was wearing autumn. My best cane, ahuehuete wood set with fire opals. Hair pinned back exactly like the most elegant ladies. All the better to impersonate someone important enough to be at a negotiation between two enemy kingdoms.

The moment I got to the edge of the woods, I saw the Adare boy— boy? Man? I still don't know. He didn't see me, but I watched him. I watch everyone.

There was nothing all that notable about him. Dark hair, gray coat, brown trousers. He had a staff with him—a nice one; even from that distance I could see the heft and the metalwork—and I could tell from the way he was holding it that he used it to help his walking, similar to how I used my own bastón.

There was something about the way he was looking around. Not like he was looking for something, or someone. More like he was checking. Which instantly made me think he was supposed to be an inconspicuous guard. Someone I'd need to avoid as I went deeper in, where half our court and half of Adare's had gathered.

I should have already had a knife out. I know that now. But I didn't. I was looking into the trees to plan my route, how best I could casually swan into the proceedings like a fashionably late duquesa.

So I didn't see him do it. But when that light came, flashing hard as sun off water, and blue as moonlight through ice, I looked back at him, and I saw.

He was holding that staff with both hands, driving it into the ground. As if he was putting all his weight and strength into keeping it there. He stared into the light like he was calling it by name. And I knew. I could tell he was the one doing this.

I reached to pull out a knife. Whatever he was doing, I knew that if I got a blade in his arm, I could probably throw his concentration enough to stop him.

But I hadn't woven them into my hair that night. I'd rushed out with them tucked into my boots, but hadn't taken the time to slip them into my braid.

If I had, I might have been fast enough.

The force following that light came hard as thunder after lightning. It went through me and knocked me to the ground. The leaves of cloth on my cape blew into a whirl. The force of that light was as hard as a current. Even with the help of my cane, I couldn't get up, not until everything had settled and gone quiet.

By then, he was gone.

What that boy did to the woods that night took our king and queen. It took my father. And every night since then I've known what we all should have known: There's no negotiating with Adare. All we can do is win.

I don't blame the boy for everything. It's almost certain that he was acting under orders.

Still, if I ever see him again, he's dead.

I slip one more knife into my hair.

The mistake I made that night, I'll never make it again.

CHAPTER TWO

CADE

I just couldn't stay away from the edges that night. I hardly ever can.

Know where your lines are. See the maps in your mind, laid out over the castle, over the battlefield, over the land. Always. If you lose track of those lines, they'll be in control, and not you.

My mother's voice, my queen's voice, as I've heard it my whole life, pulled me to the borders of our land. That night, it pulled me to her, to my father, to the Elianan ruling family and their advisors. Another negotiation. This time with its venue in the most disputed zone of the forest between Adare and Eliana.

I tried to spot one of our guards in the dark, or one of our horses. I'd have even settled for some of the Elianan contingent. Their bright colors made them stand out in moonlight. At first, all I could see were trees, and some vague movement between them.

A loud crack thundered under my feet and a burst of light brighter and bluer than sheet lightning blasted out from the forest, nearly knocking me down. I had to hold Faolan with both hands to keep steady. I felt him gripping the ground for me, keeping me upright like he does when I'm on the battlefield and about to lose my balance.

Whatever you do, don't let them take you to the ground.

My mother again, teaching me to be a warrior like her. I searched for her in the burst of light, trying to spot her or anyone close to her. But it was far too bright and pushed at me with far too much force.

As I squinted against the light, I saw a swirl of movement in red and orange, waving like the flames of a bonfire.

I focused my gaze as closely as I could. I made out the form of a person crouching, holding a staff far more delicate and ornate than Faolan. The top of the staff glinted with what looked like small flames, and I was certain that what I thought was a bonfire was actually their cloak.

I'd seen enchanters at work before, but nothing like this. One hand extended to keep their balance. The other held the staff, driving it into the ground, making the flames at the top pulse even brighter.

I knew better than to trifle with enchanters and staffs. The staff my mother carried had been passed down from queen to queen for generations. Its power was unpredictable even to its wielder. It had surprised my mother more than once.

The light intensified again, like the roots of all the trees nearby were sending veins of lightning out under our feet.

The enchanter lifted their head, dark eyes wide and fixed on the center of the light. I could see her deep red lips and long tendrils of thick black hair escaping from a twist I recognized as one popular in the Elianan court.

I memorized her face that night. And I've been looking for it ever since.

CHAPTER THREE

VALENCIA

I slip through the dark, Lila squawking behind me like I'm moving too slowly. She's been doing this since she flew out of the tapestry. The only warning I had was the sheen of her embroidered wings coming to life, turning from thread to feathers, before she fluttered right into my face.

For a quetzal who's lived a thousand years, half of it stone-still in a panel of cloth, she has no patience.

I move quickly enough that the heel of my bastón barely sinks into the night-damp ground. I may not get to use a cane where Lila's leading me, but this one gives me the best chance. Carved from palo de rosa, it's plain enough that it could belong to anyone. And when you do the kind of work I do, that's worth more than a cane set with a thousand jewels.

I pass the light-gilded windows of el palacio's main hall. Dozens of cortesanos gather under the rose-stone arches. There's one drinking from a cup bearing his family's insignia. There's another admiring his own reflection in the glass fountains. Suitors, all moving in because their families think La Princesa Abryenda is a girl in need of guidance, and they each know just the man to help her rule.

They think Bryna's weak. They think the king and queen and so many of our elders will never wake from El Encanto. They resent that we're now a kingdom ruled by a teenage queen.

The palace feels different with them here. Usually, el palacio glows with candles and marigolds. The walls shine with purple tapestries, embroidered with our green quetzals and orange ocelotls. But right now the halls smell like the perfumed coats of twenty rich young men. Among the hummingbirds and coatis that usually roam the floating gardens are the blue lizards and snakes brought here as gifts (Ondina and I *might* have stolen them from the men who consider them nothing but shows of wealth). Instead of the air spiced with mole, the corridors are sickly sweet with the pan de piña and candied roses presented to Bryna (who's going to tell them she prefers salt to sugar?).

I can see the men through the windows, raising their glasses. Arms clad in ornate sleeves lift glittering copas, and the rumble of their voices comes through the stone.

Lila's next shriek sounds annoyed, her plumas brushing the outside wall.

"My thoughts exactly," I say.

The richer the man, the more long-winded. I can walk, run, and fight just fine, but put me in a heavy dress and make me stand for the length of their speeches, and my back screams at me louder than Lila.

The moon flashes green-gold and teal off Lila's feathers, then off the brush of the fox who's out here waiting for me. I can see him, beyond the blossoming orange and lemon trees, beyond the fountains tiled in indigo and turquoise. A male, loose-limbed and swinging his tail around for balance. He's as big as a horse, and light bristles across his fur and catches on the knives of his teeth. He waits as patiently as he would for prey.

I hold out a pair of my slippers, beaded gold. His eyes light on them, teeth glinting.

He crouches, letting me onto his back. With me holding on, he bounds past the marsh reeds that whisper from the floating gardens. They're the pride of the palace grounds, half farmland, half ornament. The raised beds of earth, small islands in channels of gleaming water, hold vegetable patches and fruit trees for the palace kitchens. Marigolds, roses, and pink lavender border the vines. The best farmers and gardeners in Eliana are invited to become royal granjeros and jardineros, designing how the raised beds can be their most beautiful and fruitful.

The fox gets up to speed, the floating gardens a blur of color. I bury my hands in his fur, holding on like my father taught me. There are no weight cues like riding a horse. You don't lead a luminous fox. If you're given the honor of one taking you onto their back, they decide where you're going.

But they'll follow a quetzal like Lila, just as they'd follow one of the great cats. So we trace Lila's path of flight. The yellow of my dress streams out behind me as we leave the gilded gardens and rose-stone fountains of el palacio. We're cutting sharp in one direction, leaving familiar hills, stretches of wood, the guiding curves of rivers.

Lila is leading us into contested land, where the smell of palm and pine mix in the air. She's leading us into the woods near Adare, or at least, where Adare considers our kingdom to end and theirs to begin.

I watch the sky, waiting for it to tell me something about what our soldiers face at dawn. Certain cuentos de viejas say that the night

8

whispers the outcome of an impending battle, the moon taking on the look of blood or salt.

The sky is breathtakingly unhelpful. Just clouds against deep blue.

The fox slows and crouches, low enough that I can slip off his back. I thank him, handing him the slippers. He grips them in his teeth—those sharp, glinting teeth that make luminous foxes more beautiful nightmare than bedtime story—bows his head in farewell, and bounds off.

My blood beats in my forehead and ears, loud enough to dull the soreness in my arms and legs from holding on to the fox. I'm far enough into contested territory that the air holds that sharp smell of evergreen resin instead of the warmth of palmera fronds.

If I'm really going to do this, I'm going to need a disguise better than anything I packed in my bolsa. I'm going to need enemy armor.

I hate when I have to put on one disguise just to steal what I need for another.

I spill out my bolsa. I rip away layers of my dress until I'm down to my undergarments and skirt, my ivory bustier, my enagua. I dust my skin with paling powder and coat my hair in gold leaf. I unfold my false wings, the delicate fabric stretched over shaping wires. Once I tie their ribbons to the back laces of my bustier, I have enormous wings as shining as the surface of a fountain. Even if the corners poke me in the ribs, the ass, the hips, the back of the arms.

Last, I paint poison onto my lips. The color, deep as crushed berries, will help lure a young man into kissing me.

The poison will take care of the rest.

In daylight, I'd look ridiculous, my brown skin dusted with creamlight powder, my hair looking like gold coating that's flaking off. But the aes sídhe of Adare's stories, the sprites thought to roam the forest and the rockiest cliffs along the sea, are dreamed of in shades of white and gold, not brown.

I hear the gait of a horse. If my sense of direction isn't off tonight, the rider is going away from the camps and back toward Adare proper. A messenger, maybe? The moon shows the sheen of his armor, and I know for sure this is an enemy soldier, not one of ours. Adare's soldiers wear layers of fabric hardened with tree sap. It's lighter than our armor, and it molds to their bodies, so I'm almost looking forward to stealing some and trying it out.

I set my cane against a tree, bracing to go without it. A winged girl wouldn't need to manage how her weight meets the ground like I do; she'd barely be touching the ground at all. I ready my most delicate stride, one than looks more like wafting than walking. The horse sounds far enough still that the rider may not see me yet, but I'm not taking chances. It's never too early to commit to a disguise. My father taught me that. Never assume your enemy isn't watching.

I take another, deeper breath, and emerge from the trees. I arrange myself against the trunk nearest the road. My wings spread out behind me, my pose pinning them between my back and the tree. Leaning takes pressure off my spine while letting me play the part of a fairy looking dreamily up at the stars. By the time the rider approaches, I'm pretty enough to be painted.

The man—or boy? I can't really tell yet—halts his horse like I've startled them both.

The horse is more memorable than the rider, the sheen on the stallion's coat almost silver at certain angles. The rider looks like half the people from Adare I've ever seen, the same dark hair and dark eyes and medium-toned skin. He's not a big man, but not slight either. Nothing distinguishing.

Except for the royal crest on his breastplate.

My back rebels with a current of pain, from standing without my cane and from how tensely I'm holding my body.

Of course the soldier I've stopped is Patrick McKenna, the murderer prince. Even if I could steal his armor, what would I do with a royal breastplate? Stride around the woods pretending I'm a prince?

I breathe to slow my heart.

He stares at me.

I brace for lust to come into his eyes. Too bad there's not enough poison on my lips to kill him. Bad planning on my part.

Except the look in his eyes isn't lust.

He looks stricken, frightened by the sight of me, as though I've caught him at something. His horse even whinnies and shakes his head.

I realize what direction he's going.

Is Patrick McKenna fleeing?

The night before a battle, and Patrick McKenna is running away.

We've already won.

So why not have a little fun with him?

Should I lure him off his horse? Throw a knife at him?

Charm before blood. My father's words drift through my head, his reminder to keep my enemy closer. With a smile, you draw your adversary in. With a blade, you force him away. Choose the first, the second is still open to you. Go for blood first, and charm ceases to be an option.

I listen to my father even now that I don't have him. My father shadowed me when I was first learning the craft of being un centzontleh, telling me when I was being too hesitant or too impulsive, too brazen or too timid.

Charm before blood.

Smile and persuade first.

Fight last.

I let the wind stream my gilded hair away from my powdered face. I put on the voice of a mythical woman, a haunting song.

"You will be defeated," I say. "Abandon your plan."

Patrick McKenna regards me.

I wait for another glint of fear. I will him to see in my eyes everything he should be afraid of. Our soldados' armor, gleaming like copper. Their swords covered in obsidian teeth that break off when they strike our enemies, like a porcupine leaving quills in a predator.

Adare has underestimated us before. Let him see in my face that he shouldn't.

But rather than afraid, Patrick McKenna just looks exhausted, and sad.

"I'm not the one you need to convince," he says.

He rides off, fast as the stars winking off Lila's wings.

I know what Bryna would say: that I did exactly the right thing, and left with my life. But I'm already wondering if I could have thrown a blade precisely enough to knock him from his horse. I have them close this time, five in my hair alone.

Move on, my father would tell me right now. *Move on and keep moving.*

I still need enemy armor. That means I need to find another Adare soldier.

CHAPTER FOUR

CADE

Each torch goes out as I pass it, as if the castle is helping me cover my tracks.

I think I'm lost again, even though the corridor hasn't turned sharply, just wound around a curve or two. My armor helps hold my knee together, but it's exhausting to move in without the staff I need. I'm going as fast as I can, but with the sudden unfamiliarity of my surroundings and the weight of the armor, it feels like wading through an icy river up to my chest.

My mother's advice about keeping the map in my mind is useless these days. Our home is too confused, too pulled and prodded in too many directions. I grew up in a castle that changed slowly over the years, reflecting my mother's measured evolution as queen. Now that she's sleeping her cursed sleep in the forest, the castle's magic seems to be running wild without her. Sometimes we wake up in our own bedrooms, but in a completely different part of the castle than the night before, or there's suddenly a waterfall in the audience room that's so loud we can't hear one another.

I find the tapestry my great-grandfather wove and duck behind it.

But this time, there's nothing there. No seam in the wall, no metal owl whose beak I need to touch my fingers to, no knots of wood, no elaborate painting of my great-great-grandmother. Nothing.

I can hear Siobhán's voice through the wall, so I know they're in there. "You've put this one on top of the wrong envelope," she says.

"Ah, thank you. That would have been embarrassing." Patrick's voice is light. He can hide in there, safe, writing letters, while we all risk our lives in service of one of the worst battle plans I've ever heard of.

I pound on the empty wall. "And how in the hell does one get in there today?"

"Cade?" Siobhán asks. "What are you doing here? What's happened?"

"Either let me in or tell me what to do to let myself in," I say.

I hear some shuffling, and then Patrick's cláirseach playing the first few bars of our mother's favorite song. As he plays, enough of the stones fold away to allow me to enter. As soon as he stops, they spring back into place as if they'd never moved.

"It's the only thing that's worked this time," Patrick says as he sets his harp down.

I sigh. "Patrick, I can't be everywhere at once. If you don't put more effort into controlling this, we can all look forward to a lovely rockslide in the great hall. Or shall we just keep up the niceties and hope the castle doesn't kill anyone?"

Siobhán picks up Faolan from his spot along the wall. "Do all of us a favor and either sit down or use this." She tosses him to me. "And your brother doesn't need your threats right now, Cade. Or your tone. He's got plenty to keep him occupied."

I catch Faolan and look into the familiar owl's face that caps my most treasured possession. Faolan is my steadiness, my fighting staff. He was made just for me, after I injured my knee. Not only does he adapt to my needs when I'm getting around, his owl, normally just a decorative figure, can defend me when I can't defend myself. And if I find myself without a sword, Faolan can provide that as well, with a quick turn of my wrists.

I almost never get to have him when I'm wearing armor.

As I lean on Faolan, I look around. Almost everything here is made of stone this time—the walls, the floor, Patrick's desk, the chairs. Even the beds have stone head- and footboards.

I liked it better when this turret was the inside of a giant tree trunk. It felt like the tree house our father built with us when we were young.

I turn to Patrick. He looks as tired as I feel. And a little ashen, probably from being in this windowless chamber for two days. He's unassuming in his plain tunic and trousers. Un-princely. The tartan he wears to mark him as ruler hangs on the wall, next to the empty stand where the armor I'm wearing is stored when I'm not in it. When I get to be myself. When I don't have to be Patrick. Who, to his credit, is just sitting there. Waiting for me to speak.

"This will never work," I say.

"They've drawn the maps a hundred times," he says.

"The maps don't matter," I say, struggling to keep my voice low. "We don't have enough people. We can't hold this much ground. It's impossible."

"We risk more by not trying to take it."

"If you were really fighting out there, I would never let you do this," I say. "The chance of you being killed is far too high."

"That's your opinion," he says, too quickly.

"It is not only my opinion," I say back, one word at a time.

Patrick's eyes narrow. "I hope your soldiers can't tell how little faith you have in them."

"How could they tell anything?" My voice cracks. I don't care.

"We're too far apart to communicate. For all I know, we've lost an entire flank already!"

"Even if we have, even if we do, this could be the moment. This could be the start of us winning this war."

"Or the start of us losing it. If those advisors of yours had ever seen a battlefield, they would know that."

Siobhán sighs loudly.

"Something to add, cousin?" I ask.

"Your plans always end the same," she says. "With me stitching up a lot of people. If we're not getting on with those letters, I may as well be going."

"Cade, I know you don't agree with the advisors, but for once they all agree with one another," Patrick says. "Do you know how rare that is?"

"So all that matters to you is that they're happy?" I ask.

"Patrick, could you . . ." Siobhán tries to get his attention, but he's too busy arguing with me.

"If you want to sit in this chair, brother, be my guest," he says. "I'm only in it because you didn't want to be."

"It's far more complicated than that, and you know it," I say.

A discordant series of notes disturbs the air.

"Damn it," Siobhán says, holding the harp against her hip and looking at the wall. "It was worth a try. And better than hitting your heads together."

Patrick gets up and takes his harp from Siobhán.

"If you keep fighting each other," she says, "none of this will matter anyway. You know you can each destroy the other, so why keep talking about it? Why not find another plan you can agree on?"

"Such as?" Patrick asks her.

"Cade, what do you want?" she asks me.

"To call it off," I say. "Pull back and regroup."

"Impossible," says Patrick. "Eliana would walk away the victor by default."

"I saw a sídh on the way here," I say. "She told me, 'Abandon your plan.' How much clearer a sign could you ask for?"

"You know I don't go in for all that like you do," Patrick says.

"I don't either, usually," Siobhán says slowly. "But that would keep even me up at night."

"I can't call off an entire battle that's been planned for weeks because you saw a fairy," Patrick says.

I widen my eyes to avoid rolling them. "I spent most of those weeks telling you this would never work."

"It's too late to get word to all the flanks, even if I wanted to," Patrick says.

"Then just get word to two or three." I loosen and tighten my grip on Faolan as I think aloud. "Choose the fields we most need to hold and get word to the other flanks to fall back. I'll take one of them myself."

Patrick paces, past the stone desk and along the stone walls.

I wish, even more than usual, that my father were here. In both mind and mannerisms, Patrick and our father are so much alike. When neither my mother nor I could get through to Patrick, our father always could. He could convince Patrick what a terrible idea this is.

Siobhán goes over to Patrick's ambry and pours herself a drink. I listen to stone against stone as she sets a goblet down. Even the stopper in the carafe looks unmanageably heavy.

Patrick stops, turns toward me, and, after a deep breath, says, "I appreciate you coming all this way to share your thoughts, but we're not acting on another of your superstitions."

I press my tongue against my front teeth, but it doesn't still my anger. He had to get that one in, didn't he? Another sly remark about what I saw the night the curse fell. The Elianan woman wearing flames, swirling the enchantment around her, claiming our land for their nation and sealing our parents and most trusted advisors in a magical sleep.

He dismissed me then, so of course he's doing the same now.

I take a few steps forward, letting Faolan support as much of my weight as possible. "What happens if I die out there?" I ask him. "What will you do? Run away? Pretend to be me for a while just to even things out?"

Patrick says nothing. He doesn't seem angry, anxious, afraid, any of the things I feel. He doesn't seem anything at all.

"What is the plan for that?" I yell. "What?"

"Please," he whispers, not looking at me. "Just don't die."

CHAPTER FIVE

VALENCIA

I've done him a favor really, the wide-eyed Adare boy I lured into the woods with the promise of a charmed kiss. He'll now sleep through a battle that almost certainly would have killed him. The small dose of poison he drew off my lips will wear off, and he'll go home to his mother in one piece.

I take the armor off him and drape it over my own shirt and trousers. Now if any fleeing Adare soldiers come through here, they'll think I'm one of their own.

Faraway sounds echo off the sky. I flinch at the shouts, the crashing metal of swords. Even when we're winning, I don't relish death on either side, and from this distance, I can't hear the difference. From this distance, all loss sounds the same.

Adare armor in place (loose in some spots, tight in others; not perfect, but what in my line of work ever is?). Cloak on (the armor may let me pass as one of Adare's, but if I want to pass as a boy I need to, quite literally, cover my ass). And Lila being uncharacteristically patient in the branches overhead.

Tilde, tilde, tilde. Each item checked off the list in my head. When

I was growing up, I got distracted so easily that mi padre taught me to think in lists, so I wouldn't forget things. And right now they're buzzing inside me.

Check my bindings. Brush the gold leaf from my hair and the paling powder off my skin. Rub the poison from my lips (looking too pretty gives me away).

Weave my hair into a boy's braid, the kind that wouldn't raise an eyebrow in Eliana or Adare. Simple. Straight between my shoulder blades. Tight enough to hold the little knives I tuck back in.

I never got to tell my father how much like myself I feel this way. It's not that I don't in the gowns I wear to stand alongside Bryna; I love the flow of layered skirts. But there's another part of me that comes to life in men's trousers, my chest bound down. It mirrors the part that loves brushing rouge onto my cheeks and combing orange-blossom water into my hair.

Neither side alone is all of me, but together, they hold the light inside me, glowing like the piece of raw magic I've come out here to find.

Even with dawn seeping into the woods, I find the glow in the distance. That glow breathes beneath the earth, casting a faint blue-violet onto the undersides of leaves. As the heel of my bastón sinks into the soft earth, the glass globe on top catches the swirling light.

"There you are," I whisper.

The pressure of my bindings under my shirt steadies me. I've been raised to be at home in costumes. With the right clothes, I can be a child or a condesa. With the right stance and posture, the right paint on my face, I can come off half my age or three times it. I can tilt my voice high—flutter my eyelashes, giggle for vain cortesanos and their stupid jokes—or pitch it low enough to pass as a boy of fifteen or sixteen.

But the boy I am right now, this is part of me.

The more you get used to being everyone but yourself, the more unsettling being yourself becomes.

Lila squawks at me.

"I see it," I tell her.

Her path winds into a tight circle, weaving in and out of the branches. I lower myself to the ground and plunge my fingers into the earth, pulling aside layers of damp dirt.

It comes up looking like jagged quartz, the color of a dusk sky. Its glow dims and brightens like an ember. Bryna has pinned all her hopes on these pieces of light hiding under the ground. She keeps every one I bring back in a trunk as unassuming as a burro. She thinks if we find all the pieces, and if our monjas y brujas can seal them back together, we'll have Adare's own magic in our hands, and we'll have Adare by the throat.

Lila descends, wings fluttering in my face like a disgruntled chicken.

"Espere." I wrap the piece in heavy velvet.

She keeps flapping. And squawking.

I tuck the velvet into my bindings, between my flattened breasts, and shush her, eyeing the trees around us. My stolen armor makes me look like a boy fighting on Adare's side, but that's not going to be worth a strand of my hair if anyone sees me with a quetzal.

Her squawk turns to a shriek.

"¡Basta!" I whisper-yell. "Do you want me to get caught?"

Shapes appear against the dawn. Not soldiers fleeing the battlefield. They stand tall as the fog-shrouded cliffs they come from, blood staining their corazas. They carry the smell of Adare's lichen-damp rock fields and coastal cliffs with them, and I know.

We've lost.

These soldiers are sweeping the area. Maybe for deserters, which, at the moment, I probably look like. A boy in Adare armor hiding in the woods.

Or I would. If Lila didn't chirrup with rage and pitch herself at the biggest one's head.

The man swears as a storm of green feathers beats his face.

Really? This is the moment Lila chooses to take my side?

I trill at the back of my throat, trying to imitate the quetzal's distress call. And yes, I'm doing a terrible job, but she's going to be their dinner if she keeps this up.

Another man comes toward me, and my muscles flicker to life.

My elbow finds his sternum. He falls back. Another comes. My boot strikes his shin. He swears but gets hold of me. I jam the heel of my hand into his nose, and it drives him off.

A third comes. I grab his wrist and torque it back. It stops him for only the instant it takes a fourth to appear. Carajo, did they bring a whole flank?

They get my wrists behind my back.

They drive me forward, sending me to my knees.

I scream at Lila, my best imitation of her shriek. I may be finished, but they're not catching one of the quetzals who's lived in our tapestries for hundreds of years.

For once, she listens.

As her green feathers vanish into the sky, a great form cuts through the light.

A woman rides a gleaming horse, coat as black as my hair. Her eyes are a gray as dark as her hair is pale blond, nearly white, and she wears a braid crown so intricate she must command half the army.

The way she looks at me has the force and cold of a seawater tide.

I lower my head. If I'm lucky, if I look fearful enough—not like that

22

takes a lot of acting at the moment—she'll think I'm a boy of so little significance she might as well let me go. A boy not even worth her time.

Except that she saw Lila. Quetzals are such a symbol of Eliana's royal family, I might as well have embroidered this woman a tapestry with my confession. *Saludo, the armor I'm wearing is stolen, by all means, do apprehend me,* in gilt-thread letters.

For the first time since El Encanto took my father, I'm glad he's asleep, so he can't see what a spectacular wreck I've made of everything.

CHAPTER SIX

CADE

Now that it's quiet, the clash of metal on metal still rings in my ears. That incessant thrumming combined with the even, swinging rhythm of my horse lulls me toward sleep. But every time my head drops, the sharp cries of the dying and wounded run back through my mind like a current striking rocks and I jolt awake again.

Waking so suddenly tenses my muscles and sends flashes of pain through me. Battle has left me bruised, and riding afterward is pulling on my muscles and bones in all the wrong places.

To stay alert, I watch the perimeter of our contingent, making sure the wounded with us are still alive. I say prayers for Fergus, who is clearing the battlefield we left, and for Alma, who is still tending to the more gravely wounded and preparing them for transport. I say them again for Deirdre, who I can only hope is leading her own contingent back toward Adare, and then making her way toward us. I say them for Eamon, whose orders were to join forces with Deirdre after taking the ground between them. I say them twice for Nessa, whose orders were to hold her ground with her forces and join us after the battle. Nessa should already be here.

"Sire." The voice of one of our scouts surprises me. He looks into the distance, and I follow his eyes.

Deirdre. Riding ahead, wrapped in her breacán, looking strong as ever.

And Eamon. His height, size, and horse all apparent, even from this distance. On the horse with him, though, is a figure I can't make out. Small. Cloaked. Injured? I can't tell.

Something about this makes me nervous. I ride out to meet Deirdre and Eamon.

As I get closer, I try to peer under the hood of the cloak the figure is wearing, but their downcast head makes it impossible to see any features.

Deirdre and I both ride faster and meet alongside each other. Our horses nuzzle noses in greeting. As they pass side by side, we breathlessly clasp arms. "Thank God for your courage," I say. "Are you all right?"

"Unharmed, sire," she says. "Eamon too."

"Nessa?" I ask.

Her head drops. "No word, sire."

Deirdre looks toward the group behind me, and although her face is difficult to read, I know her well enough to see her grief, and her surprise at how small our group is.

"We took Eliana's easternmost outpost," she says, turning back to me, "but I doubt we'll hold it."

In a way, Patrick and his advisors were right. We did take much of the ground we set out to cover. But I was right too. I cried over Dermot's body. I held Cara's hand while Alma splinted her leg. I know Deirdre and Eamon have their own memories of holding our wounded and crying out for our lost. We don't know whether to grieve for Nessa and her soldiers or keep praying for their lives.

When we get back to the castle, the advisors will declare this a victory. They will laud our valor as we mourn our dead.

Eamon catches up with us. I grasp Deidre's shoulder, and she nods, turning her horse to face Eamon and the cloaked figure with him.

"Eamon," I say. I would go to him and embrace him as I did Deirdre, but he is still more than an arm's length away, and sharing his horse with whoever his charge is. His horse is nodding, surely as tired as its rider. "Who do you have here?" I ask.

"We don't know, sire," Eamon says. "But he's not one of ours."

"How are you so sure?" I ask.

"There was a quetzal with him when we found him," Deirdre says.

"And the way he moves," Eamon says. "He doesn't fight like anyone with our training."

I'm not quite convinced, but I didn't find him, and I didn't fight him. If Deirdre and Eamon think he's not ours, he must not be.

All at once, a flurry of cloak, a shout of surprise from Eamon, a whinny from his horse, flashes of metal and limbs, and the sound of a sword clanking back into its sheath.

The hood of the boy's cloak has fallen, and I can see his face and body more clearly. He looks young, but must be small even for his age. He's wearing a scout's armor, but it doesn't fit right. The breastplate is too loose despite being clasped on the tightest buckles, and the shin guards are digging into his calves even though they're on the loosest settings. I look closely at the fastenings, and it's clear this armor isn't his—there are imprints of where the buckles are normally clasped, and they're too far off to account for normal growth. Not to mention that if he'd grown this much (albeit unevenly) since he started out as a scout, he shouldn't be a scout anymore.

Eamon is holding him by the shoulders. Deirdre has managed to ride over alongside Eamon quickly enough to help him hold the boy still.

"He was cutting through his bonds with my sword!" Eamon exclaims.

26

"You don't say?" Deirdre's voice is sharp, but her eyes have a gleam of amusement. She pulls more rope from her saddlebag and ties the boy's wrists to the horn of Eamon's saddle. "Now you'll know to keep an eye on his hands."

I'm impressed the boy managed this without Eamon or anyone else noticing. I try to get a good look at his face, but his eyes still evade me.

"Who are you?" I ask him, still trying to make eye contact.

He says nothing.

"We all know this armor isn't yours," I go on. "Where did you get it?"

Still nothing.

"You must be very brave. Who are you fighting for?"

His eyes barely move. His breathing stays even. I try a new tack.

"Does your family know what you've done?"

Still no reaction.

On a whim, I try something, angling my head carefully so I can see his face and track his expression as closely as possible.

"Your ancestors must be leaping from their tapestries to see you in the armor of your enemy," I say in the language most of Eliana uses.

I see Deirdre and Eamon out of the corners of my eyes, looking first at each other in confusion, then at me as if I've lost my mind. They both know enough of the language to recognize the words, but probably not quite enough to make sense of the whole sentence.

I watch the boy's expression carefully. He keeps his head down, and his breathing doesn't change. But one corner of his mouth lifts very slightly before he can force it down again.

Whoever he is, he speaks the language of Eliana better than our general.

"What would you have us do with him?" Deidre asks, likely tiring of my battle of wills with the boy.

"We take him back with us," I say.

CHAPTER SEVEN

VALENCIA

The good news: Patrick McKenna doesn't recognize me. No sign of realizing I'm the pretty golden-haired ninfa who scared him pale as moonlight.

The bad news: He's probably going to kill me anyway.

So I'm not exactly in the mood to celebrate my own brilliance.

At least they didn't find my bolsa. A bag stuffed with a dozen different disguises is a bit of a giveaway.

My throat dries out. My bindings turn clammy against my skin. And my brain argues with itself about my chances loudly enough that I might actually yell Cállate, *Shut up*, out loud, in the language Patrick McKenna already suspects is my first one.

I go back to my lists. I let them calm me like las canciones de niños my father recited to get me to sleep. It's what's going to stop me from shaking, panicking, and all the other unhelpful things my body and brain do when I don't have a plan yet. My father taught me that the moment you stop thinking of new options is the moment you die.

Entonces, artículo uno: My hands are tied, but I'm working on that. They really thought binding them in front of me was going to work in their favor? Amateurs. I'm already wearing at the knot that tethers my wrists to the saddle's cuerno. Patience may not be one of my virtues, but even I know that I have to do this slowly, so anything I do with my wrists just seems like I'm moving with the horse's gait.

Artículo dos: The fact that I'm being guarded by a fortress door in the shape of a man.

I'll have to come back to that one.

Artículo tres, I'm on a horse. I do know how to ride a horse. Kind of. Enough. But staying up straight takes everything I have. The pain in my back is getting bad enough that it's spilling down into my thighs. Even under better circumstances, my riding has never exactly been a sight to behold. No one's going to find me gracefully jumping a horse over a hedge. I'm not Bryna, who I swear is actually talking to her mare in a way the horse understands as she braids her mane. I'm used to holding on to the glittering fur of luminous foxes, my body gripping their backs as they bound. But the foxes decide our route, not me. And I'm not used to fighting while on a moving animal. I'm used to fleeing on one.

Artículo quatro, the murderer prince. I'm going to need a moment when he's distracted.

Glaring at him gives me an excuse to watch him. Right now, he's scouting the road, eyes always moving.

At least he's not polished and smirking, smug about wearing our soldiers' blood on his armor. He doesn't look much older than Bryna, but the streaks of gray that come to all the McKennas young make him look world-weary. There's a haunted, almost mournful look in his dark eyes. Guilt, maybe? Good.

He doesn't look how I thought he would. His skin's not fair but mediano, tan either by birth or from the sun. Where it isn't streaked con gris claro, his hair is almost as dark as Ondina's. His eyes are lighter than mine, but they're definitely brown.

My father taught me that Adare was a kingdom of inmigrantes, welcoming those from any land, even ours, before the war. Los trovadores sing of how their people are as pale as the winter moon and as deep as the clearest summer night, and every shade of wheat and sand and earth brown in between.

None of that makes me feel any safer. It doesn't matter that one of the men alongside Patrick has skin as brown as my father's. Enemies are enemies, even when they look like you.

The destrier goes over a patch of rocky ground. The horse's gait falters, and I pretend to startle. I'm getting somewhere. The rope's loosening.

I'm focused enough on the rope that I don't notice we're slowing until we've almost stopped. The meadows and hillsides are still thick with the bright green of wild grass, but now we're passing cairns of stones marking distance or location, I'm not sure. And set within the green are a few stone structures that are either homes or meeting halls, I can't quite tell.

In the middle of it all is a young man who looks older than Patrick and a lot like him. A cousin, I'm guessing. I've heard about how much the McKenna cousins resemble one another, and I can see the similarity in the features, but this man's expressions twist his face into something different. Sometimes a man is ugly and you can just tell it's coming from inside, and the prettiest face can't hide it.

Or maybe I've just gotten sick of men who like hearing themselves talk.

"Today we celebrate victory over our enemies," this man pronounces, and we're getting close enough that I can see he's not alone. He has an arm around a woman who looks so loath to be alongside him that I'd think she was being held against her will, if not for her Adare armor and the braid pinned across her head.

"And today I thank each of our brave fighters"—the man goes on—"who have entrusted their lives to me and all who have led them into battle."

Entrusted their lives to me? For someone who just supposedly fought, he looks pristine. While the woman has blood freckling her face and armor, the man has no blood staining anywhere. Not even on the fine, pale shirt under his armor, which looks new, not even a scratch. Her hair is falling out of its pins, but his is perfectly arranged. She looks exhausted, battle-worn, as though it takes will to stay on her feet. He looks fresh from a night's sleep.

The families of this village are pulling back into their doorways. They're looking at this man as though he's more frightening than Patrick. Who is he?

Patrick comes down off his horse. "Nessa!" He sparks to life enough that Nessa must be a relative or a good friend. Not a lover, if I had to guess, both from how he said her name and how she's looking at him. Or the orating man whose grip she's currently escaping. More than once, my work has depended on noticing who is and isn't enamored of whom else.

The faces shadowed in doorways look almost relieved to see Patrick. Who is the man giving the speech if the murderer prince is a better option? And am I about to get handed over to him?

Pain flashes through my back again. I can ride for longer than I can stand, but how tense I am at the moment isn't helping. The longer I'm sitting, the more my body seizes up.

When it comes to working with my body, I've had no shortage of guidance. My father made sure of it. Curanderas. Hueseros. Ondina's abuela, who's used a cane since childhood. Bryna's uncle, who's used one since the last battle he fought in; he has his bastón with him now as he sleeps in the forest. Embajadores who have as much trouble sitting and standing as I do, and whose work demands that they hide it; they liked my father enough to talk to me as though I was a favorite nieta.

I learned from them not just how to work with my cane but with my body. How to strengthen the muscles that help support my back. How to stretch to ease the pressure on my spine. How to loosen places in my shoulders and legs that I don't even realize are getting pulled on until they're sore.

I can't do any of that right now. I can't do anything for my back or my body. Or my home. Or my princesa. The pain arcs through to my chest, to where I've hidden the piece I found for Bryna. Another disaster of getting caught. They'll find it on me, and they'll wring anything they can out of me about what it is, and what I'm doing with it.

Patrick embraces Nessa, and she embraces him back, and yes, I'm right. This is the hug of relatives or friends, not lovers. But Nessa cuts the reunion short and pulls away, glaring at him. Adare or not, I think I like her already.

The man whose horse I'm on stays close to Patrick, enough that I can overhear.

"Permission to speak my mind, sire?" Nessa asks as the pristine man in the background continues his speech.

"Granted," Patrick says, and he's practically laughing with relief.

But Nessa's face is hard. "I am not a prop. None of us are." She flicks her glare over her shoulder, toward the speech that never ends. "Control your cousin."

The orating man is Patrick's cousin. Another point for me.

"Perhaps he's just trying to encourage everyone," Patrick says.

"He didn't even fight," Nessa says. "And he's here acting like he led us into battle."

I'm right again. What do I win?

"Look around," Nessa says. "They're afraid of him. Maybe you should start asking why."

The man whose horse I'm on is paying close attention to this conversation. And less attention to me.

This is my chance. It would've been nice if I'd gotten my hands free first, but I can't afford to be particular.

I shove my left shoulder back, into the man's breastplate. Not hard—I don't want him on that high of a guard—just enough so he'll think I'm resisting.

On instinct, he reacts to right himself. I use that motion, driving my right shoulder back into him. This time, as hard as I can.

His effort to steady himself, and the hit from my right shoulder, and the wavering weight of his armor pitch him off his own horse.

I've thrown my right shoulder hard enough that my knee is now on the horse's flank. While everyone's reacting to the man falling, I use the leverage of my bonds to pull myself back into the saddle. The horse is whinnying and rearing, ears flicking back and forth.

I hold on with my entire body. I need this horse to believe that the chaos is not my fault and that it's in both our interests to flee. Everyone around us is getting agitated and drawing weapons, so they're making my case for me.

I think about how Bryna gets horses to move the way she wants, the softly spoken words, the clicks of her tongue, the ways she pets them to calm them. I try to sound just like her, encouraging and urging.

I may not be the best rider in Eliana, but I don't have to make this look good. I just have to get away.

The horse reacts, probably as much in fear as to anything I'm doing, and works up to a gallop so fast that the air stings my eyes. His gait is hard and thundering, not the smooth leap of a fox. I have to bow low so my body doesn't catch the wind like a sail. Pieces of hair slip from my braid and whip against my neck.

The rush of the ride dulls the ache in my back. I hold on with my thighs, working on getting one wrist free. Then the other. Nothing on my wrists except the salt-sting of rope burns.

This horse is a lot larger than any I'm used to, so I have to put my strength into cueing him with my weight, especially with how the blanket and saddle are sliding. The horse is built more for power than speed, and I don't have long until everyone else catches up. So the best I can do is take him into heavy tree cover. Part ways, climb up into the thicker-leafed trees, and hope they follow the horse instead of me.

The beating noise of another horse's gait grows louder, gaining on me. Even off the side of my vision, I can tell from the incline of the animal's head that the rider plans to cut off my path.

I slip my fingers into my braid. I bring up one of the small knives hidden in my trenza. The tiny blade won't take out a knight, but if I aim right, it might take out an eye.

My inner thighs hold to the saddle hard enough that the muscles in my hips cramp. I turn, and with a prayer to los santos, throw the blade.

The second I let go, I place who's following me. The gleam not just of the armor, but the insignia set into the breastplate.

My breath halts and burns in my chest.

As though this wasn't already a fight I had better win.

I've just thrown a weapon at the murderer prince of Adare.

I turn to ride deeper into the tree cover, whispering encouragement that's my best imitation of Bryna. Everything I'm concentrating on, Patrick is doing without even thinking about it. The shifting of weight, clicking his tongue, reading the position of a horse's ears. In Adare, they learn young. In Eliana, we guide our horses the same as they do because we once learned from them, the same way they learned from our ingenieros how to build their water systems.

A bough falls in our path, fast and sudden as if the sky threw it down.

The horse startles. Worse than startles. He stops short, trying not to get tangled in the snarl of branches coming off the bough. "Estás bien," I say, copying Bryna's gentle, reassuring voice.

But he loses his footing on the uneven ground and whinnies.

With the sudden change in speed, my grip weakens. The horse stumbles. I feel his foot catch on one of the branches, and my body loses its center. I feel the saddle sliding back. My fall is about to throw me underneath the horse by the time we both land. And for that second I feel still. I wait for the horse's weight to crush me against the ground, and the pause is endless enough for questions to crowd in.

What happens when my father finds out this is how it ended for me?

What happens if he never finds out, because they never wake up?

What happens if my father never really knows me, all of me, like I wanted him to?

What happens to Eliana now?

What happens to the princess I was supposed to protect?

CHAPTER EIGHT

CADE

That little crosdiabhal could actually get away. He'd be as fast as our messengers on the right horse, and I have a feeling he could disappear in this forest and we'd never find him.

But Eamon's horse has other ideas. He's not used to the forest at all, poor thing, crashing around in the low branches. He won't go into the deeper woods, no matter how much his rider wants him to. I duck under a low branch and it comes to me—a way to cut him off again. I slow my horse and choose a bough ahead of me, not too thick, not too long, with lots of rough branches sprouting in all directions. The leaves are curled and brittle, and the bark of the tree is patchy. I hold it tight in my left hand and strike it with my sword where it meets the trunk of the tree. Because the tree is dead or dying, it doesn't take much to break the bough loose. Once I have it, I sheathe my sword and set the branch on my right shoulder like a pike.

I urge my horse ahead, patting his neck, shifting my weight. As soon as I'm close enough, but not too close, I throw the bough as far as I can, past horse and rider and onto the ground in front of them.

But Eamon's horse doesn't rear or turn, he just keeps losing and regaining his footing in the dry branches and leaves, shaking his head. The boy isn't getting thrown and is showing no sign of trying to jump off. Eamon's horse is so big, and he's so small for a boy his age. Getting pinned would crush his leg. At best.

I'm only a few strides away now. I reach forward and grab the blanket under Eamon's saddle, closing the distance between us. I grab the boy around his whole body, lifting him free of the horse as quickly as I can. He fights for a moment, but then stops, seeing Eamon's horse land hard and heavy on the ground. I use that moment to grab the boy's leg and sit him down on my horse in front of me.

Eamon's horse rolls onto his side for a moment, whinnying and kicking as he rights himself. Then he sits. And rests. As if he was just in need of a moment's peace.

In the quiet of my horse's breathing, the boy's breathing, my breathing, I realize what I've heard. The boy's cries. They didn't sound like the cries of someone declared male at birth. Too high and too even at the same time. No cracking. No low and high tones coming together and splitting apart. And the feel of him in my arms. The way he's resisting me while protecting the whole core of his body. The curve of his jaw and the fine hairs along it. And how he is silent now. Waiting to know if I know. And I do know. I know the way only others like us can know each other.

"You drew a weapon, more than drew a weapon, on the ruler of another kingdom. I think you know how serious this is now," I say quietly, close to his ear.

"I acted alone," he says, in the deepest voice he can muster. "I'm under no orders. No one sent me."

"What do you want?" I ask.

"I want your blood, for the blood of our soldados. Their deaths are on your hands," he says, his voice raspy from exertion and being forced too deep, but calmer now. He's either a very good liar or he's telling the truth.

Harm not our own. For a few long moments, there are no more thoughts in my mind but those words, in all their versions, and the low light of the monastery's chapel when I spoke them back. The gray robes of the other monks as we knelt together, hearing only the crackling of tiny flames, one another's breathing, and the whispers of those who prayed aloud. Looking into the abbot's warm eyes and lined face, I made my vow. *I will not harm our own.*

I need to know, as surely as I can, if he really is one of our own. "How old are you?" I ask.

There's a pause, but a short one, before he says, "Sixteen."

I feel his body tense up. Maybe he really is sixteen. Or maybe he thinks sixteen is young enough. For him, it's not.

I tighten my hands around his and my arms around his shoulders.

"What is your name?" I ask.

A long pause. Too long. Maybe he picked a name, but it wasn't right, so he picked another. Or he couldn't choose one at all.

"You are not sixteen," I tell him.

"Ask my father," he says. "If you can wake him."

I squeeze my eyes shut for a moment, thinking of my own mother and father sleeping their cursed sleep with this boy's father, only a few minutes' ride deeper into the forest. I'm grateful he can't see my face. "And what name should I ask after?"

"Gael," he says. So he did choose a name.

"You may be sixteen, Gael, but no one would believe it but me."

"So you say from the wisdom of your, what, seventeen years?" he says. I laugh.

"You're more boy than man," he says. "Your crown doesn't change that."

"You have quite a way with words, don't you?" I ask. "But your voice betrays you. You are good, but you need more practice."

"Something we have in common," he says.

My heart drops, and I turn to look at him more closely. If this boy has made the same conclusion about me that I have about him, it would be from my words, not my voice. I haven't doubted its pitch or timbre for years. I know how much it resembles Patrick's when it needs to, and I know how well it marks me as a man.

When I say nothing, he goes on, "Me with my voice, you with your kingdom."

My heart's rhythm calms.

"If your father sleeps in that forest with my mother," I say, "he must be of high rank. I wonder if he would be proud to know his child is a thief."

"I am no thief," he says. "This is a war, and I have done only what I needed to do to bring you down."

I laugh, more out of surprise than amusement. "You think you can bring down a whole kingdom all by yourself, do you?"

He tenses again, surely thinking I am mocking him. But I don't mean to. I laugh only because I have been him. I have puffed myself up as big as I can in my mind, thinking that must be what makes a man. I have said I could do things I knew I couldn't, and paid for it. I have chosen a name only to abandon it and choose another. I have forced my voice too low and worn it out. I still bind my chest every day, even under armor, but I had to be taught how to do it so I could still move and breathe.

I hear noises up ahead and know we don't have much more time alone.

"I won't harm you," I say, a weak shorthand for what I wish I could say. But the part I need him to hear most, I whisper right into his ear as Deirdre approaches, broadsword raised. "But draw a weapon again and you will not survive this."

"Kill me," he says. "But don't make la princesa pay for what I've done. She knew nothing of this."

So quick to defend his ruler. I want so badly to know who he really is, how he can be so well-trained in some ways and so inexperienced in others. Whose armor he stole, and how he knew the way to move in it, despite its ill fit. But Deirdre is getting closer and looks ready to kill him as soon as he's in range. I signal Deirdre and she lowers her sword, but only partway.

"The rest of your weapons," I say, loud enough for Deirdre to hear. "Now. Slowly."

Gael slowly raises his open hands.

Deirdre comes nose-to-nose with my horse, stows her weapon, and holds an open pouch in front of Gael.

Gael reaches down toward one of his boots like he did while he was riding and pulls another knife out of a seam in the leather. When he's put that one in the pouch, he reaches for his other boot and pulls out two knives. All three are small and gleaming, their perfectly weighted handles engraved for both appearance and texture.

I wonder how old Gael was when he was first handed one. I've heard that some Elianan knife throwers are trained from the moment they pick up a twig or a spoon.

Next, Gael pulls one Elianan comb blade from his hair, then another, then another. His hair falls to his shoulders and he runs his hands through it to show there are no more blades there. They were concealed well enough, tucked under loops of his dark hair, for neither Deidre nor Eamon to catch a glimpse of them.

Gael holds up his open hands again but says nothing.

"Is that all, then?" Deirdre asks. She uses her most intimidating voice, but I can tell she's impressed.

Gael nods.

"All right," I say. "You've ridden with Eamon and tried to steal his horse, so your choices now are Deirdre or me."

Deirdre opens her arms and smiles.

"I'm fine where I am," Gael says.

Deirdre laughs.

"Very well," I say. "We've reached an understanding, have we not?" I cock my head to look into Gael's dark eyes.

He looks back, unflinching, and nods again.

"Excellent," I say.

I can't take Gael to our castle. God knows what the advisors will do with him. Especially Lowell after his display with Nessa just now. I would have no way to defend him and neither would Patrick. He tried to kill me, kill Patrick, kill the ruler of Adare. I can't keep him from the fate those actions bring with them. And I cannot see that happen to the only other person like me I've met outside of Claochlú Abbey. Someone who, if he had been there when I was, I could have studied with, shaved next to, practiced our voices and walks with, gotten to know.

For a few moments, I wonder what Patrick would do, but then I remember how angry I am at him for allowing Lowell to take credit for so much he had no role in, and for forcing me to play along or betray both Patrick and myself. Nessa was angry enough to voice her feelings to her ruler, with very little tempering. And instead of applauding her as I wanted to, I had to try to talk her out of how she felt.

My thoughts weigh on me nearly as much as my own limbs, heavy with overuse. Riding is leaving every muscle I have strained and sore. I slowly turn my horse and begin riding south. Deirdre follows at first, likely thinking I'm taking an easy path out of the woods. But when the trees thin and I keep going, she rides up next to us.

"How fortunate for you that we're all here to defend you," she says, "as you're clearly helpless against your enemies."

I laugh, grateful for her sense of humor, especially now.

"What you do seem helpless against is your own sense of direction," she says. "You do know you're riding away from the castle?"

"Yes."

"If you need something from the field, I assure you it can be retrieved for you," Deirdre says.

"We're going to Eliana," I say.

No one would notice if they weren't sharing a horse with him, but I sense relief in Gael, followed by a new tension, different from the fear and determination I felt in him before. He was ready to give his life trying to take mine. For a moment, I wonder if he was telling the truth that no one sent him, that he acted alone. Bringing him back is the best way to find out, and the best way to keep him alive.

"And why are we going to Eliana?" Deirdre asks.

"Because that is where this person came from, and that is where I wish to go." I grin at Deirdre.

"Specific as always, sire." She sighs. "Might I appeal to your radiant wisdom to reconsider taking him back to Adare instead of paying a visit to our enemies with one of their own in our capture?" She switches into the old language we rarely use. "It might seem we're gloating, and I don't trust Elianan royal tempers to take gloating well."

Deirdre is, apparently, counting on Gael not to understand our words. I'm not chancing that.

"I have a plan," I say, splitting the difference by answering in the same language, while being vague enough that my words won't be of much use.

I don't have a plan. But I have a long ride in which to come up with one.

This could be my chance to find her. The Elianan enchantress who cursed my parents. And this boy's father too, apparently. She looked like a courtier, so I might catch a glimpse of her at their palace. But what if I don't? And even if I did, what if I can't get close to her?

Deirdre signals behind her, and I'm relieved to see Eamon on his horse again, catching up to us.

Finding out how to compel the enchantress to break the curse would be much easier if I had more time, more opportunity to interact with her. Learn what she wants and how to make a deal with her. Everyone wants something.

As we ride and I feel the weather shifting, warming, my mind turns from the enchantress to Eliana's princess.

Patrick has completely ignored every invitation she has sent, as the loudest and most stubborn of the advisors have insisted. They've convinced him the risk is too great that a similar enchantment will befall more of our people.

But as long as I am wearing this breastplate, I am marked as Patrick, the ruling prince of Adare.

Every wound I have, new and old, turns to a cord of fire as I ride. I can shrug away the deep soreness in my arms and blink away the grit in my eyes, but I cannot drive away the fear that by the time we get to Eliana, my knee will not hold my weight when I try to stand.

I feel Gael's body shift, his back straightening. Only then do I realize I've just done the same thing, pulling my spine up to sit as tall as I can.

If I have to live with the consequences of Patrick's impossible battle plans, he'll have to live with the choices I make now.

I may be more guard than diplomat, more knight than prince, but if my own war companions don't suspect I'm not their true ruler, I doubt Princess Abryenda will. So long as I stay calm and keep my distance.

Patrick will surely want to have my head for this.

CHAPTER NINE

VALENCIA

I *have a plan.*

Oh, I'm sure he does. And I already know it won't end well for me. So the best thing I can do is end this now. I can't let this pendejo drag me home and bargain with Bryna for me.

Patrick McKenna isn't just evil, he's lucky. He stumbled into capturing La Princesa Abryenda's best friend.

There's only one way out of this: I have to annoy or anger Patrick McKenna enough to get him to kill me.

I should be uniquely qualified for this. Just the other day Ondina said I can be spectacularly annoying when I put my mind to it.

There's something sort of poetic about the fact that I'll die pissing off Patrick McKenna. And for once, instead of fighting the pain from riding, I get to use it. Staying in this position is wearing on me the longer we ride, but I don't have to smile through it. I don't have to bear it with the enduring grace expected of a dama.

Right now, I get to be as disagreeable as I want.

I look back at him. The small red slash on his ear is the only evidence that the knife I threw even hit him.

Let's hope I have better aim with my insults.

"You're far shorter than I thought you'd be," I tell him. (True. My father would, literally, look down at him.)

He nods as though conceding a point in a duel.

"Do you always make sure a woman's around to do your work for you?" I ask, glancing toward Deirdre.

"When she's better at the task at hand than I am, yes," he says, without bitterness.

Every time I talk, Deirdre looks over, as though to ask, *Can I kill him yet? How about now? Can I kill him now?*

Each time, the murderer prince gives a small shake of his head.

"Tell me," I say. "Are you enjoying wearing the crown of your mother's true heir?"

A shudder goes through him.

But he's silent.

I landed a knife while on a horse I don't know. Yet somehow I can't land the right words to make him draw a sword on me before we reach el palacio.

Even with the mess I'm in, I love seeing a prince and his entourage gape at the floating gardens. The bean plants and sunflowers stand as tall as any of them. The trailing vines overgrow the beds and dip their green fingers into the water.

"I seek an audience with the Princess Abryenda," Patrick says to the guards at the gate.

Tell him no, I plead with a glance when we get close enough that I can make eye contact. *Don't look at me like I matter to you or to anyone. Don't look at me like you know my father. Pretend I'm nobody. Just deny him entrance. Let him kill me.*

"Only you," the lead guard says to Patrick.

It takes all the self-control I have not to yell *no*.

"You stay out here," the second guard tells Deirdre and the man whose horse I started out on (Eamon?).

Deirdre smirks, but really, I don't blame the guards. Not just because of the braid crown that shows her rank, but because of how she looks. Maybe it's because I've grown up among people who are almost all some shade of brown, but the kind of pale Deirdre is unsettles me. Her skin, like her hair, is lighter than masa, nearly milk white.

Eamon glances at Patrick, no doubt signaling something about raising an alarm if need be. En serio? Does he really think none of the guards are going to notice that?

"Disarm," the lead guard says to Patrick.

"Any who wishes to approach La Princesa will show respect for her and her ascendientes," the second says.

Patrick McKenna is probably too stupid to realize what a favor the guards are doing him. If he walked into the room with a sword on him, a jaguar might leap at his throat.

Patrick hands his sword and dagger to Deirdre.

When I'm led through the arches of stone, it's without any rope on me. Nice gesture, I guess, but that just makes me more suspicious.

Everything familiar about el palacio greets me—the wall-mounted candles, the smell of orange oil and wet cinnamon bark, the tapestries in rust and gold. But as we walk, my back screams at me, pain twisting down into my hips and legs.

Lila squawks from her perch on a sconce, feathers brushing the amethysts and scrolled bronze.

Her cry startles Patrick, who stumbles.

I smirk at her. Bien hecho, Lila. Even in dire circumstances, she has such beautifully spiteful flare.

My heart stills as we enter the throne room, lit with even more

46

candles, bright with dyed fabric and gilded cloth. Guards stand in each corner. The air around them bristles with how ready they are.

Ferns and fronds fill tall vases, flanking Bryna. The light from the sconces gleams off the blue of her gown. On either side of her are the great cats from the tapestries outside her room, which are currently empty panels of midnight-blue cloth. The jaguar stands, silver dotting his coat. The ocelot lounges like a kitten, but she'll bare her teeth at the first threat toward Bryna. She and I have that in common.

I flick my eyes from them to Patrick McKenna. Wouldn't now be the time to go for his throat? They are, after all, supposed to be helping us. The great cats appeared, turning from embroidery to fur and muscle, in the weeks after El Encanto took our king and queen. According to las brujas, they haven't left the tapestries in hundreds of years. It's either a sign that they respect Bryna enough to guide her in ruling the kingdom, or that our ancestors think we're so thoroughly jodido they better help us out.

Bryna's face is impassive. She barely looks at me. Her mother would be proud. Nothing betrays her except details so small only I would notice them. Her tensed forehead. Two of her fingers fiddling with the lace cuff on her sleeve. The slightest gloss of perspiration along her hairline, showing more of the red in her dark hair.

My throat is as dry as the carved wood of her throne, and my spine shrieks at me. But Bryna's cold stare keeps me upright. She's not rude, but she doesn't cower. Her dress shines as much as her rose-quartz-inlaid throne. The color and embroidery of her skirt look like etched crystal.

"Su Alteza," Patrick says.

To his credit, he bows.

On trembling legs, I bow lower, despite the pain in my spine, worse for how badly I need my cane right now.

Patrick stumbles, haltingly returning to standing.

My eyes crawl over to him. *This* is Patrick McKenna? The prince known for his grace, famous for fighting a battle and then dancing the next night? This guy?

I wonder if he has an injury he's trying to hide, either from the battle he just fought in or any battle before. If stories of Patrick McKenna paint him as near invincible, he has every reason to hide evidence to the contrary. But if I can figure it out, I can use it against him. We are all one sudden movement away from this becoming a fight, and I need to be ready.

Bryna nods for all to rise, but not before looking me over, reading how I've presented myself, my bound chest, the lack of poison stain on my lips. She doesn't know that sometimes being a boy makes me feel like myself. I've never worked up the nerve to tell her. But she's used to my disguises, whether I'm a young boy or an old woman.

"You've come a long way to bring back a child," she tells Patrick.

"He's no child, and we both know it," Patrick says. "But I return him unharmed, as a gesture of goodwill."

He nods at me.

I stare.

That's it? No threatening me in front of Bryna? No attempt at using me to bargain? No Patrick McKenna flourishes, such as, oh, murdering me in front of her?

He clears his throat at me. "I'm returning you unharmed," he says far enough under his breath that I'm the only one who can hear him. He tilts his head toward Bryna pointedly.

"How kind," Bryna says, with neither sarcasm nor excessive gratitude.

I stand to the side of Bryna's throne, face still as the stone beneath us. We've all been trained well.

Except me, apparently.

Maybe my father will rise from his enchanted sleep to tell me what a disappointment I am.

"Your messengers have no doubt told you that our forces have taken the fields," Patrick says. "Down to your farthest outpost."

She flinches in a way so small I'm sure I'm the only one who can tell. But of course she feels it. How many of our cousins and friends have we buried?

"Is your bragging also a gesture of goodwill?" Bryna asks.

"I know you've lost many of your own," Patrick says, as though his thoughts have gone to the same shadowed corners as ours. "So have we. There's been too much blood, on both sides."

"Which is why I issued an invitation to negotiate," Bryna says. "Months ago."

How neatly she mentions it. She doesn't add that Adare refused the invitation. She doesn't have to. The truth hangs between her and Patrick's battle-dulled armor.

Patrick dips his head. "And for that, I apologize. Perhaps you can understand me being"—he's trying to choose his words carefully—"cautious."

Is this what ruling is? Constantly saying about a fifth of what you actually mean?

"Come to Adare," Patrick says. "We will host you and your court in the style to which you're accustomed."

Por supuesto.

Of course he put on this show of generosity because he wants something. He wants Bryna to trust him enough to bring her court to an enemy kingdom.

"This is our parents' war," Patrick says. "If you're as weary of bloodshed as I am, let us be the ones to end it."

Bryna holds his gaze. "Thank you for the invitation."

I wait for her to issue her own invitation, say, for him to become the great cats' dinner.

"I will consider it," she says.

My vision blurs, as much from her words as from the pain of standing in one place. I can't help staring at her, and I'm not alone. The guards, impassive until now, look as shocked as I am. Even the cats have turned their heads in disbelief.

"Of course, before I consider your offer," she says, eyes darting around to meet ours as if she's taking a cue, "I must ask you." She meets his eye in a way that makes it impossible for even Patrick McKenna to look away. "Did you know of, participate in, or condone any plot to curse our families?"

I could hail her aloud. This is what makes her my best friend and my future queen. She'll stare into his face and either compel him to tell the truth or see his lies for what they are.

"No," he says.

I bite my tongue to keep from laughing. Of course he knew. He probably ordered it.

"And would you consider it an insult if I were to ask that you answer the same question?" he asks.

Would he consider it an insult if I were to shove my knee into his huevos?

"No," Bryna says, still holding his gaze. "To both questions."

Patrick McKenna nods the curt single nod better befitting a knight than a prince.

Bryna's own nod—slow, delicate, commanding—dismisses Patrick. A flank of guards escorts him out.

"Leave us," she tells the other guards.

With a few steps and the swing of the doors, we're alone.

The moment they're gone, Bryna springs forward and throws her arms around me. The great cats purr. I'm flattered that the royal ascendientes care what's become of me.

I collapse into her, tired in a way that my own fear hasn't let me feel until this moment.

"Did he hurt you?" she asks.

"I'm all right." I ease away from her so I can reach under my shirt and into my bindings.

I offer her the glowing thing she sent me to find. It casts blue-violet on her face, twinkling like it holds a star.

I may not believe everything Bryna believes. But the way she looks at this blue ember between us, I almost feel it, her faith that no matter what Patrick McKenna does, no matter how long we've been without our mothers and fathers, this is a fight we can still win.

CHAPTER TEN
CADE

Siobhán fastens my last bandage into place. "If you don't stop all this on your own, that knee will do it for you."

"I know," I say.

I can't hold at bay the memory of an Elianan blade piercing through a gap in my armor. The blade only stopped when it hit the guard covering my left knee. Unlike many of my other injuries over the years, this one never quite knitted itself back together, despite Siobhán's efforts.

"If you know, why have I been saying it for months?" she says. "For the joy of hearing my own voice? And that's after you took half the recovery time I told you to take in the first place."

"I know." I ease myself off Siobhán's worktable.

The moment both my feet touch the floor, she holds up her hand.

"Stop right there," she says.

She hands Faolan to me, but doesn't let go of him yet. "You say this staff is your friend, do you?" she asks.

I look into the owl's eyes, the hematite like a deep gray river at night.

"Then use him," she says. "And take what I've told you to take when I've told you to take it. And rest. No active duty of any kind, no maneuvers, and nothing beyond conversation with . . . whoever you're conversing with these days. If I catch you doing anything more strenuous than getting up to piss, I will annihilate you."

"Not if I annihilate him first."

Patrick. His left hand is on the hilt of his sword, the way it is when someone has insulted our mother.

"Be gentle with him, Patrick," Siobhán says. "I'd hate to see all my bandaging go to waste so soon."

Siobhán pats Patrick's shoulder, then takes his goblet out of his hand and drains it as she leaves. "When you're through with him, you're next with me," she says. "I've got to make that lovely ear of yours match his."

She gestures at the bandage on my ear, where Gael's knife clipped it. Patrick may not fight in battle, but whenever I'm injured in a way that would be obvious, Siobhán duplicates the injury on Patrick as best she can. If Patrick is ever unconscious and Siobhán and I can't protect him, it needs to be as believable as possible that he actually fought in all the battles I fought for him.

When my knee was injured, he was ready to take that on too. Siobhán and I both refused. Siobhán has the same unflinching gift as her mother, the way she sees bodies as parts fitting together, but even she balked at running Patrick's knee through.

I could give Patrick an earful for not keeping Lowell in check, but instead I lean on Faolan and wait for my brother to speak first. Faolan is built to help me get around, and to change when he needs to. The tree at the center of the castle offered my mother the branch that became Faolan's staff, and the wood still grows and shifts as readily as the tree itself.

Right now, Faolan's shape allows me to hold one of his two grips, the one that functions more like a cane, taking as much of my weight as possible. I ready myself for whatever Patrick is working himself up to saying. His temper is so much like our father's, with long, slow burns, stony silences, and rare but terrifying eruptions.

He walks over to one of the walls and looks at it. "So I hear you went soft on an assassin."

"No, I turned what could have been a botched assassination attempt into an opportunity," I say. I can't tell him why I couldn't bring Gael back here, because that would break my vow too. The older monks explained to us what our vows meant, that we could not harm another we knew to be like us, even on a battlefield. And that we could not reveal the nature of their identity to anyone else without clear permission, because that could do as much harm as a strike with our hands or swords.

When Patrick says nothing, I keep going, pushing away thoughts of the abbey, and of Gael. "I saw an opening and I took it. Just as I would in a fight. Except this was to end all the fighting."

"End all the fighting. Just like that. Because it's so easy, is it?" He speaks calmly now, but with fists and jaw still clenched. "If you hadn't just been in battle, I'd challenge you right now."

He takes a shallow breath before going on. He doesn't seem to notice that the wood and stone of the walls around us are shifting, constricting. "How could you do this? Throw away our entire strategy? Risk not only the lives of some of our most skilled warriors, but all our secrets too? All at once!"

Parts of the walls are like glass now, cold and reflective. Parts that were living wood before. The floor under us is shifting now too, becoming uneven. The stones look heavier, more forbidding.

Unfazed by what now appears to be petrified wood in the walls of our tower and charred pieces of coal as our floor, Patrick goes on. "Some of those secrets are yours, Cade! What if you had been captured? You could have handed over not just your life, but our entire kingdom! In one move! What is wrong with you?"

He stares at me, clearly waiting for me to respond. I'm always surprised at how easy it is for me to reach a sense of calm when Patrick is angry. It's as if there's only enough rage for one of us at a time.

"You're right," I say.

Some of the coals under us begin to feel strangely warm.

"You don't even regret it, do you?" Patrick asks.

"I would if it had played out differently," I say. "But it didn't. She's just as much a leader as you are."

"You must not think me much of a leader if this is what you do behind my back," Patrick says.

I want to rub my temples against the headache this is giving me, but I know Patrick will think I'm trying to make a point. Every time I try to reason with my brother he thinks I'm arguing with him.

"Our advisors have never given Bryna enough credit, and I think you put too much trust in their counsel," I say. "And she's still your intended, for God's sake!"

"That was only on paper," he says. "A long time ago too." Some of the coals behind him flash orange but then burn out, smoke rising in long coils. "One of many vain attempts to broker peace."

"But what's the harm in talking with her?" I ask.

"What if we all fall under the sleeping curse too?" he asks.

"You don't really think that," I say.

"We don't know who cast it," he says. "I know you think you do, but the truth is we don't even know who would be capable of it. You could have just invited them into our home."

That was exactly the idea, but Patrick can't know that.

"I asked her directly," I say. "I looked into her eyes when she said she knew nothing of how the curse happened. I believe her."

We're both quiet. I carefully make my way over to one of the chairs at the table in the middle of the room. I have seen it as various forms of wood, stone, fabric, even metal, but this is the first time it has looked like dark glass. It's cold and hard, but it doesn't seem fragile. I sink into it cautiously, just in case. When I feel how solid it is beneath me, I let Faolan rest on the arm beside me and gently stretch my leg out.

Patrick pours two goblets of water and sets one down in front of me. He drinks from his, then sits down across the table. Perhaps he's more accustomed to the castle's abrupt shifts than I am these days. Any time I spend wearing his breastplate, he spends in this tower, seeing no one but Siobhán.

I slump back in the chair, but that puts more pressure on my knee than I expect, so I straighten up again.

Patrick takes a deep breath. "If she's coming here"—he looks around—"we're going to have to redecorate."

I almost laugh. It feels like we're brothers again, not two halves of one prince.

"Too bad." I pour some of the water from my goblet onto the floor around us. The water hisses into steam as it hits the coals. "Aren't you feeling a bit more relaxed now?"

"Not really, no," he says.

"So our castle isn't exactly a display of opulence," I say. "As long we make sure the princess and her court are comfortable, what do the details of the wall hangings matter?"

Patrick gives me a weary look.

It occurs to me that I don't know whether Patrick has been inside the Elianan palace. Wherever our castle is the greens and blue-grays of our trees, waters, and skies, their palace is bright gold and burnt orange. Wherever our stone hallways are dim, theirs are lit with a hundred wall-mounted candles, the outside a rosy sandstone.

Even if we could get the corridors and furniture to stay still, or get the rabbits and squirrels out of the indoor tree branches and shrubberies, the sight of our great hall would still hardly be a welcome befitting an Elianan princess.

"The river in the great hall could flood," Patrick says. "Or a tree could spring up in the middle of a staircase and trap some passersby, or a swarm of wasps could suddenly appear and sting everyone. Need I go on?"

He has a point. In most nations, the castle or palace or fortress reflects the ruler. In Adare, it responds and reacts to her. What she hopes, needs, and wants for her reign or her comfort, it tries to provide. The longer our mother and queen stays in her cursed sleep, the less stable it is. We often go to bed in a very different castle than the one we wake up in.

"I'll ask Fergus's sisters about the decorating," I say. "They know fashion here—and there—better than anyone."

"God help us," Patrick says. "The impression we make on a visiting princess and her court is in the hands of Fergus's little sisters."

I pull the mixture of herbs Siobhán makes for me off the table and drink a few swallows. "And you'd better show your gratitude if they agree to do it."

Patrick laughs, as if he can't help it, and the tension between us seems to have melted for now. Ever since the enchantment stole our elders, so many of us have had to face tasks we weren't prepared for, take risks we don't quite understand. We all still act as though our parents have gone away on some journey and might well be back by nightfall. Siobhán and Nessa picked up where their mothers left off in their work. Lowell, Rhys, and half a dozen more of our cousins sit proud enough to fill the seats of their advisor parents. Fergus's sisters put the taste their father taught them to making sure we don't look entirely like the country rustics so many assume us to be.

And Patrick rules in place of our mother and father. I can see it wearing on him. I think the graying of his hair has caught up to mine.

"Cade?" Patrick asks.

I meet his eyes.

"If this goes wrong, we'll have a war far worse than we do now."

I think about Gael, about how I thought leaving Claochlú Abbey meant leaving everyone like me, but knowing they were somewhere safe. This war has made it even more dangerous for people like us to live our lives in our own homes, our own nations. Even more welcoming nations like ours have grown more chaotic as the war has stretched on, and fear can easily bounce from one target to another. If I weren't part of the royal family, I would leave Adare to live as a man, and I would advise anyone like me to do the same.

I notice I've begun to run my fingers against my shirt, over the metallic beads of my rosary tattoo that lead to the cross over my heart.

I shut my eyes. "I know."

CHAPTER ELEVEN

VALENCIA

The heel of my cane taps the violet-and-blue rugs on the stone floors, as deep as the cempaxochitl blossoms are bright. It's a sound as familiar as my own heartbeat, the soft thump of wood on the woven wool, the sound of my spine easing.

Every time I get back to my room, I work the oil from the curanderas into my lower back. I heat my muscles so they stop seizing up. The lower section of my spine curves more and moves more than it should, which is great for twisting myself into odd positions. But it means that seemingly ordinary tasks like standing and sitting put pressure on my bones and wear on the surrounding muscles. There are days when I can leap onto a fox's back but can't bend straight forward enough to touch my toes. Sometimes climbing a tree is less daunting than being told to stand up straight.

My back isn't any happier about meeting Patrick McKenna than I am. Our encounter is going to make life as a demure, graceful dama painful for the next week.

Ondina catches me in the corridor. "Tell me this is all some horrible joke."

"What are you talking about?" I ask.

Ondina fiddles with her two braids, as long and thin as her body. She only ever does this when she's excited or agitated, and from the look on her face, this is squarely the latter.

"We're going to Adare," Ondina says.

"You're not serious," I say.

Ondina throws up her hands. "She consulted the ascendientes. They told her to go. Why would they tell her to go? Is this some kind of test I don't know about? Do they just give her bad advice sometimes and see if she'll take it? Is this something else rústicas like me don't get to know?"

"Stop," I say. I hate when she calls herself that.

Ondina came from los pueblos, same as my father. The village Ondina comes from is even smaller than the one where my father was born. Ondina's family rose because of her, because she helped Bryna when she was lost on the road. A storm had washed out the ground between her and her guard, and she looked so little like a princess that Ondina didn't even recognize her. That kindness, the way she held out her heart to a stranger, earned her a place at Bryna's side. And now that same kindness is what the damas take as invitation to tear her apart behind her back.

Usually behind her back. Sometimes she and I both get those charming comments about how quaintly we place the ribbons on our gowns, or digs about our family lines, or friendly advice telling us to rinse our hair with aceite de nuez because it's looking a little dull lately.

"Talk to her," Ondina says. "Please?"

"As though you could stop me." I take off, my cane sounding out my steps.

I intercept a guard on his way out of the throne room. "Tell me it's not true."

His frustrated sigh makes him look like his father. Another of our own lost to El Encanto.

"Los jaguares told her to accept the invitation," he says, with the reverence due our ancestors, but then his face changes to exasperation. "Did los jaguares also do us the courtesy of telling us how to protect la princesa in a castle that has no map? A castle that lives and breathes and changes with the seasons? No. Claramente, no."

At least Ondina and I aren't the only ones who hate this idea.

"Perhaps you'll talk sense into her," he says.

I push open one of the copper-inlaid doors to the throne room. Bryna was already on her feet, the jaguars languorous on the embroidered rug. The margays bat at the tassels like kittens.

These are the ascendientes we consult about everything from war to marriage. The ones who just told us to stroll into the court of our enemies.

I wait to escort Bryna to her room.

I wait, folding my tongue in my mouth to keep quiet. That's what it takes for me not to yell that this is an idea so bad it makes all other bad ideas look inspired. The suitor who tried to impress Bryna with some ridiculous stage play about mermaids and lovesick marineros? (The salt water ate through the basin containing the mock ocean, ruining half the rugs in the main halls.) Genius compared to this idea.

"You're accepting his invitation?" I whisper.

She nods in respect to the quetzals we pass, then turns back to me. "Do you want this war to go on forever?"

The question lands between my ribs.

My uncle and Bryna's cousin joined the ground in the same month last year.

The air in Bryna's room smells dry as winter. Everything is where it was the last time. The roselles and long green plumas embroidered onto her bed covering. The carving of palm fronds in the dark wood of her wardrobe. The gold cords holding the drapes. But it seems lonelier than the last time I was in here. None of the blossom of her usual perfume. The ember-colored marigolds she grows herself, kneeling in the earth of the floating gardens, have wilted. I wonder when was the last time she actually slept in here, or slept at all.

"It can't go on forever," I say. "We have to win. It's the only way we survive. If we leave ourselves open to them, they will crush us. It's what they do."

"Our soldiers and theirs are all out there, fighting a war none of us chose." Bryna lifts a dress from her wardrobe, the layers of gold fabric as delicate as the leaves of a book. "Do you even know how this started? Do you know how many wars start over the pointless vendettas of proud men? La nobleza on either side, feuds over land, one side strikes the other, and before you know it, feuds become wars. My own mother and father wanted to end this."

"And if they were here, do you really think they'd try again? After what happened out there? If we let them, Adare will destroy us." I offer my arm to take the weight of the dress. My instincts are always half protector, half lady-in-waiting, and I've handled that dress before. The material may be light as petals, but with that many layers, it's heavy enough that I could strengthen my arm muscles carrying it around. "This isn't just win or lose. It's win or vanish. Last time we met them halfway, literally, and look what happened."

Bryna flops the dress over one of my shoulders. "Patrick McKenna had nothing to do with that."

"Oh?" I ask. "And how do we know that?"

"I could see it." Bryna crosses the room. "He was telling the truth."

"So you're just taking his word for it," I say.

She lifts a heavy brocade from her wardrobe.

"What are you doing?" I ask.

"Packing my best." She goes back to the wardrobe.

"Bryna," I say.

"Why bother Ondina?" Bryna folds an enagua. "She's probably studying the history of the Adare coast as we speak." Bryna tucks a few jeweled hairpins into a case.

"What if this is all a trap?" I ask. "Another one."

Bryna takes a deep, steadying breath. The expression she has right now gives me a good idea of what she'll look like summoning her patience with her children. "I know what you think you saw."

This again. She sounds like las brujas. Kind and long-suffering. She doesn't think I'm lying about what I saw that night.

She just thinks I'm mistaken.

"I don't believe this is a trap," she says. "With all my heart, from everything I could see when I looked into his face, I don't believe it is. And neither do our ascendientes."

I hold my tongue as I leave her room. As I leave el palacio. As I leave the floating gardens with their scent of calendula and pink lavender.

When the luminous fox appears, teeth sharp as raw crystals but eyes curious, I hold out my shoes. She knew where I needed to go tonight before I did.

No one knows how often I go out to El Encanto. Not even Bryna. As the fox leaps through the dark, my heart turns to a thing so bitter I can taste it in the back of my throat.

Protect her.

Shield her.

Say nothing when she plans to get herself killed along with who knows how many of us.

Say nothing when I'm sure Ondina's right, that our ancestors are testing her wisdom, teaching Bryna that she will often be given bad advice, and that she must discern it from the good.

The fox leaves me, my shoes clutched between the little knives of her teeth.

The grass dampens the hem of my dress, deepening the blue field of the cloth and the gold and orange of the embroidery.

Every time, I hope this will be when I'll catch a glimpse of my father.

Ever since the sleeping enchantment took so many of our parents, the air around the woods looks dyed the deep and bright blue of an autumn dusk. It doesn't matter the month or the time of day. That color always veils it like a mist.

They're beautiful, these woods, green and rich as deepest velvet, studded with rock fields and meadows. Even before the enchantment, the trees came in rich browns and greens. In summer, the air smells like the lavender that grows wild. In autumn, falling leaves make mulch so rich it grew enough violet mushrooms for every nearby village.

I come closer to the veil of blue.

Wild daffodils brighten the forest floor. Their stems and leaves obscure the figures lying on the moss, peaceful as if they were dozing.

I try to peer deeper into the trees, hoping I can catch a scrap of the persimmon-orange coat my father wore the last time I saw him.

But I can't. I never can. El Encanto keeps them behind a cursed veil that won't even let us reach them. We can't anoint their foreheads with aceite sagrada or set the ruffled orange blossoms of cempaxochitl in their hands. I couldn't touch the hem of my father's coat even with the help of the most powerful brujas in Eliana. They've tried.

I hold my hands out in front of me until they reach the enchantment, chilled and hard as the stone of our palace walls.

Eliana needs my father right now, his skill at finding out secrets, his way of going unnoticed. And I need him. I need him to tell me how to live with the part of myself I call Gael.

What do I do with him? I want to ask my father. *You taught me what to do with my back, how to live with that part of me. What do I do with this part of me? How do I live with him?*

If my father never wakes up, he will never really know me. He will never know the part of me I never told him about. He will never know he has a son as well as a daughter.

I lay a hand flat against the enchantment keeping me out. I shut my eyes.

The wall doesn't give. It never does. But it ripples at the pressure, and the cords of scarring that cross my palm after years learning to throw knives. When the moonlight shifts, it turns the veil into a mirror.

When I open my eyes, it shows a faint copy of my own face. The brown skin, made a little paler by the moon. My black hair, my eyes almost as dark.

I try to imagine who my father thought I could become, clever and watchful, measured but fearless. Instead of how reckless I've turned out to be.

Then the first green of an idea blooms, bright and sudden as a daffodil shedding its paper shell.

I've gotten this all wrong. I thought us going to Adare was a disaster. But it's the best opportunity I could ask for.

The Adare boy I saw that night. The one who did this. I'm going to find him.

I'm going to make him undo this. I'm going to make him bring back everyone we've lost. Our king and queen will wake up, and tell Bryna that there is no negotiating with Adare.

Everyone will come back to us.

My father will come back. I can tell him everything I never got to tell him.

That boy will never see me coming. I'll look like nothing but a princess's dama, sweet and ladylike. And by the time he realizes otherwise, I'll already have him. He'll have no choice but to do exactly what I say.

CHAPTER TWELVE

CADE

T his is the only place I can know for sure that my mother is still alive.

Even though there are no windows, light sparkles through the small space. It bounces from one glittering stone to another, from one branch of the massive tree to the next.

I pay my respects to this tree and its small light-refracting globes, a constellation of them for each member of the McKenna family. Patrick's flicker thinly, like a flame without enough kindling.

As I leave, I take one last look at the many colors of my mother's royal gems, each round and smooth but different, like a cluster of grapes on a vine. When she was with us, I could hold both these things, her being my mother and being our queen. But now I miss her in two different ways. Each one is its own pull on me, and sometimes I feel them tearing me open like a seam in a lacing.

All the changes she made, all the efficiencies she added, it all continues on without her. The roads that didn't exist or were in disuse before her reign. The structures she set in place to protect farms and villages from harsh winters and scant harvests. The beacons along the coast to warn navigators of shoals. The aqueducts that were the work of engineers in both Adare and Eliana before the war.

Everything she did that the villages and farms welcomed faced opposition within the castle. So many wanted things to stay as they were. My mother either convinced them or took action anyway.

I can only hope that what I've done is the kind of bold my mother would be proud of, and not the kind of foolish Patrick thinks it is.

When I know there's no one watching, I check the wall outside my chamber. It's still solid rock, no sign of a door. When I touch a specific place, the rock shifts blue, then purple when I touch the next stone, gray-green when I touch the next. It's a pattern only I know, the change in color telling me where to set my hand. Only once I've finished do the stones in the wall pull apart. With Eliana's spies and possibly an enchantress about to cross our threshold, there's no such thing as being too careful.

Two halls away, I come upon Patrick. And Lowell, who is no doubt oiling up Patrick.

"Sire, I have heard your concerns and I sympathize, believe me, but there is no cause for alarm," Lowell says, his smooth hand on Patrick's upper arm. If I didn't know better about both of them, I would think he was trying to charm his way into Patrick's trousers. And making headway at that.

Lowell turns to me. "Cade, my good man," Lowell says. "I didn't see you there."

"Just as well," I say, looking at Patrick. "Shall we see how things are coming along?"

I sense Lowell following.

I pause, leaning more heavily on Faolan, and take the opportunity to fall back with him as Patrick enters the hall.

"How could you take credit for a victory you had no role in whatsoever?" I ask Lowell quietly.

"Celebrating victories increases morale," he says.

As we approach the hall, I hear an argument that cannot possibly end well.

"It's too frightening," one of Fergus's sisters says. "They'll expect us to draw on them at any moment! That's not how things are done there—they disarm before they enter the throne room. Everything!"

"Just because they do that doesn't mean we do," Deirdre says. Even out of resins, she still looks imposing. The three braids pinned across the crown of her head to mark her rank certainly don't hurt. "It's too great a risk for all the arms to be hidden. What if they make a threat and we have no way to defend ourselves? Our monarch?"

"The shields all stay," I say. "They are all our crests as well as shields, so they cannot be taken down. And the swords stay too."

"But—"

"It's tradition," I say. "And it can't hurt to make sure the Elianans don't forget where they are. But the smaller weapons can come down."

"Fine," Deirdre agrees.

The sisters' disbelief seems directed at both us and the swords.

"Don't blame me if they're all too frightened to dance," one of them says.

Patrick looks as though he was about to speak, but the sounds of clay flutes and many, many hoofbeats interrupt.

The full impression of what Fergus's sisters have done finally sinks in. It feels warmer from the tapestries draped over the walls and ceiling. They dampen the echo in the hall, making it feel less hollow and friendlier. They have all the colors Adare has ever used, from different eras of our history. The ranges of leafy green that have signified the McKennas over the years, the icy blue the O'Loingsighs have used in their tartans for generations to call to mind the river, the deep brown of our hills, the gray of our stones.

There are flowers everywhere. On the tables, on the walls, even float-ing in the river. There are ribbons and candles in the tree branches, and more candles than I thought reasonable on the tables as well. But none of this is any match for the retinue entering. Each of them sparkles more than the last. The women wear bright dresses, and some are carrying more brightly colored fabric folded in their arms. The men's trousers are black, shiny, and very tight. I catch some of our ladies' eyes widening.

I thank my stars this is not the fashion in my country.

That the retinue includes quetzals isn't a surprise. But the cats make me worry about the chickens we weren't able to keep out of the hall.

Princess Abryenda is close to the end of the procession, followed by intimidating-looking men who would, I'm guessing, kill me with their bare hands if they were so inclined. Her deep green dress is clearly a gesture of friendliness, and it highlights the curves of her form.

I look over at Patrick, who hasn't seen her in years. He's staring at her. Her auburn hair. Her deep brown eyes. Her skin the color of a tree trunk in the rain.

I nudge his foot with the edge of my staff, and he composes himself. We all bow deeply as she passes, and I am grateful I have Faolan when I bow this time.

A big fuzzy sheep barrels across the procession's path, followed by a small boy running after it yelling, "Adelaide!"

The Elianans smile, as if they find this charming. What seems to charm them less is the way we casually throw salt on any tapestry that starts to go up in flames. Fergus's sisters may have overdone it with the candles.

The sheep and boy are gone now, but some goats are still milling around, and they are disturbingly interested in anything hanging from the Elianans' dresses and furniture. Bows, ribbons, buttons, tassels, beading—all potential snacks.

Along a back wall, some soldiers are engaging in target practice with wooden goblets.

Fergus's youngest sister shrugs at me, as if to say, *You try making this happen in such little time.*

The castle begins to shift. A few flowering vines sprout from the trees, and the shrubs begin to blossom. Patrick has just been officially reintroduced to Princess Abryenda when a new vine springs from the floor right by her foot. The cracking stones threaten to catch her and make her fall.

Patrick reacts more quickly than I've ever seen. He moves her to his other side, lifting her by her waist and turning her across his body. As he does this, even more flowers bloom, and the light in the hall seems to shift, brighter and more glittery.

Princess Abryenda looks slightly winded, but gazes at Patrick as if he just recited a love poem. Patrick blushes. Seems having her pressed against him, even briefly, is too much for his virginal little body to handle.

This is all going far too quickly for me.

I turn and nearly stumble over a small person in a long gown. I feel the fingers on both my hands spread wide, and I know Faolan has slipped from my grasp. When I try to regain my grip, I'm holding something shorter, weighted differently. A bejeweled cane that belongs to the girl in front of me, who is now holding Faolan.

Both the gown and the lady's skin are a beautiful shade of brown, and her black hair falls in waves down her shoulders. Her large dark eyes meet mine.

Wavy black hair. A long, tasteful gown. Those big dark eyes. Deep red lips. And a cane, no less. It's her. It has to be.

I say a brief prayer of thanks and revel in my luck.

I start with a winning smile. We both laugh briefly and hand our respective canes back to each other.

"That's a beautiful piece," she says. "But far too tall and heavy for me, I'm afraid."

"Thank you," I say back. "Yours is far too sparkly for my taste. But very well made."

I inadvertently allow my eyes to run over her body as I say that last part, from her graceful neck to the curves of her hips and legs.

"Kind of you to say so," she says.

It could be my imagination, but I think I see her eyes trace their way up and down my form as well. Convincing her to break the curse could be even easier than I dared to hope. And more enjoyable.

"And whom do I have the pleasure of meeting?" I ask.

"Valencia Palafox," she says. "Dama to la princesa."

That could present some challenges.

"Cade McKenna," I say with a small bow. "Prince Patrick's half brother."

"That explains the similarities," she says.

My heart trips. Could she know about how I double for Patrick? What else does she know?

"You both work quickly," she continues.

Valencia is looking at Patrick, who is smiling and chattering away to the princess. I'm relieved, or would be if not for the image I have of her in my mind, crouched in the forest, covered in fire.

"He doesn't usually," I say. "But I do."

"Word of advice to both you and your brother." Valencia leans closer and whispers in my ear. "Ladies from Eliana value the art of subtlety."

She turns, very quickly and gracefully, and makes her way to her princess.

Now that she's not looking, I breathe heavily and lean on Faolan a bit harder.

I always wondered if the enchantress saw me. If she would recognize me if we ever met, or if she was too focused on the enchantment to notice me watching her.

She didn't react at all to meeting me. I saw nothing that would indicate recognition. No trace of fear. She must not know anyone saw her. But I did. And now she's in my castle.

CHAPTER THIRTEEN

VALENCIA

Here's something else my father taught me: Whenever you see someone, it's foolish to assume they haven't seen you.

It was half of my plan to watch for flashes of recognition, who among the Adare men might go a little paler at the sight of my face.

But now I know that the boy who cursed the forest didn't see me. Or, if he did, he didn't see enough of me to recognize me now. No familiarity showed in his face, no question, no trying to place me. To him, I was never even there.

So that's the good news.

The bad news is living, breathing, and named Cade McKenna.

I now need to charm, intimidate, and threaten the boy who's second in line to rule Adare.

Ondina's eyes follow the path I just came from.

"Who were you just talking to?" Ondina asks.

"Patrick's brother," I say.

"Judging from that sulk of yours, he must have a sparkling personality," Ondina says.

"Oh yes," I say, "younger brother is just as charming as the eldest."

"Someone's charmed." Ondina points her chin toward Bryna and Patrick. He's milking his own gallantry for all it's worth, holding her hand in his as though she might need further protection at any moment. And is she—no, she can't be—is the future queen of Eliana giggling? Bryna doesn't giggle. Even as children, when we snuck a lizard into her meanest prima's bed, there was no giggling.

"Care to wager whether they set up that little display so he could be the hero?" I ask.

"No," Ondina says. "Because I don't want to lose."

She stares into the castle's main hall, which, if it weren't ruled by a murderer prince, might be beautiful. It's as though the castle is alive, made partly of stone and partly of forest. Its colors and smells reflect where the castle sits, between Adare's forests and the rocky cliffs of the shoreline.

"Look at their sashes," Ondina says.

"What about them?" I ask.

"There are only a few different patterns," she says. "Is everyone here related?"

"Most of them are McKennas or O'Loingsighs," I say. "Patrick's both, obviously. Cade's a McKenna but not an O'Loingsigh. His mother is the queen but he has a different father. That's Siobhán, one of the court physicians. She's an O'Loingsigh, not a McKenna."

Ondina stares at me.

"What?" I lean in close enough to whisper. "You know I have to know these things."

"Your father would be proud," she says.

"After all the trouble I've caused?" I say behind a proper dama's smile. "Lo dudo."

But then I think of what my father might say right now. He'd tell me to take my victories as they come. Yes, el brujo being so close to Patrick McKenna may not be ideal. But I've already found him.

74

"Vamos," Ondina says. "Let's go pretend we're making ourselves at home."

The royal guards, los santos bless them, talked Bryna out of staying inside a castle that's constantly moving and changing, so preparations outside are already underway. The fabric of tents billows in fire colors and deep blues and violets.

We unfurl the cloth and rugs, secure estacas into the chill-hardened earth. Some of the Adare court—once they get over their shock that la princesa herself is pitching in—look impressed, as though they thought a court so finely dressed would sit around admiring our fingernails. Some even offer to help, and when any come toward us, Ondina directs them so sweetly they don't realize she's sending them away from Bryna.

The great cats weave through the grass, and the quetzals soar over the castle, green alongside the bright blue of the mariposas' wings.

Candles, floating in the stone fountains, bloom with petals of flame. Our copper trees climb toward the sky, oil running through their hollow centers. Once they're lit, flames burst from their boughs like autumn leaves, warming the air to something a little closer to Eliana.

As my hands work, I plan.

I can't threaten Cade. He may not be the ruling prince, but he's next in line. And Patrick clearly likes him, because we all know what happens to siblings he doesn't like. If Cade wasn't a favorite of Patrick's, he'd be banished to some monastery as far away as whatever convent their older sister supposedly retired to.

So I need a different plan.

Charm before blood. I breathe the words in and out, my father's reminder to think first, fight last. Men have felled kingdoms for their infatuation with a woman. A well-placed smile holds more power than an army.

I can do this. Cade McKenna clearly liked the look of me. Charming him should take less effort than unclasping a necklace.

I help with the back of Ondina's gown. Tonight we'll be wearing dresses given to us as welcome gifts. They could have done worse. Ondina's is as deep as the center of purple pitaya fruit, mine the vivid red of achiote seeds. Ondina just helped Bryna into a gown of true black velvet embroidered with vines and blossoms in gold thread.

"Good of them to ease us into things," Ondina says.

I finish the last fastening. "You mean before tossing McKenna green and O'Loingsigh blue at us?"

"I give it a few days," she says.

As I change into my dress, pain goes through my body. The marigold orange of the tent lining blurs. I double over, bracing on one of the trunks.

Ondina hands me the oil next to my bed.

"Thank you," I say. I rub aceite into my lower back, feeling the warmth of the hierbas sink into me.

"Travel?" Ondina asks as she fastens the back of my dress. "Or a parting gift from your little adventure with Patrick?"

"Both," I say. "But mostly the latter."

Since that performance on horseback, my spine has been more off than usual. It's even worse right now, like pain is running through my blood. I have to stop thinking about it. It feeds off me thinking about it.

"Adelante," I say. "It always takes a little while to work. I'll be along."

Ondina knows me well enough not to ask if I'm sure. Whether my body is making me slower against my will, or I'm pulling back on purpose to sneak into somewhere unnoticed, I'm often falling behind.

I brace against my bed and gather myself. I run through the different signals our guards use and how to give them. Cipactli, for the hopefully unlikely event that any of us spots one of Adare's fabled sea monsters. Xochitl, to signify Bryna, the flower of Eliana. Ocelotl, for anything related to the great cats.

The pain fades but still feels hot. Tomorrow I'll see the curanderas, but for now, I have work to do.

With a new coat of poison on my lips, and a little color on my cheeks, I'm every inch a princesa's lady. I fix my hair, setting it in place with all the knives that will fit.

Appear harmless, my father taught me. *Be deadly.*

I grab my ashwood cane. I grit my teeth through the pain that's starting to feel like part of my skin.

I don't realize until a few minutes later. I don't realize until I'm lost inside the castle and I can't tell if the walls are moving or if they just look like they are.

But in a rush of heat over my back and chest, I know.

It's not my spine.

It's my dress.

The dress I'm wearing is poisoning me.

I reach for the smallest knife in my hair, the one that might spark me back to life, the one with the right remedio inside the hollow blade. But my fingers can't grasp it. I try to pull at the lacings of my dress, but my hands are too numb to loosen them.

An enchantment over a forest.

A poison dress.

I was so sure he hadn't seen me.

I was so sure he didn't recognize me now.

I underestimated him.

I won't make that mistake again.

CHAPTER FOURTEEN

CADE

"He wouldn't listen to me," Nessa says. "He just completely ignored me and went on as if I hadn't said anything."

"I'm so sorry," I say, and I mean it more than Nessa can know. To be Patrick, I thought I had to ignore her or risk revealing too much.

"You can make this right," she says. "You can convince him to listen to me. To everyone."

"You really think I have that kind of sway over my brother?" I ask.

"If you don't, who does?" she asks. "This is getting serious. People are concerned he'll let Lowell take over. Run everything."

"All right," I say. "I'll do what I can."

Nessa nods and turns back toward the hall. I keep going. I need some time away from the festivities.

It's quite early for someone to be completely intoxicated. So when I see the Elianan girl slumped against the stone of the wall and floor in the corridor, I know something is wrong. As I move toward her, I recognize her. The enchantress. Her black hair is styled for the party and her ornate cane is beside her, but she's breathing heavily and her skin is blotched with red, close to the color she's wearing.

"You," she rasps, glaring at me while pulling at her dress. "Get away from me."

She maneuvers out of it, leaving just her underdress. She says something under her breath, and though I'm not sure of the exact translation, I'm fairly sure it's an insult. I don't care. If she dies, the curse could last forever.

"Stay here," I say. "Don't move."

Don't die.

I lean on Faolan as much as I need to as I work up my pace, the closest to running that I can muster these days.

Her blotched skin, bloodshot eyes, and the sound of her breath, like knives scraping stones, make me suspect poison.

Why on earth would someone want to kill Valencia? Did someone else see her that night?

By the time I get to the great hall, my head is spinning and my thighs are burning as much as my lungs. The party is at full pitch. The musicians are playing a lively jig and the middle of the floor is a blur of fabric and hair in various colors.

I still can't find Siobhán, but Patrick and Bryna are impossible to miss. Patrick is clearly enjoying looking at her. His gaze follows the pattern of embroidery that flows over her dress. He's wearing his royal pins in his hair, decorated with some of his gems from our tree room, and the sparkle seems to be drawing Bryna's eyes.

The princess appears to be in excellent form and health, but I still pull Patrick aside as casually as I can.

"Keep a close eye on her," I say.

"Why?" Patrick asks. "Is something wrong?"

"What?" I ask. "As though you'll find watching over her a hardship?"

He glares at me, but goes back to take her hand.

I finally spot Siobhán, wearing a dress with thin twists of black and gold cloth filigree forming the shoulder straps, tracing over the bodice, and then trailing off into the billowing skirt. She's taken to Elianan fashion quickly.

She's also leaning against a pillar, draining the goblet in her hand. My stomach drops.

After taking a deep breath, I make my way around the edges of the crowd, weaving through both friendly and unfamiliar faces. When I reach Siobhán, her face lights up.

"Cade! Where have you been?" She doesn't wait for an answer. "Have you come to dance?"

"I need your help." I try to get her glassy eyes to focus on mine, and I tell her, as quickly and quietly as I can.

"Poison. Excellent," Siobhán says, a bit too loudly. "Just the evening I had in mind."

CHAPTER FIFTEEN

VALENCIA

Voices float through the dark. My eyelids feel heavy as the tent panels.

"You must sleep," I hear Ondina say.

"I can't," Bryna says.

"You've been up all night," Ondina says. "Staring at her and worrying isn't going to help."

"This was all a mistake," Bryna says. "I shouldn't have brought us here."

Good. If I had to be poisoned to turn us back around toward Eliana, I'll take it. We'll go home. Far enough from the ocean that we can't smell the salt of Adare's coastline. We'll get Bryna as far away from the McKenna brothers as our borders will let us.

I fall back under.

CHAPTER SIXTEEN

CADE

Just as I've finished a set of exercises, Patrick sweeps into our hidden chamber. It's back to being like the inside of a tree trunk again—unfinished wooden walls with knots and hollows, all wooden furnishings, lichen and moss on the floors and walls. And as Patrick crosses the threshold, a path of flowers appears in front of him. Blooming vines spread out along the walls.

"You have outdone yourself, brother," I say.

"What do you mean?" he asks.

"The flowers?"

"I'm not doing this," Patrick says. "It's just happening."

I start another set. "If you say so."

"I'm not!"

When I hear the tone of his voice, one that reminds me of when we were young, I reach up to the bar with both hands to pull myself out of my odd position. "It's not an accusation. It's just so obvious."

"I don't mean for any of this to happen."

"Have you ever tried to *make* anything happen?" I ask.

"Our mother's not dead," he says. "We can't inherit power that's still hers."

"She doesn't have all of it," I say. "We've had some since we were born. You may not like that, but you know it. You play the harp, the wall opens. You stop, it closes. You come in here and flowers bloom everywhere." I pull myself up a few more times. "What if you just tried? What's the worst that could happen?"

"Don't you think we should have tried such experiments before a large contingent from Eliana was camped on our grounds?" Patrick asks.

He has a point. Once when I was practicing as a child, I got frustrated that I couldn't change the walls of my chamber to McKenna green and accidentally carpeted a staircase in moss. My mother gave me a long lecture about the potential for unintended consequences when trying to control the castle.

"Just something small," I say, hearing her voice to me then. "Something in here. That's how I started."

"You really think I've never tried that?" Patrick asks. "With all the time I've spent in here alone? I've never so much as changed the color of a stone. I can't control the castle, I can't fight in battle, and I can't figure out which of the advisors to listen to when they don't agree."

I drop from the bar to my feet, favoring my right leg but still allowing my left foot to land, distributing the pressure of my weight back up through my body the way Siobhán taught me.

"You saved my life," I say. "Twice. You could fight, and you *can* rule. You are ruling already." I remove the lacings from my wrists and run my fingers over the calluses that cross my palms, from fighting, training, and using Faolan. "And you can learn to move the castle, to work with it, but it may take you more time."

He appears to be suppressing an eye roll. If he's already in a sour mood, I might as well bring this up now.

"Nessa told me about Lowell taking credit for the victory," I say. "As if he'd led the charge himself."

"He just got overly excited," Patrick says.

"Did you know about that?" I ask. "Did he tell you he was planning it?"

"No," he says. "When I talked with him about it afterward, he said he was just overcome with joy at our success and wanted to celebrate our soldiers."

"Nessa's concerned you'll let Lowell take over ruling. And from what she tells me, she's not the only one."

"Lowell wants to rule," Patrick says. "Neither of us do."

"You can't let him," I say. "He's only out for himself."

"Who isn't?" Patrick says. "Besides, I have worse problems right now."

"Worse than a cousin who wants to take over our home and could easily run it into the ground?" I ask.

"One of the princess's ladies was just poisoned while a guest here," he says. "You think they're not going to blame us for that? I'll be lucky if they don't pull out of negotiations." Patrick looks at me, serious. "If you have such strong views about all of this, why do you not wish to rule? Do you want to go back to the monastery?"

"Those are two quite different questions," I say. "One I don't know the answer to yet, and the other I'd say is obvious." I can't help looking down at my chest.

"I know you're not who they're expecting, but you're still you," Patrick says. "You could tell everyone who you really are."

"And maybe get us both killed in the process," I say without thinking.

Patrick doesn't look shocked, but does look like he's hunting for the right words. I save him the trouble.

"I know there's no law against who I am here," I say, "and I know there are others like me living, presumably happily, in our kingdom. But do you know who they are?"

Patrick thinks for a moment. "No," he says. "Not for certain."

"Exactly," I say. "That's exactly the point. You don't know, and no one else knows but people they really trust. Their closest friends. Maybe a wife or husband. Children if they have any or take any in. They came here as they are now, and no one remembers who they used to be. That's what the monastery is for, at least for some of us. To give us a chance to start a new life and choose a new home. But I didn't choose a new home, just a new life. No one like me has ever ruled Adare. At least not that anyone remembers. They've always been like Mother, or Grandmother, or Deirdre. Or they've been like Father, like you. You can do this, Patrick. It has to be you now. It's not the right time for someone like me."

"Why not?" he asks. "When would the right time be if not now?"

"I don't know," I say. "I wish I did. I just know it's not now. If our parents, their key advisors—if they had thought I could rule someday, they wouldn't have led us here. Boxed us into this story that I'm your bastard half brother. Told us all to lie."

When Patrick says nothing, I try once more.

"Lowell will destroy all the progress our mother made," I say. "And he'll start by making the taxes his personal coffers."

"You're speaking from rumors," Patrick says.

Siobhán bursts in without warning. "What are all the flowers about? Fergus's sisters haven't been in here now too, have they?"

"Of course not," Patrick and I say in near unison.

Siobhán looks at Patrick. "They're waiting for you."

He groans.

"I know." Siobhán adjusts his tartan and the stones in his hair. He looks good, shiny.

"Don't make a prácás out of this," Siobhán says. "Unless you'd like to ride out into battle, of course, because if I have anything to say about it, he's never doing that again."

"I know," Patrick says.

I take a few swallows of Siobhán's herb mixture and salute her with the bottle.

If Patrick can take matters into his own hands, so can I.

CHAPTER SEVENTEEN

VALENCIA

T he next time I wake up I hear Ondina's voice again, in a distinctly louder register. "Like hell he is!"

The moment I remember the poison, I bolt to sitting up, and instantly regret it.

The last time I woke up this miserable was after a visiting duquesa convinced us all to drink iztāc octli and mezcal in the same night. She sold it with one hell of an old wives' tale, some cuento de viejas about how the combination would make us all beautiful at a hundred years old. *The maguey looks green and lively at a century old, so it makes sense, doesn't it?*

The next morning, we were all hiding from the sunlight, decidedly less beautiful than any maguey, and swearing never to listen to her or any other duquesa ever again.

The pain that morning was a throbbing weight in my forehead. Now every vein in my body feels like lightning, ending in a hot ember.

"His Highness only wishes to pledge his dedication in bringing the poisoner to justice." I think I know that voice. The man giving the endless speech next to the cairns—Lowe? Lowen? "And I'm sure he would welcome the chance to say so himself."

A chorus of profanities dances through my head.

No. Patrick McKenna cannot come in here. He cannot see me up close, without my face made up. If he does, chances are uncomfortably high that he'll remember holding me on his horse.

"I don't care what he's prince of," Ondina says. "He's not calling on one of la princesa's ladies when she's in a state of undress."

Ondina is pretty and tall and thin as a hollyhock, but anyone who thinks she's fragile hasn't heard her yell.

The tent panels rustle.

"Drink this." Ondina holds out a cup of what smells like one of her sisters' tonics, all roses and lemons and spice. A little bitter, but easier to swallow than my father's remedios.

She pours some water. "You're the talk of the whole court."

"Just what I need," I say.

"And Patrick"—Ondina sprinkles a few flower petals into what I'm drinking—"he's pledged to stay by Bryna's side as her personal guard until the poisoner is caught. And his brother, after so gallantly coming to your aid, has taken it upon himself to search out your poisoner. How chivalrous they all are."

Perfect. The very boy who poisoned me now looks like a hero for helping me.

If I'm going to stay ahead of Cade McKenna, I need to work faster.

"How much time have you spent around the cortesanos here?" I ask Ondina.

"Enough to know there are as many boring conversationalists in Adare as there are at home," she says. "Why?"

"What do you hear about Cade?" I ask. "He's second in line after Patrick. Does he want to rule?"

"Hardly," Ondina says. "From what I hear, he's happy to be Patrick's henchman."

I'll bet.

"Every McKenna cousin thinks they should be granted a higher position," Ondina says. "They all think they'd do a better job at ruling than Patrick. Except Cade. They say that if you wanted him on the throne, you'd have to tie him to it. He's not interested."

"How do you know all this?" I ask.

Ondina's smile is shy but proud. "You're not the only one who can overhear things."

I bow like a boy, deep and appreciating.

"Muchas gracias." She curtsies, just as theatrically.

So Cade's loyal to Patrick.

That means he could be doing all of this at Patrick's behest.

"It must be nice for Patrick," Ondina says. "To have someone close who doesn't want your throne, but who can do all the things you don't want to do, or that you can't be seen doing."

"Like getting your sister out of the way to clear the path to the throne?" I ask.

"Are they serious?" Ondina says. "That story about a convent? She still had to choose her name."

"What are you talking about?" I ask.

Ondina sighs. "You haven't reviewed your Adare history lately, have you?"

"I'm too busy learning about its present," I say.

"Then it's time for your first lesson," Ondina says.

I press a hand into my lower back. The band of pain just below my waist tells me how restless I was last night. "Can I stretch during the lecture portion?"

"You think I've known you this long and expect you to stay still?" Ondina asks.

I pull my knees into my chest.

"Karlynn's heir should have at least come back to choose her name when she came of age," Ondina says. "It's a tradition that goes back as far as Adare's line of warrior queens."

"And there I'm already lost," I say. "Because why would Patrick think that they'd accept him when he has an older sister?"

"They've had generations of queens in Adare," Ondina says. "But it doesn't mean a king can't rule. Adare's throne, like many, traditionally passed from eldest child to eldest child, regardless of gender. And then we come to a part of Adare's history they don't much care to brag about, because hundreds of years ago, even when they claimed it was eldest child to eldest child, what do you think happened when that eldest child was a daughter?"

I bend one leg over the other. "Her younger brothers and primos thought they should rule instead of a woman?"

"Exacto," Ondina says. "Men deciding they should rule even when there was an eldest daughter. Hence the staff Karlynn had with her in the woods."

I feel my spine easing. "What does the staff have to do with it?"

Ondina shifts her angle so we can still look at each other. "For generations that staff has been passed down only from McKenna woman to McKenna woman. Rumor is it's enchanted, that a very talented bruja crafted it specifically so McKenna men would stop trying to undermine their queens."

"Is it?" I ask. "Enchanted?"

"I don't know," Ondina says. "Maybe. Since that staff came into the family, they've certainly ended up with more queens, so it's enough to frighten brothers and cousins away from interfering. Well, until Patrick."

"No," I say. "I mean, is it enchanted in a way that could help us?"

I sound more hopeful than I want to, and Ondina's face is near pitying. She knows what I'm thinking. If Karlynn sleeps holding an enchanted staff, maybe it could wake her and everyone else. We would just need a way to stir the magic within it, like signaling fireflies.

"Not that I've heard," Ondina says. "It's possible, but I don't think that's the point. I think the rumors about its magic are part of its power. It's meant to declare that McKenna daughters have just as much right to rule as McKenna sons."

"Well, it worked," I say. I know enough about Adare's recent history to know they've come to favor queens.

"Which is why what Patrick is doing is so brazen," Ondina says. "Sin vergüenza. Karlynn is one of the most loved rulers in memory here. Everyone was hopeful about her heir. What did Patrick think, that no one would notice his sister's birthday going by? He may think we're stupid, and that his own people are stupid, but we're not, and they're not. Patrick might as well make a royal announcement that he had her killed or banished. And if he'll do anything to get his own sister out of the way"—Ondina's pacing now—"what might he do to Bryna? It's all roses and azahares between them now, but what if she disagrees with him on something? What if he thinks she's inconvenient?"

"I know," I say, and the words don't come in the clear resonant voice damas are trained to speak in. They're frayed, pulled thin. "Why are we the only ones who see what a bad idea this is?"

"I don't know." Ondina lets out a disbelieving laugh. "I really don't. If he'll interfere with his own family's line of succession, what's sacred to him? If you're a prince, you don't meddle with that, no matter how much you want the throne. Just like if you have any sense, you don't meddle with fairies, no matter how convenient a disguise." She gives me a pointed look.

I try not to let my eyes widen, but I know I look caught.

"Do you think I don't know what you pack in your bolsa?" she asks. "You take your fate into your hands when you open those wings and dress up like las hadas."

"Don't tell me you believe in Adare bedtime stories," I say. "Next you'll be telling me about sailors and sirenas."

"Fairies are in our stories too," she says. "And when they come wanting penance for you impersonating them, I'll be the first to say I warned you."

"What's next?" I ask. "You want me to watch out for sea monsters?"

"Yes, and since we're on the subject of poisonous things from Adare," Ondina says, "please tell me you're going to watch out for Cade McKenna."

"I'll do better than that," I say.

I go back to my father's words, like a torch illuminating the ground in front of me.

Charm before blood. I can't fight Cade. He's twice my size, and besides that he could probably turn me into a hand mirror or a crayfish. I need to get him to negotiate with me.

And to do that, I need something that Cade McKenna wants.

CHAPTER EIGHTEEN

CADE

Nessa guides me to the center of the village, a grassy square that looks more suited to outdoor games than speeches. The river coils around, a shiny blue stripe through the thick grass. Wearing Patrick's tartan, I say a few words in his voice to reassure the village, trying to explain why Lowell took it upon himself to make a victory speech.

But I've barely begun when questions hem me in.

What are you doing to continue your mother's work?

Have you handed over your power to your cousin?

For each question I try to answer, more come. Sharper. Angrier. Worse.

Why have you invited a contingent from Eliana when your own house isn't in order?

How do you know they won't curse you all?

I stop hearing their words. All I can hear is the sound of their voices, the accusation, the anger, the fear.

To them, I have no authority, no place to be speaking as if I know anything. And because I'm currently Patrick, that means Patrick doesn't either. I feel, far more than I usually do, that Patrick and I are both here at once, and that we've both been deemed poor substitutes for our mother. However much trust Adare may have in her, they don't have it in us. And I don't blame them.

When I hear their words again, one question slices through all the others.

Where is your sister?

A loud splash echoes behind me. I turn to see a looming green figure, smooth and shiny. Its head has fins on top and both sides, flapping gently in the air. Its large fins are spread wide along the bulk of its long body. It screeches, showing the blades of its teeth.

For a few moments, I wonder what I've done to suffer this fate despite my allegiance to Saint Marinos. Maybe it was letting things get this far with Patrick and Lowell. Or failing to help Patrick claim the power I can't inherit. Or not stopping Valencia from casting the enchantment. Or not insisting on going with my mother and father that night.

But none of those will be the story told about me. This sea monster will gobble me up in front of a gathered crowd. Before it spits out my bones, everyone will figure out I was impersonating Patrick. And I will forever be the bastard prince who playacted his brother, and was devoured for it. I will become a story of warning, a cautionary bedtime tale.

As I'm bracing for the sea monster's teeth, I hear another loud splash. I open my eyes in time to see it jump back under the water and swim away.

My relief doesn't last.

If I didn't know this was a warning, I would from the way Nessa and everyone else are staring at me. I cannot and do not want to fathom the rumors that will come of this, or how they'll spread quick as sea aster across the salt marshes. I can only hope Patrick is too distracted to hear them.

I need Valencia to break this curse. I need my mother to return and set everything right again. I need her to do what Patrick won't and I can't.

CHAPTER NINETEEN

VALENCIA

Cover my poison burns with as much makeup as it takes.

Straighten the waves out of my hair.

(The best thing about everyone thinking I'm sick? No one will expect me at any of these ridiculous gatherings. They'll all think I'm resting.)

Slick back half my hair.

Flatten my chest with bands of cloth.

Put on a tunic and trousers.

A little paling powder and shadowing powder in the right places, to bring out the angles in my face and to make my eyes and lips look smaller.

Within less time than it takes Ondina to help Bryna from a day gown into a complicated evening dress, I turn myself from Valencia into Gael.

I may not be completely steady on my feet yet, but I'm not missing a chance like this. I need leverage on the one person who can get my father and our king and queen back. And the best leverage I can think of are the only jewels the McKenna men value more than the ones in their trousers.

No better time than now. Not only will everyone expect me to be in bed, they'll be distracted with today's negotiations. If Patrick gets riled up enough, it'll throw the castle into chaos. No one will notice Gael sneaking anywhere.

I can practically hear both my father and the curanderas telling me to slow down, to do this right and prepare. I set hot cloths against my muscles, loosening them enough that I won't tense as much. I rub aceite into my back, getting my body ready to leave my cane. I don't want to, but I do. Using my cane could mark me as Valencia.

Forget el Diablo. Deception is in the details.

I slip as many knives into my hair as it'll hold. Not as many as when I have the complicated hairstyles of a proper dama, but as many as I think will fit. Then one more, to follow my father's first rule. And as I sneak into the castle's inner halls, I'm following his second and third quite admirably, if I do say so myself.

Always be ready to become someone else.

Wait until you have the perfect plan, and you'll never do anything.

As I slip down the stone corridors, the castle rattles, the walls shifting.

Clearly negotiations are going well.

I'm smiling even as I pass the tapestries, which get creepier the farther in I go. Yes, they're beautiful, all deep greens, blues, and golds. Whenever the ache in my back flares down into my leg, I touch the walls to steady myself, and I can see the gleam of the fine embroidery.

But the renderings of the sea and river monsters—with their forked tongues, their tails looking as sharp as swords, their silver teeth—make me shudder. Ondina told me that, years ago, anyone suspected of treason to the crown was sent before them. The great animals would turn their shining, scaled backs on the innocent while eating the guilty in a single bite. A little like how our great cats used to tear any traitor to Eliana limb from limb.

If everyone figures out that Patrick murdered his sister, do we get to watch him be eaten by both sea monster and jaguares?

A boy can dream.

The castle keeps shifting around, stone grinding against stone, river water trickling between walls and over the floor. All I have to do is move, patient and unseen, toward the center of the castle.

I'll worry about Patrick later. Right now, I have another McKenna boy to deal with.

Cade McKenna took our families.

It's time to take some pieces of his.

CHAPTER TWENTY

CADE

I'm on my way to the room set aside for negotiations, moving as quickly as I can while still appearing calm, or so I hope. The castle is wavering, unsettled, as if it isn't sure which hallways to connect to which rooms. I feel fine, so it must be Patrick.

Not that I blame him.

The irony of Patrick negotiating river access in a room decorated with our most impressive tapestries of sea monsters. The Elianans are concerned, and rightfully so, that even the ones in our shared rivers are on our side and will kill any Elianans that get too close. Patrick is surely trying to convince them the monsters will not kill anyone who has done no wrong. I wonder how *that* explanation is going.

I try not to look at the tapestries. The embroidered sea monsters seem to be glaring at me now.

"My good sir," Lowell greets me, bowing low. He must want something.

I bow stiffly, not bothering to really make an effort.

He puts his hand on my arm and turns me away from the door to the negotiation room. My arm muscles tense under his touch, but I don't resist him. His expression changes slightly. He smiles but leans back, looking both impressed and nervous, which I hope means I reminded him how much stronger I am than he is. I could snap him like a twig, and I've often wanted to.

"Have you noticed how troubled your dear brother seems lately?" he asks, his voice hushed, and his face far too close to mine. "I hope you'll support me in my efforts to lighten his burden."

"Support you how?" I ask. "I don't decide these things. You know that."

"No, you don't," Lowell says. "But there's no good reason you should be barred from offering your opinion."

He knows my opinion. My opinion is that every responsibility Lowell already has, he handles badly. Our roads were so much of my mother's work, and from what I hear, the stretches under Lowell's control are already falling into disrepair. There are even rumors that he uses them to seize property at random, and worse.

I grit my teeth. "Just tell me what you want."

Lowell's sly smile, his real smile, creeps across his lips.

As the corner of his mouth rises, I feel the floor beneath me undulate. There's a snap like a fresh sheet flying over a bed or a starched tablecloth being laid.

I land on my knees and right hand. My left hand still grips Faolan tightly, but this was too fast for even him to catch me. His wings are spread and his head is lowered. He was caught as off guard as I was.

My breathing is heavy, likely visibly so.

Lowell smiles down at me. But within a second, he's offering to help me up.

"Clearly you're as tired as your brother," he says. "I've never seen you lose your balance like that."

"Don't you dare touch me," I say.

Faolan seconds me with a quick shriek.

Lowell steps back. Faolan's shrieks have that effect on people.

Faolan and I both relax. I lean into him and he helps me back to my feet.

I hear solid footsteps behind me, followed by Fergus's deep voice.

"Are you all right, sir?" he asks.

"Just lost his balance for a moment," Lowell says. "It must be difficult, living without the battle skills you used to have."

I'd like to show him a few battle skills. Lowell and everyone like him are why so many of our injured soldiers no longer live near the castle. They choose existences away from those who smile while insulting us.

"Sir, we must speak," Fergus says, stepping between Lowell and me.

"Of course," Lowell says.

He turns, takes a few steps, and then turns back.

"Cousin, I do hope you'll reconsider," he says, his eyes finding mine over Fergus's shoulder. "I'm very concerned about your brother."

I watch the edge of his brocade tartan as it disappears into the negotiation room.

"Sir," Fergus says again.

"I appreciate you extricating me from that particular conversation," I say.

"I wish it were of my generosity," Fergus says. "But we need permission to enter the room of the tree. Now."

"Why?" I ask, my nerves already mounting again.

"We think someone might be in there who shouldn't be," he says. "We saw someone slipping between the walls near there while the castle was shifting."

Of course someone would take advantage of the castle's movements. And of course Patrick's lack of understanding about the castle, and his role in it, would land us here.

Or worse, Lowell could be exercising his newfound power.

"I'll take care of this," I tell Fergus.

"Be careful," he says. "From what we saw, his clothes and hair, we think it's a young Elianan boy. Maybe as young as thirteen. He could be a noble family's son they brought along. He could just be poking about. No nefarious intent."

"He seems to be a young boy?" I ask.

Fergus nods.

"Does he move well?" I ask. "Gracefully?"

"Yes," Fergus says.

"I will take care of this," I say. "Right now."

CHAPTER TWENTY-ONE

VALENCIA

In a perfect world, I'd find whichever stones in this massive tree belong to Cade.

But in this world, I just need to steal enough of them that Cade will do anything to get them back.

I climb the boughs, leaves whispering around me. Curls of wood grow from the branches, each ending in a tiny sphere as gleaming and polished as a drop of amber. Some are blue or green, like olivine or emerald. Some are more purple or red, like amethyst or garnet. But they all make their own light, and together they give the tree the effect of being sprinkled with an impossible number of stars.

Each time I ease away a stone, a delicate stem of wood comes with it. Supposedly the wooden stems merge back with the tree when they're returned, so I pull each one away quickly, before the tree can take them back. And I handle them carefully. The stems are sharp as pins, and if I'm not careful, they're going to stick little holes in my palms. Leaving my blood on an enchanted tree seems like a ruinously bad idea.

A knot near my shoulder blade seizes up, a section of muscle that's trying to compensate for muscle lower down. How flexible my lower back is means I can contort myself into strange positions, moving from one branch to the next. I keep my movements gradual, steady.

Maybe I'll recognize the McKenna brothers' stones as soon as I see them. Maybe they'll be white as death, bleached as bones in the sun, stricken by their own ascendientes. Patrick banished his sister, or killed her, or had her killed, so he could reign. Cade cursed our families and his own in the process. How could their own ancestors not denounce them?

The heavy door creaks.

I peer through the leaves.

The silhouette against the door throws me back to the day I met Patrick McKenna. I have the feeling of being not on a tree bough but on an unfamiliar horse, one Patrick pulled me onto.

The noise of wood on stone sounds, the rhythm of a boy walking with a staff. Each strike vibrates through the floor and up the tree trunk, through the boughs, into my body. That, together with the fact that this boy is a lot sloppier-looking than Patrick—messier hair, shirt carelessly tucked in, boots shined in a half-assed way instead of gleaming—tells me exactly who this is.

I stay absolutely still.

"I know you're here," Cade says.

No, I'm not. I most certainly am not.

If I think it hard enough, maybe he'll think it too.

Cade comes close enough to lean a hand against the trunk.

You can leave now, Cade. Nothing to see.

The leaves whisper against one another, even though I'm still.

Pain shimmers across my body. Why does it feel like it's gathering in my hands?

Then I feel it for sure, the stones searing my palm. I open my hands, and they look coated in frost, so cold they're burning me. They're leaving tiny rounds of frostbite on my hands. Like they know I'm a thief.

The owl head of Cade's staff pokes up through the leaves.

I grip the bough I'm on harder and wrap the frozen pieces into the folds of my pockets. Even through the cloth, they send needles of cold into me. I wish I wasn't a boy right now. If I were dressed as a girl, I could tear away layers of my skirt and wrap them around that piercing cold.

Every time Cade shoves that stupid owl up here, I scramble away. Each time I skitter onto another branch, I get a face full of leaves studded with another set of gems. Caray. How many McKennas have there been?

That serious, slightly pissed-off-looking owl bobs up and down through the foliage.

Why do I always have fewer knives when I'm a boy? I do my best, slipping them in like pins, but the hairstyle that makes me look most like a boy just doesn't hide as many.

That owl head pokes up through the leaves again. I scramble out of the way. Another face full of leaves. Another constellation of stones growing from curls of wood.

But the ones that are less than a hand's width from my face are different. They flash from one color to the next—green, blue, deep red, violet, white—like certain stars in winter.

I don't know whose they are, but they look important, worth the potential frost burns. I take them and slip them into another pocket.

"If you come down now, I might not kill you," Cade says.

I wonder how many people have fallen for that line.

I have seven knives and no desire to fight this boy. He's about twice my size, I don't have my bastón, he has his, and I saw him curse an entire forest.

A rope of pain goes through my spine. If I weren't in a tree that rustles every time I move, I could shift my weight. But thanks to the branches and leaves, he can hear everything I do.

Seven knives.

All I have to do is get out of here, lose him, and change back into Valencia. The faster I can get to the door and start running, the better. As long as I have to stay still, he has the advantage. My bones and muscles declare this. Loudly.

When you live with pain, you learn to block it out, to distract your brain and body. I run through the guards' signals. Rain. Rabbit. Wind. Deer. I try to guess which luminous foxes might be the parents of which kits I've seen this season.

But that doesn't mean the pain's not there. Even if I manage to ignore it, it affects my aim, my speed. I'll have to concentrate to make up for how it's throwing me off.

Cade goes back toward the door.

Something about how he's moving catches me. Suddenly, the loudest thing in my brain isn't the pain in my back. It's the thrill I get when I notice something I can use.

The official information on Cade McKenna says he injured his back falling off a horse in battle. But the uneven way he's walking, the tentative way he puts his weight down, tells me he's lying about where he's injured. He may have fallen off a horse. And his back may be a problem for him. But it's not the only problem.

He's most hesitant about and most protective of his left knee.

But why lie about that? He'd need his staff either way.

I slip a knife from my hair. Even the small motion makes a new bolt of pain shriek through me. I hold the noise I want to make, the profanities I want to yell, at the back of my throat.

I aim for his arm. Like I should have the night I first saw him.

I check my grip, and my line.

The moment I let the blade fly, I sense the shift in Cade. He can feel that I'm striking, and steps out of the way.

The knife hits the floor, wedging in the border between two stones.

I pull another knife from my hair and throw. Fast.

He moves just enough that it goes into his staff.

Carajo. What kind of brujo is this boy? He curses forests. He poisons dresses. And even though he's twice my size, he's outmaneuvering me.

Everything I learn about him makes me like him less.

Cade looks at the staff, then pulls out the knife. He pockets it and says, "You know it's cowardly to throw blades from corners."

Not as cowardly as what you did.

I hold the next knife, and I'm back in that forest, on that night. I throw again like I can stop everything that happened. I throw it like I can do that night over.

This one lands, getting him in the back of his shoulder.

The blade goes in. It sticks out from him like it did with the staff.

He just looks over his shoulder. "Huh," he says, like he's only now noticing the knife, like he didn't even feel it. He pulls it out.

Living with pain written into your body changes how you react to it. I've been bitten by a snake and just sat there, silent, through the remedio. Considering what I know about Cade, about the battles he fought in, about how he moves, he has a higher pain tolerance than I do.

I understand this. But that doesn't mean it doesn't terrify me. He just drew one of my knives away as though brushing a pine needle from his shirt.

I shift position, inhale, and breathe out as I throw my fourth and fifth knives.

Even with my spine protesting, I find my aim, the humming sense of feeling a knife's path before I let it go. Both get him in the chest.

He hardly reacts. This is more than pain tolerance. The blades barely penetrate. What does he have under there? Are all Adare guards wearing some kind of castle-specific protective gear? Some lighter version of what they wear into battle?

Cade pulls the knives out. "You're just giving these away now."

I pause. I need to get one of his forearms, his hands, something that'll throw him off enough that I can get out of here.

I slip my second-to-last knife out of my hair and aim. Maybe I can't go back to that night and stop him, but I can land a blade in him now.

It sails right by his wrist and lands in the door. But it doesn't rattle him like I thought it would. He just looks at the blade like it's something interesting, a conversation piece.

My lower back feels as brittle as dried-out wood.

Cade pulls my sixth knife out of the door. It goes into his pocket with the rest of them. I swear he's enjoying this.

I cannot let him catch me. If he heard a good enough description of the boy assassin to recognize me, he'll bring me to Patrick, and if I'm dressed like this, like Gael, Patrick will know exactly who I am. Even if Patrick doesn't, who knows what Cade will do with me? I saw what he did to his own mother, and I can't exactly argue with Ondina's theories about what he probably did to his own half sister.

I hold the last knife in my hand.

Cade keeps a hand on the door and shuts his eyes. This is it, the perfect chance to throw.

Except for the way he has his head bowed.

Is he . . . praying?

No. He can't be praying right now.

Everyone from my father to my ancestors to los santos, to, oh, you know, God, might object to me throwing a knife at a praying man. They'd never bless my aim. The blade would never land.

Or is there some loophole for boys who curse forests and their own families?

The door disappears.

It's just gone, with stone in its place.

Did he really do that? And did I really just think he was praying when he was actually talking to this possessed castle?

I'm not waiting for him to open his eyes.

The moment I let the last knife fly, Cade opens his eyes. The knife rushes alongside his head.

He leans his weight on the door, and I know from his posture that I have him. I may be out of knives, but he's afraid. I can tell from his breathing.

He comes closer to the tree. I can see the effort he's putting into his posture. He wants this to seem threatening, like he's challenging me. But I know he wants to be able to hear me better.

"Now that you can't leave"—Cade twirls one of my knives between his fingers—"you might as well come down."

Maybe there's no door, no path out of this room. But the moment you stop thinking of new options is the moment you die.

And I know my best option right now.

Give Cade McKenna exactly what he thinks he wants.

CHAPTER TWENTY-TWO

CADE

I hear Gael drop out of the tree a moment too late, and he's on my back, landing as forcefully as possible.

"That's not exactly what I had in mind," I say.

I feel him pressing down, and my knees begin to buckle. I brace, leaning on Faolan.

I reach up to Gael's left arm with my own, holding on tight. Instead of fighting the force of him pressing down on me, I follow it. I bend lower, quickly enough that I send him over my shoulder. Then he's on the ground, gasping.

I'm about to grab him and restrain him. But he grabs a long branch that fell out of the tree along with him. When he uses it to try to sweep my legs out from under me, I pin the branch under my left foot.

"I can see how you almost got away from my brother," I say.

"I *did* get away from your brother," he says.

Gael isn't letting go. So I get Faolan under his right arm and push him away from me. I change my grip. I hold the part I use when I'm holding Faolan as I would a cane.

Gael goes along with the momentum and gets to his feet. I get to mine too.

"Did he send you to finish his work?" Gael asks.

"More or less," I say. I need to choose what I do next carefully. I could kill him, oath aside, but he's much more use to me alive than dead.

I swing Faolan at his hip, but he spins backward out of my reach. He's behind me now, and he gets the branch against my throat. I work my left arm up enough to grip the branch, and I push down as hard as I can. I'm stronger than Gael, but he is stronger than he looks. He doesn't let go.

"And what other work has he had you finish?" Gael asks.

In a split second, he changes his grip, and the branch is across my chest and under my left knee.

"A lot," I say. "Why do you ask?"

Before Gael can pull me into him any tighter, I turn toward the branch, leaning heavily on Faolan, and switch my footing. Putting my full weight on my left leg is always dangerous, but I have no choice.

"Is this what you wanted all along?" I ask. "To get into our tree room?"

I push Faolan into Gael, but he barely flinches.

My left knee won't hold me much longer, and Gael has my right pinned against him.

I let myself fall on Gael, my full weight on him as we go down. I can even make use of the fact that he still has my right knee pinned against him. I push the branch into his left shoulder, just under his collarbone.

Gael thrusts part of the branch at my left thigh, and I pull back a bit, instinctively protecting that knee. The hesitation is just enough to allow Gael to roll me off him.

"If you can find what I've taken, you can have it," he says.

I wonder where he's hiding them, and how their searing cold isn't tearing through whatever he's put them in. I can feel the temperature in the room dropping, the tree's protective instincts kicking in. Soon those stones will be cold enough to put frostbite on fingers through anything but battle gloves.

A loud crackling, like a fire made with sap-soaked wood, catches both of our attention. I know even before I look that the door to the room has returned. It flickers in and out for a few moments, and then stays. I've gotten tired, and all my focus has gone into the fight. I couldn't hold the door away anymore. But I'm getting to know how Gael moves, and I think I can get him to react the way I want him to.

I charge at him with Faolan, trying to make it seem as though I am forcing him straight back when I really want him to turn. He does, right into the tree. The tree moves, cracking as it stretches. It pulls the branch away from Gael, reabsorbing it.

I use Gael's moment of confusion to pin him against the tree with Faolan and my own weight. Even caught off guard, Gael is fast, and pushes back against Faolan, his hands in fists.

"I may be smaller than you," he says. "But I bet you'll get tired before I do."

As I'm pushing Faolan into his chest, he tries to kick me with his left leg.

"I have plenty of fight left in me," I say.

I grab his thigh.

"You'll need more than you have," he says.

We both look into each other's eyes. I feel him breathing, and I know he can feel me breathing.

I'm certain I see the spark flash across his face, making him blink and hold his breath.

"I intend to surprise you," I say.

The floor underneath my feet suddenly feels much colder. I can see both Gael's breath and my own.

The ground has turned to a layer of ice. Gael sees it too.

He pushes off the tree with his right foot, sending himself over my shoulder and down my back. When he drops to the floor again, he slides on his hip all the way to the door.

Even with Faolan, it's difficult to keep my balance on the slick stone. I switch my hand position to one that allows me to lean on the extended part of the grip, holding Faolan like a cane again. But by the time I get to the door, Gael is nowhere to be seen.

I don't go after him. I get to the negotiation room. I enter quietly, but I needn't have bothered. Everyone is yelling at one another. Elianans at Adarans and vice versa, but even more disturbingly, Adarans and Elianans yelling among themselves.

I spot Fergus and beckon him out of the room.

In the hall, where it's quieter, I tell him, "There's an Elianan assassin on the loose in the castle."

"I'll pull in everyone I can," Fergus says.

Fergus clears his throat and gestures with his chin a bit behind me. I turn and see Patrick, just standing there.

"Good Lord, brother," I say. "Does no one miss you in there?"

"I doubt it," Patrick says. "I gave up my own yelling, but all of them are still going. What are you two whispering about so urgently?"

"We needn't trouble you with it," I say.

Patrick stands there staring at us.

"You're not going to like this," I say.

"I wouldn't expect to."

I tell him.

Patrick's eyes flare. "Their princess must answer for this," he says, his voice deep. "She swore that boy would never leave Eliana again."

Patrick turns and bursts back into the negotiation room. I hear him yell "Silence!" in his most powerful voice before the doors slam shut.

I lean against the castle wall.

"This can't possibly go well," Fergus says.

He's right. The negotiations are about to end. Badly. The Elianans will gather around Bryna to defend her against all of us, here in our home, or they will all march out of our kingdom insulted. Either way, the war will go on, with no end in sight. Either way, Patrick was right.

This was all a terrible idea.

CHAPTER TWENTY-THREE

VALENCIA

I run, with those points of searing cold needling into me. I run, send-ing my gratitude toward the sky that after crouching in that tree, my body can still run right now. My back and my lungs feel like fabric rip-ping apart, but I make it out of the castle and to the edge of our camp.

I've got to turn back into Valencia, fast. Half the Adare royal guard must be looking for Gael.

Unfortunately for me, the tent I share with Ondina is nearly in the middle of the courtyard. I can see the red edging through the trees I'm hiding behind, and there are dozens of eyes ready to spot me. I may be good at hiding, but I'm not stupid enough to think a strange boy can sneak into damas' quarters without attracting attention.

And now that both Patrick and Cade have met Gael, I've effectively burned this disguise for the time I'm in Adare.

Too bad. I think Cade likes me. Gael-me, not Valencia-me. I felt it from the way he had me against that tree, how he was holding my thigh, like he was hesitating about his grip. And I saw it in his face. Whenever I find a look like that, I can use it against someone. But Gael's not using anything against anyone for a while. He's getting packed away along with my trousers and shirts until we get back to Eliana.

Between the trees, I spot the wardrobe tent. Inside, it's crowded with gowns we brought and the dresses the most prominent families in Adare have given la princesa and her damas. Ones the blues and greens of the nearby sea, the rich grays of the coastal cliffs, the bright colors of the flowers in Eliana. Right now, I'd wear a gown of McKenna green itself. If I can throw on a dress, I'll swoon all the way back to our tent. I can count on Ondina to take my cue and make a big show of it. *Valencia, you're ill, what are you doing out of bed? You can't just wander about! You must rest!*

"Gael!"

The voice that calls my name chills every knob on my spine.

I know that voice.

I grew up with that voice.

I serve that voice.

And that voice sounds exceedingly pissed.

"Gael Palma!" Bryna calls out.

She just invented a last name for me.

Whatever she's doing, she has a plan, and I have to trust her.

"Show yourself," she says.

Now I see her. She stands in the middle of the courtyard, the dyed cloth of tent flaps fluttering around her. The wind ruffles her skirt like it's made of the sea, and everyone stares.

"Do you defy your future queen?" she yells into the air.

I have to obey her. I have no choice. Thanks to me, the entire Adare court thinks she brought a boy assassin along. If I don't go out there, I'm making her look even worse.

I breathe out, ready as I'll ever be for half the Elianan court to see me as Gael. I stand up as straight as I can, trying to look like I don't want, don't need, would never use a cane. Any hint of a problem with my back could connect Gael to Valencia.

Spine as upright as I can make it, shoulders squared, I walk out of the tree cover like the man I'm still too young to pass for. I probably come off as exactly what I am, a boy trying to look like a man, but I'll take it.

Adare guards come toward me.

Bryna lifts a staying hand.

They all freeze. Even though she's not their princess, they hold where they are. Bryna's anger has that effect on people.

I face my future queen, her dress billowing around her in the colors of fire. Curls of gilded embroidery catch the light like embers.

"Kneel," she says, the word sharp.

Half the faces watching—including a number from the Adare court who've come out to see the show—wince. They probably think she's trying to frighten me, to lord her power over me. *He's a child*, they're probably thinking. *Is this necessary?*

What they don't know is she's doing me a favor. I won't last long kneeling, but it's better than standing, and she knows it.

I kneel.

"I sent you back to your family," she says. Her rage pushes her words across the courtyard, a hard wind in a sail. "And he spared your life"—she looks toward Patrick—"and you've squandered both his mercy and mine."

The light makes the edges of her dark hair brilliant red, the brightest autumn leaves.

She goes on about my crimes, my sins. It's all for show. I have to trust her. She will get me out of this.

I can practically hear the sound of her thoughts, like the slight noise of her moving a fire-opal chess piece into checkmate. I thought, when we began playing together as children, that I'd have to let her win or risk her parents' wrath and my father's post.

116

But I never had to. I couldn't have won if I'd tried.

A low growling pulls my attention.

I know better than to disrespect Bryna by looking away while she speaks. But as the growling gets louder, shades of orange fill my peripheral vision.

A flank of great cats stalks into the courtyard. I place each one—the muscled shoulders of a full-grown jaguar, a maracayá and jaguarundi who are both little bigger than house cats, an ocelot with eyes shining like blown glass.

The Adare court scrambles backward.

Really? All their tapestries about knife-toothed sea monsters and they're afraid of our cats?

"For your treachery," Bryna declares to me and to everyone, "you are forbidden ever again to approach this land. Your own ancestors will chase you from it"—the great cats come closer, baring their teeth— "and should you ever come near Adare or its people again, they will have your life for it."

She can't mean this. No one faces the judgment of the great cats unless they're suspected of the worst deception, the most ruthless acts. And it's been years since it's happened at all. I only know how it works because of stories about them leaping from the tapestries, standing in front of the innocent to protect them, tearing the guilty to pieces.

Our ascendientes know about the sleeping enchantment. They can't run me out of Adare just when I've found the boy who did it. They can't expect me to leave Bryna and Ondina here with the McKenna brothers.

Even the Adare cortesanos look horrified.

I try to catch Bryna's eye, looking for the tiniest shift in her expression, however she wants to say *trust me*.

But her impassive face regards me as though I'm a sea's depth beneath her.

Bryna shakes her head. "May el cielo have mercy on you."

The cats' growls sharpen. They shift their weight backward, readying to lunge at me.

And I do the same foolish thing as anyone who's ever faced their scorn.

I run.

CHAPTER TWENTY-FOUR

CADE

W hen I find Patrick, he greets me with a very different impression of Bryna's actions than I have.

"Did you see how commanding she was?" Patrick asks.

He doesn't even seem to realize that the terrain under our feet is different than it was a day or so ago. More uneven. Some of the Elianan tents look lopsided. I've rarely seen the castle's changes have an effect this far from its walls. I wonder if Patrick is causing this or if I am.

"How she looked with those majestic cats on either side of her?" Patrick asks. "How deep and powerful her voice was as she read that assassin his crimes?"

How can Patrick be so happy?

I'm terrified. I was sure this would change his mind about the princess, but it seems I was entirely wrong. Bryna just ordered Gael into exile, on pain of death by ancestor, a form of punishment they haven't used in decades, maybe even centuries. It was nearly the equivalent of Patrick ordering the sea monsters to dispatch someone the way they did in ancient times.

If our tales are to be believed, the sea monsters were once Adare's judge, jury, and executioner. People suspected of crimes were sent to face these supposedly infallible, all-knowing animals. If the person was guilty, the sea monsters would rear and hiss at them before they struck. If the person was innocent, they would bow their heads in apology for frightening them. When one burst from the river to loom over me, it was as clear a warning as a sign from the sky.

"Wasn't the princess stunning?" Patrick asks.

The metallic taste in my mouth intensifies. I cannot have this conversation with Patrick. Not that he needs me for it. He goes on about their plans for the day without waiting for me to answer.

I make my way to my chamber. As I touch the precise stones that will open the wall, I wonder if Patrick is still talking to himself, extolling Bryna's virtues.

The wall doesn't give. I hear a sound like a lock catching, and it stays solid.

I try again. I touch the exact place on the wall I did last time, the exact place I've touched every time I need to open the wall to my room.

The rocks flash blue, like light glancing off ice, but then back to gray before I can touch the next stone in the pattern.

That's when I know exactly who to thank for this.

I run through the progression again, faster this time. But I get it wrong, and the wall flashes green, as though making a point of how wrong I've gotten it.

She's doing this. I know it.

I take a moment to breathe before trying another time.

I touch the stone that tints the wall blue, then the next, and it shifts purple. The next, and it tints dark green. The rocks edge apart.

Nothing in the space looks different. Nothing disturbed. If I had to say by instinct, she hasn't even been in here. But the relief barely touches me before my unease shoves it aside. Patrick and I have so little hold of the castle that an enchantress from Eliana can disturb its magic.

She's trying to unsettle me. And it's working.

CHAPTER TWENTY-FIVE

VALENCIA

The sting of running flames through my lungs and out through my body. Pain cracks up through my leg and into my back. It trips me, and I stumble over a root, landing in the underbrush.

The cold of the stolen stones bites into me.

I can hear the great cats gaining on me. I get to my hands and knees, trying to show them that I'm still running away, that they don't need to tear me to pieces. But before I can get my breath back enough to yell *I'm leaving, I'm going,* they've caught up with me.

The first cat is on me. I shut my eyes and brace for teeth tearing into me.

But the sensation that comes next isn't teeth. It's a wet, rough grain.

The cat isn't biting me.

The cat—I'm just opening my eyes enough to see the jaguarundi— is licking me.

The maracayá joins the jaguarundi, nuzzling into my hair. Then I hear the ocelot's purrs, louder than the blood rushing through my brain.

The jaguar's shadow deepens the tree shade. She stands over us, looking weary and disapproving, as though the four of us are tiresome kittens.

From my viewpoint she's upside down, and I should probably get up to pay my respects, but the three smaller cats are still crawling on me, purring against my hair and licking my poison burns like they're wounds that need tending.

A familiar laugh glides through the trees, followed by an even more familiar voice.

"You should have seen your face," Bryna says.

"Glad I could amuse you," I say.

She slides down from her horse. The coral of her skirt flows down the mare's flank like the veil of a waterfall. It slips alongside a bright yellow riding cape, draped over the point of the horse's hip.

Bryna strokes the mare's mane and crest and then draws her riding cape down toward her. She murmurs something to the horse in a gentle voice. The mare goes off toward a clearing to graze, tail flicking.

Bryna turns to me. "You didn't really think I meant it, did you?"

"Well," I say. "Yes."

"You're your father's child." She tosses a cane toward me.

I catch it. The cats don't flinch.

"Neither I nor them"—Bryna nods reverently to the ascendientes—"expect you to stay away from an enemy kingdom."

I plant my cane, my body easing with the familiar comfort of having one more point to root against the ground. It's one Bryna gave me, rosewood, with a bloom carved at the top, the petals edged in gilt.

"Here's the problem, though," Bryna says. "The entire purpose in us being here is so we can cease to be enemy kingdoms. And you're truly not helping. What were you doing?"

"Learning about the McKenna family," I say. "I thought you wanted me to take an interest in Adare history."

Her stare burrows into me.

Fast as a flinch, I try to work out how to lie without lying. If I lie too much, she'll know. The trick with someone who knows me as well as Bryna is to make sure I only lie a little.

"I was trying to figure out something about the curse," I say.

"Not this again," she says.

"I know what I saw that night," I say.

"You know you saw someone from Adare, maybe, possibly, out there, that night," she says. "It doesn't mean he was to blame. By the same logic, an entire village could have seen you out there and everyone could have blamed you. It was the most impressive heights of stupidity that you chose to go out there that night—"

"You thought you should be there too," I say.

"The difference is my parents told me to stay at el palacio and I did," she says. "Your father told you to stay and you followed him. Thank your stars no one saw you and recognized you, or you might have had two kingdoms declaring you a bruja mala."

This is exactly why I haven't told her about recognizing Cade. She didn't believe me that the boy I saw cast the enchantment. Neither did los astrónomos, who looked at me as though I was a troublemaker and a liar, or las brujas, who nodded with gentle patience as though I was insisting a nightmare was real. *I believe that you believe it, mija.*

Bryna looks at me, considering.

"What is it?" I ask.

"How did you cover the poison burns so well?"

"Makeup can do a lot more than make a girl look flushed and flirtatious," I say. "You know that."

"You do make a handsome boy," she says, objective as though observing a painting.

The part of me that is Gael lights up, like the flame leaves blooming on the fire trees.

I raise an eyebrow. "Interested?"

She smiles. "You're not my type."

"Who is then?" I ask. "Patrick?"

"Perhaps you should try getting to know him," Bryna says. "Instead of you and his brother throwing each other into walls."

"I think if he sees me now, he'll ask the sea monsters to do what our ascendientes didn't." I give a reverent nod toward the great cats.

"No, he won't," Bryna says. "Wash your face. The stream's just over there."

"Full of sea monsters, no doubt?" I ask.

"Oh, very funny." She throws her yellow riding cape at me. It spreads out between us, unfurling in a great flag of gold.

Not a riding cape.

I grab it out of the air to catch it.

Them. It's not one piece of fabric. It's a dress, a shirt in the same fabric, and a pair of dark trousers.

"Am I meant to wear all of these at once?" I ask.

"No." Bryna sounds hesitant. "I just wanted to give you a choice."

This is it. This is my opening. This is when I could tell her that Gael is as much a part of me as Valencia.

But I'm the gallina who couldn't even work up the nerve to tell my own father.

When I get her mother and father back. When I get Cade to wake everyone up. That's when I'll tell her. That's when I'll tell my father. I just need to set things right, to fix what I didn't stop that night, and then there'll be space for Gael.

"Both yellow?" I ask, holding up the shirt and the dress. It's a shade that looks as awful on me as it does luminous on Bryna and Ondina. The one thing I did right the night I met Patrick McKenna was lose the dress I was wearing and now Bryna's gotten me an even brighter replacement. With a shirt too, so Gael can look as awful in this color as Valencia does.

"After what you just did," she says, "you'll wear any color palette I ask."

I go to the water and come back with my face damp, the gold and orange of the skirt fanning out around me.

I present myself with a gesture of my hands that's more Gael than Valencia. I catch myself, startle, pretend it never happened.

"Me parezco a un huevo frito," I say.

"Then you are the most fetching fried egg ever known," she says.

"Oh, muchas gracias," I grumble.

"Truly," she says. "The poets will sing of nothing else."

"I'm glad you're enjoying this." I bend down to pet the maracayá, who's rubbing her face against my leg. "You didn't by any chance bring—"

Bryna tosses me agua de rosas, cheek powder, crushed-raspberry blush that shows up on the brown of my skin.

"Of course I did," she says. "Do you think I've learned nothing being your friend?"

She even hands me the vial of poison she pretends not to know is poison, the dye that doesn't do anything to me except deepen my lips to a plum red.

All the things that make me look more like a love-flushed girl than a well-trained centzontleh.

Appear harmless. Be deadly.

CHAPTER TWENTY-SIX

CADE

"Yes, just like that," Lowell says. "Steady, even, consistent."

I watch as Lowell encourages Patrick and as the wall in front of them changes from deep gray stone to golden polished wood. The transformation is a bit tentative and doesn't look like it will hold. But it's the most I've ever seen Patrick do.

A new strand of rage coils in my chest. This one is different, worse than when Lowell moved the floor under my feet.

Lowell has no right to teach Patrick this. He has no right to teach Patrick anything. He's not our mother, who felt the castle as closely as if its rock and her bones were the same. He's not our father, who could do what neither my mother nor I could do, whose words always met Patrick where he was.

But I can't say any of this aloud. Especially about our father, who, as far as Lowell or anyone else knows, isn't my father.

"What's going on?" I ask.

As soon as Patrick turns to me, the wall changes back to stone.

I expect Patrick to look caught. But he looks proud, even defiant.

"I hope you don't object," Lowell says, and the look he gives me says what we both know, that it doesn't matter if I do.

I leave before I say anything I'll regret or Lowell can use. If I do what I want to do to him right now, he'll have everything he needs to declare me a bad influence on Patrick.

Outside, as the dawn light shifts from pink and orange to yellow, the differences in the castle are stark, glaring, frightening. Our gardens have expanded to include the Elianan encampment, our lichen-covered stone walls and patches of overgrowth springing up among their orderly tents and fire pillars.

Our colors and theirs blend together. I can no longer tell the difference between the purple of our morning glories and the purple of their tapestries, the orange of our clay dirt and the orange of their striped cats, the green of our vines and the green wings of their quetzals. This is certainly not my doing.

It could be Patrick's, however unwittingly, his feelings for Bryna blooming like the flowers that seem to follow him everywhere now. This could all be his desire for her, our worlds growing together as he wants to grow closer to her.

Or it could be something far worse.

I can't help but wonder what Lowell might gain from all this, the appearance that Adare is opening itself to Eliana's influence. And I can't help but wonder if I was too quick to blame Valencia for my trouble getting into my chamber.

Lowell is gaining power, which means we are losing it.

There's only so much castle to care for, my mother used to say, like it was a good thing. She was telling me that I could handle it. I could learn more, grow stronger. But if there's only so much castle, and Lowell can control some of it already, there's less for Patrick and me. And I know how Lowell works.

Once he has some, he'll strive for more.

CHAPTER TWENTY-SEVEN

VALENCIA

I slide away the knots of wood in my bedframe, revealing one hollow at a time. Thank los santos for Eliana's royal carpenters. Cade could turn over this entire tent and find nothing.

Holding each McKenna jewel by the stem, and not by its blazingly cold point, I slip them into the hollows and slide each knot back into place. In those dark niches, they look like stars made of ice.

Once Cade realizes they're gone, he'll think Gael stole them.

And I'll sweep in, the girl who can get them back from the boy assassin.

For a price.

I leave the tent, making a point to look tired and fever worn. Every dama I pass greets me with well wishes. *How lovely to see you on your feet again. Pobrecita. So good to see your color coming back. How awful that was, but how beautiful you look now, mija.*

Every smile I have to give tastes sour. Not because I mind any dama more than any other, but because the castle seems to be enveloping the courtyard, and our tents with it. A low stone wall, greened with moss and lichen, appears to be growing out of the ground. Adare lilacs blossom alongside pitaya, the cups of the blooms fringed with ray-like leaves. Flowering vines snake between the rocks, interspersed with the kind of salt grasses that grow along Adare's shores. Stone fountains push up through the earth between fire trees. They look a little like our fountains back home, scrolled and elaborately carved, except in the deep gray rock of Adare instead of our blushed stone. There are flashes of silver and pale blue in the water, the flitting of little fish that stop the mosquitoes from taking over. And worse—how is this getting worse the longer I look?—young willow grows alongside ahuehuete, the trees that anchor our floating gardens.

I sculpt my face into my best impression of a smile. I am a pleasant, well-behaved dama, fresh from sleeping off a fever, ready for the task at hand.

If the Adare court was surprised to see Elianan ladies help with staking tents, I wonder what they think about seeing everyone—even our own princesa—grind masa in the courtyard. I can't wait until they see us dredging fibrous plants from the floating gardens. Back home, Bryna had no hesitation about rolling up her sleeves, pinning up her skirt, and wading right in. She'd displayed her mud-covered hands to her suitors, offering, by way of explanation, that the plants could be used for their fibers but would choke the canals if we didn't clear them. But I know she relished the horror on their faces.

We all get on our knees in front of stone metates, and Bryna runs the mano over the corn with the same determination she brings to negotiations. Elianan queens take as much pride in their calluses as they do their jewels. Preparing the masa is the one shared task that not even the richest families would pay someone else to do. To anyone who touches my hands during a dance, I'm simply another dama with a set of well-earned calluses.

The rhythm of our talk spurs our rolling the mano over the corn.

We speculate about who's making a certain seamstress blush. A dreamy-eyed cook tells us she knows what phase of the moon her baby will be born under. The ingenieros who tend the fire trees tell us how they build them to work without setting fire to anything other than the oil, how they turn the flames purple as Bryna's jewels or gold as cempaxochitl.

I kneel alongside the other ladies and take hold of a stone mano. And when they speak in scandalized tones of that boy, I ask, "What boy?" as though I've never heard of Gael Palma.

CHAPTER TWENTY-EIGHT

CADE

Even as the chapel door closes behind me, I say one more prayer that either our ancestors will keep the castle in line, or God will help Patrick and me do it. I try not to ask too much of God at once, and I've been asking a lot lately.

I hear voices down the corridor and see a flash of skirt around a corner. My cousin Rhys is at it again. I can see him advancing, leading with his hips. I can't see the woman, only the edge of her dress. The skirt echoes both the color and shape of mallow flowers.

I hear him say, "Doesn't matter to me, as long as you can still kneel."

Something long, thin, and shiny hits Rhys squarely between his legs. Hard. He groans and crumples to his knees. I stifle a laugh. Serves him right.

I see the woman more clearly now. She's facing away from me, her free arm extended to balance the one knocking out Rhys's magairlí. Her dress exposes part of her olive back, which looks both soft and muscular, as do her arms. Her dark hair is piled on her head and adorned with jeweled combs. Valencia.

I hear her say, "¡Mire! So can you," in a biting tone.

I'm nearly even with them now.

"Do allow me to interrupt," I say. "I apologize on behalf of my brutish cousin, who I believe may be unable to do so for himself at the moment." I glare at Rhys, who is still on the floor. "May I escort you to your destination?"

"How kind," Valencia says, but her expression is difficult to read. I'll just work on being extra charming.

We begin making our way toward the hall, leaving Rhys to hopefully learn his lesson. Although he's perhaps the least likely among my cousins to do so.

"I'm glad to see you feeling well enough to join us this evening," I say, using the voice I normally reserve for seduction.

"Thank you," she says. "For how you helped me. I'm sorry I was so rude to you."

"You needn't apologize," I say. "Pain often makes us say things we regret."

Her fingers almost touch the deeper burns that reach up from the neckline of her dress toward her shoulders.

"You don't need to hide them," I say.

"Some of them might scar," she says. "So I'd better get used to them."

"Scars aren't a bad thing," I say. I run through my mental list of which scars belong to Patrick and which belong to me, and which of mine would most impress a princess's lady who also happens to be an enchantress. I finally land on one that wraps around my forearm and show it to Valencia.

"I got this one in a practice duel with my brother," I say.

"You're a man," she says. "And a soldier. It's different."

There's no trace of lust or admiration in her voice or manner. I hope Rhys didn't sour her on the whole McKenna family.

As soon as she sees the princess in the hall, she's off.

Patrick is in his element. He's gesturing at various features of the castle: the sparkling lights, the indoor flowering vines. He shares pieces of Adare history. He laughs at Elianans' jokes at just the right volume and tone.

I, on the other hand, am already tired, and feel even more exhausted when I think about how many hours stand between me and my bed.

Suddenly there's a goblet in my hand. Siobhán's delicate fingers are still gripping the top of it. "Drink this already, will you? You look like someone stole your favorite sheep."

"What is it?" I ask. It smells deep and flowery.

"Haven't a clue," she says. "Apparently it's an Elianan delicacy. Patrick has had three and is more sparkling than ever. And I've had four and I'm not the slightest bit drunk. So, whatever it is, you'll be fine."

I take a tentative swallow. The dark brown liquid is thicker than I expected and has a strong aftertaste. It's rich and spicy, and tastes like the orange blossoms I've smelled in Eliana.

"Now go dance with someone and stop drawing attention to your attention," Siobhán says. "You can't guard Patrick all the time."

"I thought you wanted me off my feet," I say.

"Dancing is good for you," she says. "As long as you've got the right brace on your knee." She glances at my leg pointedly before asking, "Do you?"

"Of course," I say. I may not follow as many of her instructions as she wishes I did, but I wear the braces and supports she tells me to wear, when she tells me to wear them, at the tension she tells me to use.

"Good," she says. "Then you can do as I say and enjoy yourself. You never know who you might meet while you're at it. I've got my eye on that fellow over there." She raises her eyebrows in the direction of a strapping young Elianan with long dark hair. He's dressed in fine clothes, but looks a bit nervous, like it's his first time at an event this important.

"You won't give me chase, will you?" Siobhán asks.

"He's all yours," I say.

"Good," she says. "Lord knows I'll have enough competition as it is." She eyes the ladies gathered around the young man. She turns to face me and hoists her corset up, adjusting her breasts to accentuate her cleavage. "How do I look?" she asks.

"I'm not a mirror, Siobhán," I say.

"Fine," she groans. "I'm going now, and so should you."

I wave her off and get up with some effort, leaning on Faolan. I make a great show of stretching out my back to disguise gently stretching my knee.

I begin walking along the edge of the crowd, keeping an eye on Patrick, who is deeply engaged in conversation with Bryna. Her laugh is low and musical and Patrick beams in response.

In the periphery of my vision, I see Valencia. I notice again how the low neckline of her dress shows the curves of her breasts. The waist nips in briefly before blossoming out again along her full hips. The almost shimmery fabric looks thick, but also like it's right against her skin. I can't tell what, if anything, she's wearing underneath.

I'm feeling inspired to try again with her.

"Let me guess," she says as I approach. "You, your brother, and the entire Adare council all demand I apologize to your cousin."

"I doubt this is a story Rhys will want making the rounds," I say, "and I don't intend to tell anyone."

"I take it he's not your favorite cousin," she says.

"No," I say. "One of my least favorites." I see a flash of Lowell's coat and add, "Though he has strong competition."

I wonder why I shared this so easily, almost unthinkingly. Have I fallen under some kind of spell? I take an involuntary step back from Valencia, looking her over, as if I could somehow see whether she was enchanting me.

My eyes are drawn up to a high voice saying, "Valencia, ¡mira! Tan lindo."

The tall lady to whom the voice belongs is by the rivulet flowing through the hall. She reaches toward the flowers floating in the water.

Valencia bends low next to her.

There's something moving along the edge of the river, near the stone of the floor. I see its little bluish-green shape, and make out the fins on the sides of its head. This is not good.

The sea monster is little, a baby, and barely resembles the ones in our tapestries, but is no less deadly for being so small. Its big blue eyes stare up at the two ladies in rapt attention, and it wiggles its thick tail.

Nessa is faster than I am. She reaches the river's edge in seconds.

She deftly holds the tall lady by her shoulders and moves her aside gently, wordlessly.

"Step back from the river," Nessa says. "Now. Slowly, please."

"We have rivers in Eliana." Valencia sounds amused. "Damas don't dissolve in water."

In seconds, the baby sea monster has vaulted onto her head.

"Don't move," I say, approaching slowly.

Quite a lot of eyes focus on Valencia. No surprise. If an Adare sea monster bites and kills an Elianan lady, the same one who was poisoned before, no less, that will surely be the end of our negotiations. And even if no one else knows about her casting the curse, I've got to keep her alive. Again.

"What is wrong with all of you?" Valencia asks. "You've never seen an axolotl?"

The little creature is wiggling its fins, looking distractingly joyful.

"Sabe," she says. "A salamander."

"No," I say. "It's one of our sea monsters. It's a baby, but it can still kill you."

I say the last part in as soft a voice as I can muster while beginning to coax the little creature off Valencia's head. Given my last interaction with one of our sea monsters, I'm even more careful than I already would be.

Valencia's eyes are wide, but she's keeping still.

"Come here, little one," I say. "Let's get you back in the water."

I manage to get it into my hands, and back into the rivulet. I make sure it's headed in the right direction, out of the castle and hopefully back to its pod.

There's a collective sigh of relief among the people watching. Most go back to what they were doing.

"That was," Valencia says, "a baby version of los monstruos that used to be in charge of Adare's executions?"

"Yes," I say. "Very much like your jaguars."

Some of the guests still have their eyes on us.

"Was that your doing?" Valencia asks.

"What?" I ask.

"You seem to have a talent for orchestrating things that make you look like the hero," she says.

We could talk past each other all night.

Instead, I offer her my hand.

"What are you doing?" she asks.

"If we're dancing, people will stop staring at us and we can speak more freely."

I try not to take personally the way she sighs, as though I am the most unpleasant company to be found in two kingdoms.

"Fine," she says. "Momentito."

"Where are you going?" I ask.

"This is so we don't draw attention to ourselves, no?" she asks.

"Yes," I say, hesitating.

She comes close enough to talk under her breath. "You may know how to dance with your cane, but I don't know how to dance with mine. So if you want us not to draw attention, I don't think you want mine knocking into yours every third count."

I realize how thoughtless I've just been. Since I was a child, I've seen those with canes dance. Those who fought in the war. Leaders from the villages who come here for ceremonies. Farmers and craftsmen who gather for festivals and celebrations. In Adare, we learn modified versions of dances. They're passed down. We teach them to one another. We learn to switch hands or change angles. We make adjustments that let us keep one hand free. One hand holding our partner's hand, the other on a cane instead of in the air or behind our backs.

It took me months to get the feel of it, the instinct for shifting choreography. But now it's built into my body. For all I have to do as Patrick, I wouldn't know how to dance as him. When I dance, I'm Cade.

Val leaves her cane propped against a wall.

"You'll be all right without it?" I ask when she comes back.

"How much standing around does this one involve?" she asks.

"Some," he says.

"More or less than one of your cousin's average speeches?"

I laugh. "Less."

"I'll be fine."

She accepts my hand and we join the other dancers. Or we try. Valencia keeps as much distance between us as possible. She pulls away. She stumbles back, recovers, slips back into the dance. When I try to turn her and she resists, I realize. She's avoiding Faolan as though

138

I'm using him as a weapon. Why is the enchantress who plunged our families into cursed sleep on guard against *me*?

"Do you think I'm trying to attack you?" I ask.

"I've never danced with a cane," she says. "I've never danced with someone who is using a cane, and I don't know this dance very well, despite Ondina's best efforts. So I apologize if I'm not a portrait of grace at the moment."

"Just follow what I'm doing," I say. If she stays this tense, this conversation will go nowhere. If she lets me lead, she'll stop watching everyone else for what to do, and she'll dance with me.

I look at her, trying to keep her eyes on me. I dance like I've learned to dance. I anchor when I need to. I switch Faolan from one hand to the other fast enough that I barely have to pause. I lift Valencia with one arm around her instead of with two hands, a little off to my side so I can still hold on to Faolan. In each moment, I choose the hand that's most important so my other hand stays free.

I lift Valencia up onto her toes as she leans on my shoulder with her forearm. Our height difference allows me an enjoyable view. Her breasts are held tightly in her dress, pressing against the lowest point of the neckline.

I turn Valencia and pull her back into my arms.

From the look on her face, I've surprised her. In a good way, for once.

"You find me impressive, do you?" I say.

With Faolan's help, I lift her against my hip, her arm draped across my shoulder. Valencia's leg arches out, and as I lower her to the ground, her back is against me.

She looks at me over her shoulder. "I find you impressed with yourself."

I take her left hand in mine and spin her again.

Valencia steps forward and stumbles, but recovers so quickly I can't even offer my hand. I'm guessing her shoes aren't helping. They look new, not yet broken in. The thread of the embroidered flowers and vines isn't worn or frayed.

We drop our hands and face each other. Her eyes flash to my side. She's tracking where Faolan is. Again. As though she thinks I intend to fight her, or that she might have to get out of the way if I suddenly start fighting someone else. On that point, I can't blame her. Officially, I'm one of Patrick's guards.

Valencia steps out for the next turn and slips. I catch her to keep her from falling. We end up with her back to me, our bodies pressed together. I run my hand down her side. When I reach just below her rib cage, a flash of a memory comes to me. The forest. A chase on horseback. My hand has been here before. Holding a reluctant rider on my horse in front of me. The shape of her body feels different but still recognizable.

The knife thrower.

The Elianan boy like me who tried to kill me. Twice.

CHAPTER TWENTY-NINE

VALENCIA

4^{00.} I grew up knowing that the number 400 stands for that which is innumerable. There's a reason they call anyone like me centzontleh. One who possesses 400 tongues, 400 voices. My task is not just to have any tongue or voice I must have. It's to have innumerable voices, innumerable tongues.

And I can tell by the way Cade McKenna is holding me that I've just failed to keep two of my voices far enough apart.

But then, so has he.

Cade McKenna has been doubling for his brother.

El brujo malo has been doubling for his brother.

Patrick McKenna has never seen me this close.

Because the Patrick McKenna I met was Cade.

I've just placed him.

He's just placed me.

And if he hasn't, a tiny blade falls out of my hair, right on cue. It pings to the floor.

No wonder his face betrayed nothing of him recognizing me. He's as practiced at being someone else as I am.

I look for any of Bryna's guards who might be looking. I drop my hand to my side, so my fingers can signal.

Cade's grip tightens. Behind me, he switches his staff to his left hand. Fast as how he moved in the room with the tree, he gets his dagger to my back, so smoothly that no one around us stops dancing. We look like we're in some kind of flirtatious embrace.

Hoping someone is watching closely, I flash my whole hand for the number five. Twice more, plus three fingers. Tecpatl. Flint. Knife.

"I wouldn't," Cade says.

The point of his dagger digs into the cloth of my dress. He holds it so precisely I can picture it, the metal against the pitaya pink of the bodice.

Every detail of this room heightens. The smell of honey and spice. The texture of moss dripping from the sconces. The red of the amaranth and the blue of the corn. The salt turning the fires violet or richer orange. The texture of the hierbas scattered on the ground, leaves letting off a green scent as polished shoes dance across them.

I drop the signaling.

"We're going to take a walk in the gardens," Cade whispers, "calmly, as if we are the best of friends."

With the trembling inside his voice, a crack of light finds its way in.

He feels threatened.

I can work with threatened.

Before he leads me out of the hall, he stops near one of the doors, right by where I propped my cane.

He waits. I wait. If this is some kind of trick, it's not an especially clever one. If he expects me to grab my cane and start fighting him in front of everyone, if that's his plan for revealing me as more dangerous than I appear, I'm about to disappoint him.

We stay there, neither of us moving, his blade at my back.

He sighs as though losing patience. He tilts his head toward where my cane leans, at a seam in the stone.

I turn my head slightly, trying to read his face without looking back at him. Is he truly giving me access to something I can use as a weapon? Without making a scene about it?

This is either a trick, or he's stupid enough to underestimate me. Worse than stupid. Reckless.

He's still waiting.

I step forward. He stays close, the blade close.

I reach for my cane, and he doesn't stop me.

The globe of cuarzo rosa, cool under my palm, lets me breathe.

"How chivalrous." I let sarcasm coat each word.

"Chivalry has nothing to do with it," he says. "It's going to look odd if we go for a walk and you don't have it. Now you do. So let's go for a lovely evening stroll, shall we? You really will love the gardens." He's stopped whispering. He speaks loudly enough to be overheard. "Eamon's always telling me I don't appreciate them enough by moonlight."

I go where he wants. He barely has to touch the dagger to lead me. If I'm going to fight him, I'm not doing it here, not where everyone around us could get hurt. Not when he could use me to threaten Bryna, just like I feared he would when he brought me, Gael-me, back to Eliana.

He holds me close enough that by the time we're out of sight, everyone probably thinks we're lovers.

The castle shifts, the colors of the walls turning. The light has a redder cast, and the fires seem to be burning hotter. The flowers shift to red and white. The cleansing salts turn the flames blue and green, and the fires flare as though breathing out. I haven't heard of ancient animals emerging from tapestries here like they do at home, but I swear the sea monsters on the walls and shields look like they're snarling.

As Cade takes me toward the gardens, my head is so full of thoughts they crash into one another. How often does Cade play Patrick? Does Patrick ever play him?

Is this part of why Cade helped clear Patrick's way to the throne?

Is this why they sealed their own mother and Patrick's own father into an enchanted sleep?

Is this why Cade plays so indifferent toward the thought of ruling?

Is their plan to rule together?

No wonder Cade has to hide that his knee is the problem. That injury probably supposedly happened to Patrick, in battle, when Cade was fighting in his place.

The scent of apricot blossoms and spring wood brightens the air. The light the fire trees cast on the gardens would be beautiful, if a murderer prince's equally murderous half brother didn't have a dagger at my back.

But then he withdraws it. He lets me go. He moves so he's in front of me, so I can see him return it to the sheath on the back of his belt.

"So," he says. "Now we talk, yes?"

I'm through with charm.

I shove my cane against his chest.

He catches it, fast—how is a boy who has so much height and weight on me so much faster than I am?—and pushes down on it.

He sighs. "Must we?"

I lever the cane into his left shoulder. He gets his bastón under mine, then up and over my arm, shoving me down to the grass.

Fine. I can fight from down here.

I grab his leg—his uninjured one, because I am both a lady and a gentleman—but before I can get him off-balance, he just turns and steps out of my hold. Quick and smooth as a dance.

He stands over me. "Are you done?"

I swing my cane, trying to sweep his right leg out from under him. He grabs hold of it. But I spin under it so he has to let go unless he wants to sprain a wrist.

This time, I go for his head. Neither my most ladylike nor most gentlemanly move, but I'm not gonna kill him. I am calibrating carefully enough to knock him out. I just need enough time to figure out what to do, and I can't get it as long as he's conscious and looking out for my next move.

Cade blocks from above with his own bastón. I keep hold of mine, spinning under to disengage.

I pull back.

"Had enough?" he asks.

I alternate between wielding my cane and using it to steady myself. "Who are you?" I ask.

"Who are *you*?" he asks.

"I promise I don't matter as much as you do," I say.

"I think you do," he says.

He missteps in a way that's not about his knee. I can tell. He seems . . . twitchy.

Then I put it together.

And I laugh.

He jerks at the sound. "What?"

In the same way we don't drink much alcohol in Eliana, I've heard that Adare cortesanos aren't overly familiar with plants that rile you up, that make you more awake.

"First time having xocolatl?" I ask.

He stares at me.

"Feeling a little"—I take my time, enjoying this—"jumpy?"

"No." How quick he says it just makes it funnier. "Yes. Why?"

The next time I come at him, I think about how I can use this. I try

145

to fake going one way, and then go the other. I try to use what's working against both of us. Every time one of us can't have our cane as a point of contact with the ground, we have it against the other, leaning on each other. This is a fight where we're taking each other's weight, so whenever I can get him down on the ground, I'm not only taking strain off my back, I'm taking some of his size advantage.

When we're both on our knees, he tries to pin me. He's so quick about it he almost does it, almost gets hold of my hands so I can't fight back. But I come at him with my cane again. And when he tries to deflect it, I lever the end of it right at his crotch.

Harder than I mean to.

If he was a sparring partner, this is when we'd break apart and I'd offer a hundred apologies.

But he's not. He's Patrick McKenna's shadow. He's the brujo who put my father an enchantment away from me.

So no apologies. When a man takes our families, I go for his huevos.

Cade still holds on to me, so I can't disengage. But his whole body buckles with the impact.

"And how are the crown jewels?" I ask. My voice may be shaking with effort, but I'm still smirking.

"Fine," he says, voice strained.

He recovers fast enough to knock my cane out of my hand.

I feint trying to get past him, grabbing my cane and getting up as though I might run.

And of course, he doesn't let me. He blocks me with his staff. Good. I use how he's pushing on me to spin into him. Then I throw my cane toward his shoulder, trying for his head again.

He blocks with his staff from underneath.

But I can work with this. I lever my cane under his armpit. He presses down on his staff, which is—how did this happen?—now bearing down on my left shoulder. My back can't take the pressure for more than a minute, so it's strangely good news when he pulls me into him, his staff across my collarbone.

We're off-balance right now. He can feel it. I can see it in how his eyes are wavering. So I consider it squarely his fault when he doesn't let me go, and we fall. Or, more accurately, he falls on me. His staff ends up between us, across my body, the one thing stopping his chest from lying fully against mine.

I have both my hands on the wood, pushing it and him off me.

"I don't want to hurt you," Cade says.

Sure he doesn't.

I try to hit him with my right arm. He blocks with his forearm, both of us pressing into each other.

We're both breathing hard, his exhale tracing the curve of my neck. I move my mouth and tilt my chin up like I might kiss him, and his inhale sharpens.

Boys, even brujo boys, are so delightfully stupid.

I buck my right hip, throwing my body and his own staff into him. But the second I scramble on top of him, he steadies himself with his back in a way I can't. He pushes the staff I'm still holding on to, and—in a show of strength that would impress me if it wasn't getting used against me—he flips me over him.

I get a single jagged moment in which to realize that:

First, when I land, the back of my head will hit the ground.

Second, the earth under the grass is still hardened with spring chill.

Third, I've lost this fight to Cade McKenna. Cade McKenna, who is sometimes Patrick. I've managed to lose to both McKenna brothers at the same time.

CHAPTER THIRTY

CADE

Did I just kill an Elianan? And not just any Elianan—the enchantress whose curse could now keep my parents and our best advisors asleep for eternity?

And who also happens to be very close to Princess Abryenda? And, in case all that wasn't enough, also quite possibly a brother I vowed never to harm?

Not only is this a potential disaster between our kingdoms, one that would be entirely my fault, it might also mean my parents never wake up. I sorely wish I could take back the last four or five moves in this fight, even if that would mean losing.

I check for blood, breathing, twitching. Nothing.

Can I feel a pulse? My hands are shaking too hard to be sure, and all I can hear is blood rushing through my ears. I put my hands on the ground and look for Faolan. I feel him in my hand again. I pet the owl's head, right between his notched brows, and he helps me up.

The Elianan in question is still just lying there, not moving, cane thrown aside. I nudge the cane farther away to see if there's any reaction. Still nothing. But also no blood.

My knee is destroyed again, so Faolan helps me slide down onto my good knee to scoop Valencia up, gather Gael over my shoulder. I have to bring her to Siobhán. Now.

Hands on my ribs, crushing in. Knee under the softest part of my jaw. Teeth strike against teeth inside my mouth.

When my back hits the ground, all the air comes into my lungs again and I'm back up, sitting, looking. But Gael is gone. Nowhere around.

I listen for Valencia, but hear only wind, distant music, laughter, and something crackling. I watch the owl fly off, shaking out his wings. He's circling, looking too.

But where's the rest of Faolan? I pat the ground, check my shoulder holster. Jump up. But my knee won't hold and I'm down again.

Not just my knee. The boy again. With Faolan's staff and sword pinning my right arm and her own cane against my chest. All three of those hard lines press against me, trapping me in one position.

The owl swoops down, landing gently above my head, bowing to my victorious opponent. My heart is beating hard enough to rattle through the ground under me.

I stare into Valencia's fiery brown eyes. I've spent time with people who haven't quite landed on a name yet, or whether they want to live as women or men or neither or both. I've talked with them, and muddled my way through talking about them when necessary. You would think that would prepare me for situations like this, for interactions with people like this Elianan. But I have no idea how to refer to this person.

"Who are you?" I manage.

"Wake them up," Valencia demands.

"What?" I gasp, staring even deeper into the dark eyes that have bested me.

Gael presses his cane harder into my chest. "Wake them up."

"Wake them up?" I repeat, sounding as stupid as I feel.

"I saw you. I saw you do it. I know it was you."

Suddenly things make much more sense. And also much less.

"That night," I say. "You think I did it."

"You wanted to get acquainted. Here's something you need to know about me." Valencia pulls a thin knife from her hair and jabs it into my left shoulder. Hard. Fast. It's so small I hardly feel it, but I see the blade come out again in her hand. "I am not a patient person."

My eyes can't quite focus with the shine of the tiny blade, the shine of my blood, and the shine of those dark eyes behind the hand holding the small hilt.

"The moment you bring them back," Valencia says, "I give you the remedio for this."

Poison.

"And I assure you." Valencia sits up, weight moving lower, toward my stomach. I find myself wishing Gael would go back to pressing my chest into the ground. "Whatever magic you have, it can't save you." Valencia cleans the knife against her dress and tucks it back into her hair. "Only I can."

CHAPTER THIRTY-ONE

VALENCIA

"¿Qué demonios?" Bryna says the moment she sees me.

I hadn't expected to run into her out here. The look on her face tells me that the moon and the light from the fire trees are doing nothing to flatter me. My hair is more tangle than trenza, and I'm sweating and streaked with dirt.

"You look awful," she says.

"No," I say. "Tell me what you really think."

She looks so crestfallen I wish I could take back the sarcasm. I've turned her from love-blushed princesa to worried friend. During el baile, the embroidery on her dress looked pink as summer roses and bright as ripe oranges. Now they've faded along with her smile.

"This is my fault," she says.

"No," I say. "Te prometo. It's not."

"Yes, it is." She lowers her voice. "I asked los gatos to chase you, and then I expected you to join in for dancing. You should have been in bed resting."

"As though that was going to happen," I say.

"Sometimes you act as if you're indestructible so convincingly that

I believe you." She comes closer, enough that I can smell her agua de rosas. "We're going to find them."

"Who?" I ask.

"Whoever poisoned you," she says. "Patrick has committed to it. His closest cousin is leading the effort."

Oh, well, if the McKennas are on the task.

Bryna's face turns impassive, and I can imagine her making men twice her age relent during negotiations. "And if I need to, I will personally tear their hearts from their chests."

"Patrick and Lowell McKenna?" I ask.

"Very funny," she says.

"I wasn't trying to be," I say.

My back prickles with the impression that there are more people outside than when we started talking.

Bryna and I both turn. There's a crowd gathering, with more streaming out of the castle.

They're looking toward a contingent dismounting from their horses. Their clothes look made of heavy cloth, the kind that can withstand riding, and they wear sashes patterned in ways I can't make sense of (Bryna could probably name every family they stand for).

But that's not what I'm most interested in. Between them, they look like the trovadores' songs about Adare. Some are pale in a way that's a little startling, but just as many have dark skin. One has the black hair and deep brown skin of our queen. Another has eyes as wide and dark as Ondina's.

"We weren't expecting you until next month." Patrick, who before looked golden with infatuation, now looks pale as the tips of his own fingernails. "But, of course, we're honored to receive you early. Please join in our festivities. We are humbled to be hosting La Princesa Abryenda and her court at our castle."

The men and women give Bryna respectful nods, slight bows, but their lack of interest in her is blatant. At first I'm insulted on her behalf, then relieved. The way these men and women hold themselves, the lines etched on their faces, the pins on their sashes, make me suspect they're important, and they don't look happy. I'd rather they be unhappy with someone other than my future queen.

Within seconds, they all seem to exchange glances. And then, like a flock of wings finding a common branch, all eyes land on Patrick.

The woman standing in front says, "We need to speak with your sister."

CHAPTER THIRTY-TWO

CADE

I make my way toward Siobhán's chamber, left leg dragging despite Faolan's help. I knock on her door and lean my head on the frame. I tuck Faolan in toward my chest and he nuzzles my shoulder, wings fluttering gently against my collarbone.

My fight with the boy left the grounds full of deep furrows and mud rivulets. But the castle itself is solid and steady. The pine of Siobhán's door is just the right temperature and texture against my throbbing head, but it doesn't stop my thoughts from swirling.

If Valencia didn't cast the enchantment, who did? I can see why she thought I did it. Same reason I thought she did. We were both there to watch, to eavesdrop on a conversation we weren't invited to join. And we saw each other. But now Valencia is convinced I cursed everyone, and that I can fix it. Not to mention Valencia is also Gael, who seemed to be an entirely different person with his own agenda, one that threatened our throne, or at least our most treasured royal symbols. So what was that about?

Worst of all, I can't tell whether what I'm feeling is aftereffects of our fight, perhaps combined with a bit too much of that unsettling

Elianan drink, or the early signs of poison taking effect. All my muscles are sore, and I'm clenching my teeth against the sourness rising from my stomach.

When Siobhán opens the door, she does so only a crack, shawl pulled tight around her neck.

"What happened?" she whispers, seeing the state of me. "I thought you went with Valencia."

"I did," I say. "This is what happened. Can we go to the tower room?"

She looks over her shoulder. "Just give me a moment."

I had assumed she wasn't alone. She almost never is after a party. At least half of what I know about romance, she taught me.

After she eases the door shut, I roll my back along the cool stone wall, resting my head against it and closing my eyes.

Siobhán comes out wearing a simple utility dress and tartan wrap. She closes the door gently and slips under my right arm to help me and Faolan.

"Did you leave a note?" I ask.

"Cade," Siobhán says, a slightly sharper whisper.

"What?" I ask.

"Nothing," she says. "Where are you hurt?"

"I think I might have been poisoned," I say, "but I'm not sure."

She stops us right where we are and puts her left hand on the back of my neck. With her right, she gently pulls down each of my eyelids and quickly checks each of my ears and hands. Next she puts her right hand over my heart and her left hand at my back. Last, she sets her ear against my side. Like always, I do my best to just be still and breathe.

"Well, we needn't run there as far as I can tell," she says. "But I am concerned. What happened?"

"Valencia and I had a fight," I say.

"And she poisoned you?" Siobhán casts a wary glance back toward her room. "What don't I know about Elianan courtship?"

"She has combat training," I say. "I put it together while we were dancing. She stabbed me with a comb blade and said it was poisoned, but I'm not so sure. She could have just been angry I found her out."

"I wouldn't chance it," Siobhán says.

The sunrise comes in through one of the corridor windows, pink shifting to yellow. I hear voices and the shuffling of feet. Siobhán and I are no longer the only ones nearby, and whether I'm slowly dying or not, I can't alarm anyone.

I stretch my back dramatically against the wall, yawn, and let off a belch. Siobhán laughs. She can tell this little display was for the benefit of our impending audience.

That audience has very much arrived, in the form of my brother with the princess on his arm, surrounded by a contingent from both Adare and Eliana.

Patrick looks disturbingly like our father. Tall, focused. His figure complements the princess's, their arms linking at just the right place to accentuate her curves. The deep colors of her dress even seem well matched with the winter-river blue of his O'Loingsigh tartan.

To top it all off, along with the jaguars and quetzals that accompany Bryna's retinue, a little flammulated owl has joined their procession. On Bryna's shoulder. Swaying along with motion of her gait, and seemingly enjoying every moment of it.

When I look over at Siobhán, even she is in a dead stare.

As I'm shaking off the thought that perhaps the princess already bedded my virgin brother, I hear familiar voices. Ones I haven't heard in a long time. I smell stronger lichen, pine, lye, seawater. The village representatives have come early.

I see Nessa and Fergus in the procession and slip in alongside them. Fergus nods at me, but Nessa raises an eyebrow.

"Where did you come from?" she says. "You look a mess."

"What's going on?" I ask. "Why are the leaders here?"

"We're all about to find out," she says.

As we approach the great hall, I hear Patrick trying to herd the village leaders into our audience room and Lowell trying to persuade the Elianans not to follow. As usual, Lowell has the easier job. The leaders are all talking at once, insisting to be heard immediately.

"You cannot hold us off any longer," one says. "We demand an audience with the queen's firstborn."

"We must hear what she thinks of your plans to carry on your mother's work," another says.

"Inform her we wish to speak with her," a third says.

The leaders want my sister's blessing on Patrick's rule.

And of course they had to ask for it in front of the Elianans.

Princess Abryenda looks impassive or perhaps slightly irritated, judging from the hard set to her lips. Valencia is standing next to the princess, taking this all in.

I deepen my voice as much as possible before I say, "I'll do it."

"Cade, you can't," Patrick says, quickly covering with, "I can't spare you. Not right now."

"I'll go, then," Lowell volunteers.

"No," Patrick says even more quickly. "Cade, you're right. It should be you. She knows you better."

We're truly doing this. We're not only talking about a completely fictional princess, we're discussing who's closer to her.

But I nod with a small bow, hoping I come up with a way to produce our imaginary sister.

CHAPTER THIRTY-THREE

VALENCIA

I would say my prayers have been answered, but I wouldn't have even dared to pray, hope, or dream of this.

Ondina hovers over me as I search through a wooden trunk.

"You know I don't like to ask you favors," she says. "But this may be our one chance to find out what's happened to Karlynn's heir. Her real heir. Not Patrick"—under her breath, Ondina mutters an expletive too unladylike to say in front of anyone but me—"McKenna."

"You're wondering if I can follow Cade?" I sling my bolsa onto my shoulder. "I was already going to."

Ondina looks as touched as if I'd brought her abuela flowers. "Sometimes you're worth the years you take off my life."

"That's all I can hope for," I say. "Can you explain my absence?"

"Claro," Ondina says. "You overexerted yourself at dancing, before you had truly recovered from the poisoning."

I wish it was a lie. But since we left Eliana, I've barely been keeping ahead of my own body. I've been leaning up against the frame of my bed at every angle the hueseros taught me. I've been using heat and cold. Aceite goes on my back before I sleep and when I wake up.

"So you're resting," Ondina says. "I'll make a whole spectacle of saying that I told you so, that Bryna and I both told you to take care of yourself, that this time I'm ensuring you comply with las curanderas' orders, and Bryna's."

"What would I do without you?" I ask.

Ondina hesitates.

"What?" I ask.

"There's something I need to tell you."

I nod.

She looks at the woven rug at our feet. Her eyes follow the gilt thread running through the green and scarlet.

"Don't take any chance you don't have to," she says. "If Cade was part of getting his own sister out of Patrick's way, there's no telling what he might do to you. And even if he had nothing to do with it, he may not come back alive. If you're too close to him, neither will you."

"You think Patrick would have his own brother killed over this?" I ask, not in disbelief. I ask in wanting to know the opinion of the one friend I have who thinks I'm right about the McKennas.

"Princes have done worse over less," Ondina says. "So be careful."

I nod. "I'm careful."

"No," Ondina says. "Not the way you want to be careful. The way your father would want you to be careful."

I know she doesn't mean them to, but her words catch me in the center of my chest.

Maybe my father would want me to be careful, but I lost him because I wasn't quick enough. Because I didn't act fast enough. Because I couldn't throw a blade at Cade McKenna in time, I lost my father. Bryna lost her mother and father. We lost our king and queen. And so many more lost so many others.

This time, I'll be fast enough, and I'll be ready.

CHAPTER THIRTY-FOUR
CADE

If my mother were here, I'd ask her what to do. But she's not, so there's only one place I can go. The place that taught me to be a man. The same place that gave me my Saint Marinos tattoo, oak leaves and acorns and water inked into my side.

I don't want to think of my mother right now, not when there's so much else I need to figure out. But I can't help it. Every time I take this road, I think about her. She's the one who first sent me to live among the monks who would become my brothers.

My mother saw me as I was, and she told me I could be who I was. But she didn't see everything.

Once my mother knew who I really was, she told me I could still rule one day. *They will accept you,* she told me. *They are ready for a prince and king like you.*

I asked her what would happen if there were people who weren't.

My mother wasn't one for lying, even when I was a child, and she didn't lie then. She didn't say everyone would accept me.

There are always challenges, she told me. *In every generation—yours, mine, the ones who came before and the ones who will come after—there are those who want things to be different and those who want things to stay the same.*

But as she said those words, all I heard in my head were the arguments about her reforms. Advisors telling her she was changing too much, too quickly, and that people would rebel if pushed too far.

I was sure I would be that final push too far, and that she would be blamed for who I was. That there would be a price for me living as who I am, and that my mother would have to pay it. Everyone in Adare would have to pay it. If my mother fought for me, she'd lose somewhere else. She'd have to concede, to lay aside reforms Adare needed.

My mother set herself in the space between tradition and change. She held close this castle, the tree with our family's gems, the lore of the staff passed down from queen to queen. But I couldn't live in that space with her, no more than I could turn myself into a queen who could inherit that staff. No matter what ancient stories I loved, no matter what traditions I held on to, I would always be too much change, too quickly.

My mother had more faith in who I could be than I did. She didn't realize that everything about me would mean choices, trade-offs, things lost.

Before she lost anything else because of me, I had to choose between who I was born to be and who I truly was.

When I told my mother I didn't want to rule Adare, she asked only once if I was sure.

When I said yes, we never spoke of it again.

CHAPTER THIRTY-FIVE

VALENCIA

I keep my distance, whispering to the luminous fox carrying me on her back. The velvet of my bolsa lies deep blue against the thick gray of her brush. Even with as quickly as I packed, it holds a dozen different versions of me. A sprinkling of metal dust on my forehead and limbs can give me the look of a skilled worker. Gray to coat my hair and a tincture from green plants that puckers my skin can make me look just like my abuela. A length of plain parchment, and I'm a messenger boy. A boiled-down syrup can pass for blood.

And always, the poison I paint onto my lips.

I stroke the fox's side. The luminous foxes are no one's pets, teeth more threat than smile, but this one is young, with the echo of a kit's build.

"You're going to be a magnificent one, did you know that?" I ask. She has big, questioning eyes, and golden red touching her ears and ruff. The points of light are just starting to come into the tips of her fur.

When I look up, I've lost sight of Cade McKenna.

"¿De verdad?" I whisper to nobody but myself and the luminous fox.

This forest looks so different from the ahuehuete trees I grew up beneath. I only recognize some of the plants here, the crowberry bushes, and the kind of green artemisia that grows in Adare. So many trees here are dead, standing alongside the bright green of living ones. Some are dry and hollowed husks, looking as though they might turn to dust and ash at any moment. Others are bright with what grows on them—green moss, the deep red of thin-edged mushrooms, the poured gold of witch's butter, so ruffled it looks like marigolds turning to liquid and light.

I duck under a branch, following a stand of trees. The leaves tint the sunlight bright green.

Then the luminous fox is nose-to-nose with a warhorse twice her size. And I'm face-to-face with Cade McKenna.

"I had a feeling you'd be a problem," he says.

"A feeling?" I ask, stroking the fox's side. I don't want the destrier intimidating her. "Just a feeling? I'm hurt."

"You're a problem," he says. "Are you happy?"

The curious fox brings me closer to Cade.

"It must really bother you that you tried to kill me and failed so spectacularly," I say.

Cade's eyes turn hard as slate. "If I ever meant to kill you, you'd have been dead before you even knew my name."

That look, that tone, shuts me up. I forgot that Cade's not just the brujo I saw that night. He's also a soldier, and far more used to killing enemies than overpowering them alive. Adare isn't much for taking prisoners. They leave you be, or they leave you dead.

But Cade looks nervous, the stallion taking the cue and backing up. He eyes the fox as though she might drink his soul from his body.

"Are you scared of her?" I ask.

"No," he says, and the lie is so bad that I can guess how he sounded as a little boy, promising that he wouldn't get into fights.

"She's very friendly," I say, and I can't keep the wicked mirth out of my voice.

With a curious flick of her ears, the fox looks up at Cade, as though she might want to learn his scent, set her nose against his hand. Or bite it off.

"Unless she gets her teeth into you," I say. "But that shouldn't be a problem for you. You can just enchant her, can't you? Charm her into being as harmless as a kitten?"

A bristling goes through the fox's brush. Is she frightened of him? She lets out a little squeal, and I wrap my arms around her, protective, calming. Luminous foxes don't bark or whimper or chatter half as often as their smaller, more numerous cousins, the red or desert foxes who wander through woods and farms and the floating gardens. Luminous foxes speak most loudly with their silences, or an occasional yawn of irritation. But this one's upset, and I don't blame her. She can probably sense the thorned heart within Cade McKenna's chest.

I pet her brush, trying to calm her.

Then I hear a voice that belongs neither to me nor to Cade nor to the fox.

"Take her too."

Hands, gloved in green-dyed leather, pull me off the fox's back.

"And the animal," the same voice says.

"No," I call, an instinctive cry. "Leave," I yell at the fox.

The fox blinks at me. Why is she still there? Usually they're quick to bound away. They're not fighters, not any more than they have to be to defend their kits. And these men are reaching for her.

"Run," I yell.

The fox's pupils contract into vertical slits and she leaps away.

In the moments I fight the green-gloved hands, I spin through what might be happening. Did Cade do this? No. One of these men said *take her too*.

Too, like I'm an afterthought.

They've come for Cade.

Whoever they are, I need him more than they do. They're not getting him, and they're not getting me.

I elbow the man holding me. He tries to flip me toward the ground, but I go limp, my body dead weight. I lock my muscles back up in time to collide with another of these men, knocking him forward.

The man holding me just used me as a swinging weapon against one of his friends. Whoever they are, Cade and I can get out of this.

The one in the green gloves grabs at my skirt. He gets a solid grip on the top layer. But I pull out my dagger and slash enough of a cut that I can spin out. The top layer tears away, leaving nothing but a length of fabric in the man's gloved hands.

Amateurs.

I take hold of that length of fabric he's still gripping and pull hard enough that he tumbles forward.

Then it happens. A fist, or a heel, or an elbow. It doesn't make much difference. Whatever it is drives into my lower back. Hard enough to knock my dagger off my body.

The sound I make would be a scream if I could get a full breath. Instead it's a desperate gasp for air before the whirlpool drags me back underwater.

A lightning storm of pain spiders through my back. Then out through my limbs, trails of heat blazing like stars. It snaps all the way to my fingertips, and I can't feel my own body enough to fight back.

Gloved hands bind my wrists.

Between the slashes of searing light, thin breaths get in, cool slices of calm dark.

One lets me move my bound hands up to my head.

Another lets me pull a knife from a twirl of hair.

A third gives me the space to stab this man's arm.

He yells, calls me names I choose to take as compliments. While he's busy with the tiny knife sticking out of his arm, I get to the nearest tree.

I loop the rope over one branch, then the next. I climb a skeleton of bleached-out wood, a dead tree among the deep bark and green leaves. Pieces of the trunk come off as I scramble up. Splintering wood will rain down right into the eyes of anyone coming after me.

Two bodies crash into the base of the tree. The force rattles up through the branches, more splinters tumbling down.

One of the men has Cade cornered. Cade's holding him off, but I can tell from the angle of Cade's body that the man is putting pressure on his injured leg.

I have just enough slack between my hands to climb down to a lower bough and throw the rope around the man's neck.

I wrench my hands back, putting pressure on his throat until he goes limp and falls away from Cade.

"Pull your hands apart," Cade says.

"Why are you bothering with me?" I ask. "Do something to them."

"Like what?" Cade asks.

"Oh, I don't know," I say. "What you did to our families. Do that to them."

"Just"—he lands hard on each word—"hold your hands apart."

I know what he's about to do.

I don't know him well enough to let him.

But I have no choice.

I pull my hands apart.

Cade swings a blade.

I shut my eyes.

With the rasp of metal against rope, the tension between my wrists vanishes. Rope ends trail against my forearms.

I open my eyes.

"Stay up there and do what you do best," Cade says.

I pull a blade out of my hair. "Throw knives at people I don't like?"

Cade nods up at me. "You got it."

CHAPTER THIRTY-SIX

CADE

I already wasn't at my best, I might be poisoned, and now one of the largest men I've ever seen has one of his massive arms pulling my wrist up to the back of my head. Of course.

By breathing fast, like Fergus taught me, I prepare, mentally and physically, for something I almost certainly can't do while making him think he is getting the best of me.

I give Valencia a look.

The fire in her dark eyes and the set of her jaw show me she is ready. As she pulls more knives from the seemingly endless supply in her hair, I pull down as hard as I can on the man's arm while bending forward and letting out a battle cry. I try to roll him over my right shoulder, but I crumple under him, tiny knives raining down around us.

He tries to get up, the bulk of his weight lifting off me just in time to grab his leg. I'm angry enough to stand up and have a height advantage. But if I want to keep it, I'll have to brace against something. I spot the nearest tree just behind me and wrench his leg backward until I hit the tree, hard enough to rebound off it. As he resists and I stay still, I hear his hip socket snap.

Just as I think I've gotten him down, I hear wild crackling. Flames are consuming the trunk of the tree Valencia is perched in, set by the man I just took down on his way to the ground.

Or maybe by the guy flying toward me with his sword at the ready. I hold Faolan's grip in my right hand and lower down the staff in my left, listening to the unlocking mechanism twist and click. Faolan's owl flies away to circle while I unsheathe the thin blade hidden inside my staff just in time to meet my opponent's sword, my staff a ballast in my left hand to keep my weight off my knee.

Patrick is much better suited to this type of swordplay than I am. I prefer the thicker, wider blades of short swords and broadswords. But I revolve the hilt of the thin blade in my hand like my father taught me, circling my sword around my opponent's. That usually disarms a less experienced sword fighter. This man's blade might as well be welded to his hand. But he becomes less cautious with the line of his body. I lunge forward quickly, piercing the left shoulder falling into my strike range.

From the sound he lets out and the blood, it seems fatal, but right now Valencia and I can't afford to be anything less than sure. I stab him once more where I gauge his liver to be, just like my mother taught me.

With Faolan's aid, I advance as fast as I can, my right leg leading and my left dragging, to the tree going up in flames. The dead, brittle wood won't last much longer, and the flames are eating their way closer to Valencia's branch. She's been sending knives down at our remaining opponents the whole time, but I can tell she knows she needs to jump.

Her eyes are bouncing from tree to tree as if she's trying to find a bough she can grab on her way down. But I don't think she can make the jump without her back getting even more damaged than it already is, and I have an idea. I sheathe Faolan and offer her my open right hand, just as I did when I asked her to dance. When her eyes meet mine and I see her smile crack even in the midst of all this, I know she's ready. I tuck my left arm behind me so Faolan can latch to my shoulder holster and help support my back. I'll need both my arms for this.

As Valencia lets herself slip off the bough, she turns, gripping the branch with her hand as it comes down.

Her left hip lands against my right shoulder, just below my collarbone, and she plants her left hand. I slip my left hand down her hip to her inner thigh and spin her as hard as I can to the left, in line with our momentum. Her right leg arcs out like when we were dancing, but this time, she kicks the closest of our opponents hard enough to send him spinning. She presses her hands into my shoulders and kicks him again. He goes down, sending a reverberation through the forest.

Valencia's weight lands against my chest. My hands are still on her hips, and her hands are still on my shoulders. As I lower her down, her hands slip to my chest. Her hips run down the length of my torso.

We're both breathing hard, and the racing beats of our hearts seem to match as they run past each other. As her face gets closer to mine, I feel the warmth of her breath on my cheek. From her expression, I think she's feeling at least something like what I am. When her feet touch the ground, she runs her hand through my hair, and a sharp sigh escapes from my mouth. Her eyes widen. I think our lips are about to meet when she whispers in my ear.

"Stay still."

She pulls a knife out of her hair, shifting her body to my left. I run my left hand up between her shoulder blades and hold her left hip tighter to help protect her back.

Once she's thrown the knife, I look over my shoulder, but all I see is the empty forest.

"What did you throw at?" I ask.

"I saw the third one again," she says. "The smaller one. I think I got a better hit this time."

She hasn't straightened up her spine yet.

"How hurt are you?" I ask her.

"It's been worse," she says. "You?"

"Bruised. Winded. Bit dizzy," I admit. "But nothing serious."

We both look around. The forest is quiet except for the crackling of the fire through the dead tree, flickering out. We look at each other and then slowly move toward the two bodies. Their neutral clothing makes it difficult to place them, and I wonder if anything else on them or with them could explain why they came after us.

As we come up even with the body of the large man, I feel a tug on my right ankle, strong enough that it pulls me off-balance. I fall forward onto my stomach, gasping when I hit the ground, my left arm and Faolan pinned under me.

The man climbs up my back, grunting with the effort.

"May your brother enjoy the throne while he has it," he says.

I hear Valencia cry out and the man's breath catches. Croaks escape his throat and I know Valencia must have stabbed him. When I manage to roll over onto my back, I know he's dead.

This is all my fault. There's so much doubt in Patrick's rule, and I must have something to do with that. The sea monster threatening me is proof.

Blood rushes down my arm, soaking my sleeve and the ground around me. The air smells metallic. I can hear distant battle cries and swords clashing. For a moment, I know that must be my imagination, but the sound grows more and more real. It fills my ears and my brain. It drowns out everything around me, just as it did on the battlefield.

CHAPTER THIRTY-SEVEN

VALENCIA

There's a reason I don't often use my dagger.

There's a reason I prefer to throw knives than to stab them into people.

There's a reason I work with blades small enough to wound and halt, but not kill.

Despite Gael's growing reputation as an assassin, I don't like killing people. In that way, and so many others, I am my father's daughter and my father's son.

I had just found my dagger in the underbrush and I didn't plan on putting it into a man's back. But that man had a meaner blade aimed at the base of Cade's neck.

You never get used to the feeling of a blade you're wielding sinking into someone else's body. I doubt our soldados get used to it either, no matter how many battles they've fought. With my hands trembling now, I feel for them, how they've had to wound and kill so much more than I have, just to stay alive against our enemies.

Except right now, my enemy is also a boy who saved my life and whose life I just saved, and who I need if I'm ever going to see my father again.

I kneel next to him. "Cade?"

This boy might be the brujo who sealed our families in El Encanto. But I need him to answer me. I need to get him away from here before the man I hit with a knife regroups and comes back.

"Cade?"

He stares up into the sky like the clouds have teeth, like there's venom dripping from the leaves above us. At first I think he's wary of the burning tree, but the dead wood is almost out now, smoldering into embers.

A flare of red deepens the hem of my skirt. Blood, coming from his arm.

"Cade, look at me," I say, even though I'm not looking at him, I'm tearing a layer of my skirt. Then another one. I can use the linen of my enagua to bandage his arm and tie it back, keep the wound above his heart. I'll also have to wrap some kind of brace across his chest to keep his arm still. Probably? Forget every time I've ever complained about how much fabric our skirts are made of, how heavy they are. I'm going to be down to a layer of slip by the time I'm done with him.

With a strip of cloth in one hand, I reach for his arm.

Cade's eyes snap open. He holds his staff between us, and the owl's metal face twists. The owl's wings lift and spread out, a defensive posture.

I'm no expert on owls. And certainly not an expert on enchanted owls that live as statues atop royal canes. But I've gotten the general impression that this owl is some kind of extension of Cade, and even though Cade doesn't have wings he can puff up, he and the owl are both staring at me with equivalent expressions of *Don't you dare get near me.*

Really, Cade? Really, Owl That Likes Cade Better than Most People? I back up.

If Cade doesn't want my help, fine. I'll leave him here. If that owl can tourniquet a wound, he can be my guest. I'll even leave behind the cloth strips that used to be my skirt, as my gift.

My cane is currently in splinters across the ground, so I grab a staff one of the men brought with him. It's heavier than I'm used to, and it makes me feel lopsided. A staff made just for fighting is weighted differently than one that doubles as an aid for walking and standing. But it's the best I can do right now. Once the rush of this fight wears off, my spine will scream at me again.

Twin blooms spread through my chest, hope and dread. If Cade dies, does the curse on the forest end? Or does it mean it never ends? Should I be cheering right now or trying to save him?

Brushstrokes of light swim through the trees, like swarms of fireflies. The proud head of a luminous fox comes into view, this one grown, as regal as Bryna's mother. I'll go back with her. I'm not taking Cade's horse. That's fair, no? He's on his own because he wants to be, and he has a way back. Kind of. If he can get on the horse in the shape he's in. And I don't know why I'm even wondering, because this is distinctly not my problem.

The luminous fox blinks, the amber of her eyes vanishing and then reappearing. At her feet is the bolsa I brought with me, where I keep the gold leaf, the paling and shadowing powders, the metal dust.

"But how . . ." My protests sound even more pathetic out loud than in my head.

Who exactly could I turn myself into that Cade wouldn't wield a staff against? He knows me as a boy. He knows me as a girl. He's fought me as both. Maybe I could be an old woman? Surely he wouldn't curse a kindly vieja right out of a storybook.

The luminous fox nudges the bolsa.

A corner of tulle and copper wire sticks out.

"No," I say.

The luminous fox blinks at me. A brighter shimmer dances along the tips of her fur, a warning.

I don't like this. That warning tells me that she knows more than I do. If I let Cade die, maybe we never get our king and queen and my father and everyone else back. Maybe I never get to fix what I got wrong that night.

Maybe I never get to tell my father everything about who I am.

"If this doesn't work"—I pull out a pair of violet beaded slippers—"and he turns me to mushrooms or rocks or something"—I hold them toward her—"it's on your head."

CHAPTER THIRTY-EIGHT

CADE

Sparkles swim along my vision. Sunlight trails through the leaves, bouncing off raindrops or bits of dust. The air is warm, wet, soft. I wish I could take more of it into my lungs, but it catches in my throat.

The sparkles come closer, moving like a deer. She comes into the center of my vision. The fairy. The same one who warned me off when I was trying to stop Patrick's absurd battle plan. Glints of fairy dust puff from her hair as she moves.

She is close enough now to whisper in my ear. She strokes my neck. I can't understand what she's saying, some secret language. Maybe she's healing my battle wounds. They were all burning earlier, even the oldest scars. But now I can hardly feel them.

I want to touch her, but my arms are so heavy. My shoulder jerks when I try to lift my fingers to her face.

She feels me trying to move and pets me. "Rest now, Cade," she says. "Let me take you."

My heart stops jumping. My breath stops clicking in my throat. I let her take me.

CHAPTER THIRTY-NINE

VALENCIA

Cade's horse is glancing back at me with a snort that I swear means, *Qué carajo are you and why are you with my person?*

Getting Cade onto a horse and keeping him here is a lot harder than I thought it would be. And really, that's my fault. I underestimated Cade's muscle mass, which means I underestimated how heavy he is. I already knew Cade has a lot on me in height, weight, and strength (and, as grudgingly as I admit this, speed, in everything except actual running).

But under the weight that softens the edges of him, he has a hard pack of muscle I didn't know the depth of until I felt it, or, really, until I tried to move him. Cade's not conscious enough to engage it like he does when he's alert. So this is a little like moving an iceberg.

And I could do it, I could hold on to this iceberg of a boy, except that he wouldn't let me come near him until I put on this ridiculous outfit. So lucky me, I get to deal with the (surprisingly dense) bastard prince of Adare while I'm wearing this contraption made of wire, sheer netting, and gold leafing.

I bent the wings so they wouldn't poke the horse, which doesn't seem to have raised his opinion of me. All I get for my trouble is the wire frame jabbing into my ribs.

If I could, I'd swear my annoyance right up into the sky. But I can't, because I am supposed to be a fairy. A disguise that's only working because Cade is suffering from blood loss, and if I start yelling, it might rouse him into taking another look at me.

The ache in my body is an echo of the last time I was on a horse with him, and I cannot believe I am on a horse with Cade McKenna, again, this time by choice. And this time with him in front of me so I can hold on to him, and so he can't look at me too closely.

I nod at the glimmer of light in the corner of my vision, the luminous fox watching us. A true nod of thanks, no sarcasm—she nosed Cade awake enough to help me get him on this horse in the first place, and she's sparkly, so she looks like a fairy's companion.

Cade lolls, and I know he's drifting off. I stroke his hair with as many free fingers as I have and put on a voice as delicate as silver bells.

"You're safe," I say.

"Am I dying?" he asks.

What do I say to that? *I hope not but no promises?*

And what answer would make him easier to handle?

"Where do you"—my voice comes out too hard, like Valencia, and too low, like Gael, so I clear my throat—"Where do you wish to go?" I whisper, breathy as leaves rustling.

He comes back toward consciousness. "Claochlú Abbey," he says between hard breaths. "Please. That's where I belong."

Excellent. If we're on the way to a monastery, maybe he'll be in the mood to confess a few sins. Unburden his soul about his half sister, and El Encanto, and things neither Ondina nor I have even suspected.

The horse cocks an ear back, paying attention to anything that might be a weight cue from Cade.

But he's not shifting his weight. He's listing to one side.

"Cade?" I say in my fairy voice.

He slumps, and I have to hold on to him harder.

"Cade?" I say, louder, my voice no longer fairy-delicate.

He doesn't answer. He doesn't straighten up.

"No," I say under my breath. If I can get him to a monastery, they can help him. He's lost a lot of blood, but the wound is clean enough that if it's treated correctly, it'll heal fast. But if he goes all the way out, I won't be able to hold him on this horse. And I used the leftover bands of cloth to strap him to me, so if he falls, I'm going down with him.

My fingers comb through my hair for one particular blade. The one I was looking for to bring me back to life when the dress was poisoning me. The one I couldn't use on any of our opponents in the forest because it only would have helped them. The tiny hollow needle of a knife my father taught me to carry whenever I could.

I find the rounded bead of its hilt, slip it out of my hair, and stab it into Cade's uninjured arm.

The extract of the hierbas, concentrated into that narrow blade, hits his blood fast. He wakes up, sits up straight, and looks around. He takes in everything, from the trees going past to his bandaged arm, his wrist fastened behind his back to keep the wound higher. I can feel his nerves crackling with those reflexes I've had to go up against every time I fought him.

Before he can use them on me, I say, "It's okay. You're all right."

In my normal voice.

Caray.

He looks back at me, taking in my face, placing me as Valencia, as Gael, as the fairy who bandaged his arm and calmed him with the soft blush of her voice.

"Oh, please tell me you are kidding," he says.

"You're welcome," I say.

"I can't believe you did that," he says.

He sounds annoyed. Time for a subject change.

I touch his back, feeling the thick layer that protects his body and stopped my little knives from going into him.

"How much armor are you wearing?" I ask.

"More than it looks like I'm wearing, which is exactly the point," he says. "Now, returning to the previous subject."

So much for that.

"That was you back there?" he asks. "Pretending to be"—he takes in the makeshift white dress, the gold leaf—"this?"

I'm still holding him on the horse, so I don't really have the hands free for a proper shrug. "Lo siento."

He looks forward again. "Apologies sound more believable when you mean them, you know."

He sounds tired in a way that goes deeper than his wound. It's a kind of worn out that sounds woven into his heart, his bones, his being.

Before this moment, it hadn't occurred to me to wonder why Cade cast El Encanto. Now I'm beginning to. Cade is second in line to the throne, and he's proved himself more adept on the battlefield than Patrick, even if no one else knows it. He's half brother to a prince who's unsure of himself and his rule. Insecure men tend to lash out, and when insecure men on the throne lash out, it usually means someone's head. Cade's is a good candidate. If Cade wants to keep it, that probably means doing whatever Patrick wants, even if it's fighting in his place.

Even if it's casting an enchantment over his own family.

I can't get soft with Cade McKenna. But if I understand him, I have a better chance of getting what I want from him. And I understand him enough to know I wouldn't want to be him.

"Speaking of apologies"—I need him not to give up once the hier- bas wear off; I need him to stay with me—"I didn't poison you."

He doesn't look back. "I know."

"How?" I ask.

"Why would you bother helping me if you had?" he asks.

The smell of his sweat is like moss and the sea air along the Adare coast, and I'm guessing it's one the horse is used to. They seem to know each other well, the horse taking his rhythm, following a route they both know by heart. Gracias a Dios, because with Cade awake, there's no way his horse would follow my cues.

"Thank you," Cade says.

"No hay de qué," I say as I notice the grade of the terrain increasing. "So what's at Claochlú Abbey?"

Cade leans his head back. "The place I grew up."

"You grew up in a monastery?" I ask.

"I did," he says. "Why?"

"Nothing," I say. "You just don't seem like the kind."

"What kind do I seem like?" he asks.

"I'm not getting within a field's distance of that question," I say.

Cade laughs. It's a sound as unexpected and comforting as the fox's gait through the woods.

The grade gets steeper, the woods turning to rocky terrain greened with shrubs. Cade and I both instinctively lean forward as we climb. I worry for the horse, especially with me as more weight than he's used to. But even with the trees getting sparser and the rocks taking over the landscape, the horse doesn't falter.

I look toward the direction I last saw the luminous fox. She's gone, leaving a trail of light behind.

The land opens toward neat orchard rows and the low stone profile of the abbey.

Before we get to the vine-covered gate, I feel Cade breathe in harder.

"Our bodies will be as our hearts," he calls out to no one. And with enough effort that he gasps to get his next breath.

A few voices answer back: "And we will be called awake."

Cade says, along with all of them, one word:

"Incorruptible."

Monks in storm-gray robes help Cade off the horse, unlashing him from me, making sure his staff doesn't hit his arm. I still look enough like a fairy that the younger ones regard me in disconcerted awe. The older ones take me as no more remarkable than the abbey walls. How many fairies have they seen?

A couple of the monks seem familiar with Cade's horse, and from the tilt of the horse's ears, he's familiar with them. They lead him away while the others take Cade.

I slip away toward the orchard, cursing in a distinctly un-fairy-like fashion when I realize I've lost the staff I picked up. And my back lets me know it. So do my thighs and knees from being that long on a horse, especially one that size.

Staying still is worse than walking, so I change while walking. Out of what's left of my enagua, the pale linen slip I wore to play a fairy. Into trousers and a shirt. Wings folded down and away. Brush off the paling powder and the gold leaf. Slick my hair back. Shadow under the angles of my face to bring them out. Pinch my cheeks to look like I'm flushed.

Time to give another magnificent performance.

I run to the abbey gate, feigning complete panic as I ask after Patrick McKenna's brother.

When they tell me they have him, I act the part of the relieved guard.

When they ask me my name, I lie.

I give the name of Ondina's handsome cousin, the one I pattern my features after when I use shadowing powder to look more masculine. I can't be Gael right now; anyone who knows Gael knows him as an assassin. But if anyone checks up on my fake name, they'll hear about a real person. "The prince has sent me to follow his brother, to ensure his safety. I must send word."

Pain shocks through my back and I stumble.

One of the monks comes alongside me. "Let's make sure you're all right before we commence the letter writing, shall we?"

I nod, acquiesce, show just enough reluctance.

Someone just tried to capture or kill Cade. And if they succeed, we may never find out how to lift El Encanto. If I want my father and Eliana's king and queen and everyone else we lost back, I have to keep him safe.

I don't have to like Cade McKenna. I just have to protect him.

CHAPTER FORTY

CADE

My eyelids are still heavy, but the smell of gently burning spices pulls me from sleep. I know where I am. The low lights of wall lanterns and the deep humming stillness are proof. I let my eyes close again.

The colors of the fox's fur rush across my field of vision, followed by golden dust from the fairy's wings. Next is dancing with Valencia, then chasing Gael through the forest. One moment I'm chasing him, the next I'm chasing Valencia, her fuchsia skirts flashing against the browns and greens of the trees. She's looking back at me and laughing. A tree blocks my path. Its leaves are hair and its branches are arms. It hits me hard across the shoulder blades, knocking me down. When it comes at me again and I stab it with my broadsword, it bleeds and sputters, just like every soldier I've ever had to kill.

I gasp awake, heart pounding.

I hear bells pealing. Birdsong. Laughter, footfalls, voices cracking during chanting practice. I'm still here, I'm still safe, and it's morning.

But when I try to move, what stops me isn't a shock wave of pain through my spine, or a sharp pinch in my knee. It's my left side. When I leaned on my left hand.

I run my fingers over my left collarbone. I loosen my robe and see the silver circles of my rosary tattoo. They look as I remember them, the light and shadow of the stones, mineral dust mixed in with the ink to make them sparkle—no damage. I straighten my spine and feel the intricate cross they lead to, on the left side of my chest, over my heart. It looks unscathed, and there's no pain when I touch it. But as I work my way across the morning glories on my ribs, I find bruising. I lift my arm to look more closely and feel tremendous weight, dull and pulling. The pain in my arm and side worsens as I try to lift it to an even height with my shoulder. I give up and let my arm land on the bed.

Just as I'm closing my eyes to say my prayers, to tell God I'm grateful to be alive, Brother Peter enters.

"You're up," he says.

"Barely," I groan.

"I brought your favorites." He settles a basket next to my right hip, and the air turns tart with lemon and raspberry. "I'm under orders not to tell you all the goings-on until you eat and drink."

"What goings-on?" I ask.

"What did I just say?" He hands me a cup of water from the table beside me.

According to Brother Peter, the abbey is abuzz about my arrival nearly dead ("I'm nearly dead, am I?" "Who's telling this story, you or me?") and the arrival afterward of a beautiful Elianan my brother sent to make sure I was all right.

I listen, wondering if Patrick has really gotten himself in so deep with Bryna that her emissaries are checking on me. Or checking up on me.

Brother Béla comes in, singing whatever Alleluia they were practicing last. He sets a little jar of flowers on one of the wall shelves, puts a basin next to me, and hands me a sea sponge.

"Wash, my brother!" he says as he pours water in, and then flits away, Brother Peter right behind him.

As the water is splashing my face and I'm running the sponge over my ears and the back of my neck, Brother Silas comes in.

"Good to see you moving," he says. "I thought you might be done in this time."

I glimpse the version of him that terrifies new postulants. The piercing gray eyes. The serious expression.

"Where did all my lacings end up?" I ask.

"We had to use the quick releases," he says. "In a hurry. And there was a lot of blood. Might be time for some new ones anyway." He eyes me up and down.

"Not everyone is built like you," I say.

He leans back and his hands rise a bit.

"Just stating a fact," he says. "Those lacings served you well."

I realize I must still be glaring at him when he goes on.

"I worry for you," he says. "You seem . . . unwell. Not just injured. Damaged. The kind of damage that takes time to heal. How long can you stay?"

"I don't know. Not long. I'm worried about Patrick."

"Let Patrick worry about Patrick," he says. "I'll see if we can fit you with some temporary lacings. Let's get you up on your feet again."

CHAPTER FORTY-ONE

VALENCIA

T hanks to the monks, I have a borrowed cane. I pace one of the abbey corridors, the wood striking the stone.

Two of the monks sit on the low wall between arches. They have a book between them—La Biblia? Scripture of some sort? Some other scholarly text? I can't tell.

"Don't lead with your hips," one says without looking up.

I stop.

He closes the book. "You're leading with your lower body." He sets the book on the stone gently, reverently, as though placing a jewel. "If you're going to lead with your lower body, lead from your huevos. That's where men lead from."

I glare and call him a name unbefitting our sacred surroundings. Where does he come from telling me to lead with anatomy I don't have?

"Good." He smiles with an older-brother smugness. "Now insult me again, from deeper in your chest. You're not using all of your lungs."

"How would you know?" I say, except now that I am thinking about my lungs, my voice is coming out lower. Deeper. Richer.

If I wasn't currently so annoyed by Brother Opinions-I-Didn't-Ask-For, I might say something nice about his hair, the way it's shaved in some places and long in others. And the intricate tattoos I can just see the edges of at the hem of his sleeves. Los monjes can do that? Wear their hair however they want and have ink pressed into their skin?

"This charmer is Jeremiah," the second monk says. "I'm Owain." He looks over his shoulder as though searching for someone. "Have you met Peter? He's usually around here somewhere."

I don't even try to press the sarcasm out of my voice when I say, "Is he the one in the gray robe?"

Brother Jeremiah says to another monk, "Oh, he's funny, this one."

The simple syllable—he—catches me in the chest. I'm dressed in boys' clothing, so they call me *he*, and it gives me a painful amount of hope, this possibility that I could be called *he* when I'm a boy and *she* when I'm a girl.

The monks are staring at me.

"What?" I ask.

"You should try wearing a flowy shirt," Jeremiah says.

"He's right," Owain says. "You're not doing yourself any favors with the tunics. If you tuck in a billowy shirt, it'll make you look taller."

"If you shut up for the next five years, it'll make you sound like less of an ass," I say.

They look at each other and laugh. Not at me. More like I've gained the respect of a couple of men in a tavern.

"Apologies," Owain says. "You look like maybe you're trying to seem older than you are. We thought we might help."

What kind of monastery is this? Our Brothers of Grace and Elegant Dress? Do they venture to palaces in every kingdom and try to blend in with the cortesanos, catching eyes with their style and hearts with their lessons of kindness and gentleness? Not a bad strategy. But I wish someone had told me what I was walking into.

Before I can properly storm off, my curiosity gets the better of me.

"Why would tucking in my shirt make me look taller?" I ask.

"A billowy shirt will help your line," Jeremiah says. "Not that there's anything wrong with being short."

"Why do you look at me when you say that?" Owain asks.

Bells ring out, the approximately thousandth of the day. At the sudden noise, I nearly jump high enough to clear the stone arch into the courtyard.

Jeremiah and Owain don't startle. They rise from where they're sitting, nod their farewells, and make their way to whatever it is monjes do on the thousandth bell of the day.

Out of the corner of my eye, a flicker of light dances between stone pillars. Like embers or fireflies, but in shades of purple and blue instead of white and gold.

I turn to find it, but the brightening and dimming flits into the corner of my vision again.

Not a luminous fox. Something else. The blue and violet is so familiar, I practically hear Lila's calls and see the green of her feathers.

The light settles near the ground, bright as the glow off a candle. I kneel in the courtyard, dig my hands into the chilled earth until I find that shard of glowing glass. But this time it's not a shard. It's a globe big enough to fill my palm, nearly smooth except for the broken base. It hums like distant lightning. It turns warm and cool in my hand, the changes in temperature strong enough that I can still feel them even as I wrap it in the pocket of my cape.

The high tone off it, the ringing like the echo from a far bell, sounds like a warning. Like the fraying sound of Lila's distress call. And under the smell of lichen and lemon blossoms is something sharp, metallic. Something about it reminds me of that night, the first time I saw Cade.

Magic. Monjes. Monastery.

How did it take me this long to put it together?

A monk whose name I've been told is Silas—a monk who looks more imposing than any man of the church should be allowed to look—crosses the courtyard. Cade is with him.

Cade is looking better. He's working up a good walking rhythm, and his wounded arm seems relaxed.

The two of them notice me at the same time.

I don't like the way they're looking at me.

I don't like the way anyone here is looking at me.

My heartbeat flickers from my chest into my throat.

This isn't just where Cade grew up.

This is where he learned everything he knows.

Including how to do what he did to our families.

My hand finds my dagger.

"Gael, no," Cade says.

But I've already drawn. "Stay back."

The fevered gray of Silas's eyes bores into me. "You will lower your blade," he says with a voice as measured as the water in the fountains.

The steps of gathering monks echo through the courtyard. From the disjointed sounds of them shuffling, I can tell some are nervous, and some have come to watch the show.

"You will lower your blade," Silas says as levelly as the first time.

Cade and Silas trade a look. I shouldn't notice that. It gives Silas the split second he needs. He comes toward me and grabs my hand, pinching a tendon between two of my fingers in a way that makes me loosen my grip. That's enough to get the dagger away from me.

"No one draws on his brother in my priory," Silas says.

I reach for the tiny knives hidden in my hair.

Cade grabs my arm. "Please."

But I already have two out, the filigree hilts between my fingers. "Come closer. I dare you."

"Gael, please," Cade says.

"Do they know?" I ask. "What you did that night?"

"Don't do this," Cade says.

"Would they condemn it if they knew, or did they bless it?" I ask. "Did they teach you exactly how to do it? Or did you twist what they taught you?"

"What is he talking about?" Silas says.

But Cade's eyes stay on me. "We would never hurt anyone."

My laugh is bitter on my tongue, and I hold my blade-wielding arm straighter.

"Including you," Cade says. "Especially you."

My fingers tremble, and the tiny knives with them.

Cade looks around at the faces staring into the courtyard. "Did anyone tell him what we do here?"

Los monjes are silent.

"Did anyone explain to our guest who we are?" Silas asks.

Murmurs ripple through the assembled monks.

"Gael," Cade says, low enough that the muffled conversations around us don't stop.

I turn to face him, but keep the knives ready.

"They would never hurt anyone like me or like you," Cade says. "They taught me how to be a man."

"Tearing families apart?" I ask. "Cursing your own mother? That's what makes you a man?"

"You're not listening," Cade says. I think he's looking down out of embarrassment, but then I place the nature of his glance, an involuntary surveying of his chest.

"They taught me"—Cade's saying it slowly this time, emphasis and pause on each word—"how to be a man."

Like the convergence of stars, things I know but did not understand rush together, throwing off bursts of light.

The monks here offering me advice on how to walk and speak.

The soft version of armor Cade wears under his shirts.

How Cade placed me as someone declared a girl at birth but didn't mock me or scorn me for it.

He didn't make fun of me because he is a boy who was once considered a girl.

And these monks, his brothers, taught him how to live as who he truly is.

I look around at them.

Something in their identical expressions leaves a different cast on them, like a veil of water lifting between us. I notice the things I've missed by seeing them all as one, as a set of gray robes, instead of each as their own man. Yes, some of it is their bodies. How their faces are softer than most men's. The way most of them are a little shorter than most men I've seen in Eliana or Adare. But more than that, it's their expressions, the shared way they look at me and my wide hips and my bound-down breasts and my boys' shirt not in judgment but in understanding.

Their eyes don't say *What are you?*

Their eyes say *We have been where you are.*

It's only with the delicate clatter of metal against stone that I realize I've lost the feeling in my fingers.

I've just dropped my knives.

CHAPTER FORTY-TWO

CADE

When Gael flees, I know I should let him go. Every time he appears, he brings chaos I don't need.

I don't realize Silas can tell I'm wavering until he nods, as though telling me to do what my instincts are saying. So I follow Gael into the orchard.

I call his name when I'm within earshot.

He turns to me, a knife flashing in his hand. Not a chance that will stop me now. I've picked up speed going downhill and he's finally stopped running.

I reach under his elbow and grab it, turning his arm in an uncomfortable direction. He doesn't drop the knife, but he does pull back.

"Do you know what the worst part of this is?" he asks. "My father will never know me."

The grief in his words intertwines with how much I miss my mother. It draws me years back, into remembering how much I wanted to tell her who I was, how much I never wanted her to know, how much I wanted her to know without me having to tell her.

Gael advances, knife pointed at me. "Because of you."

This time I slip Faolan under my arm. Even with one arm in a sling, I need both hands. With my left, I grab Gael's wrist. With my right, I lock onto his elbow. It sends burning pain through my left arm and down my side, but I manage to get the knife out of his hand and into mine. I tuck it in the back of my waistband.

He produces another knife easily.

"You really think I'm responsible for the curse?" I ask.

Gael moves toward me again, this time less directly.

"Even now that you know what we do here?" I ask.

"That makes it worse," he says. "You realize that, right? You had this place. Everyone here was there for you when you needed them. And you took people that other people needed."

He's raising his voice, and without meaning to, I raise mine to match when I say, "I didn't."

"How could you do that?" he asks.

"I didn't." By now, I know I'm yelling. I don't realize I'm holding on to Gael's arm, making him look at me, until we both freeze.

Gael has finally stopped fighting with me. There are no knives in his hands. It's as if I can hear his brain working all this through. It sounds like water and polished glass being poured into a wooden trough.

I let go of him. But neither of us steps back.

"I saw you that night," Gael says, quieter now.

"I saw you too," I say, quieter along with him, ready to air all that's been unspoken between us.

"I know," Gael says. "That's why you wanted me dead."

"What?"

"The dress. You poisoned it."

This hits me more squarely in the chest than any blow either Valencia or Gael has landed on me.

"No," I say. "I would never do that. I've been trying to keep you alive."

"And why would you do that?" he asks.

"Because I knew if you died, everyone in the forest could stay that way forever," I say.

Now Gael does step back. "You think *I* did it?"

"You were on fire," I say, still agitated. "Of course I thought you did it."

"They were pieces of fabric, which were distinctly not on fire," Gael says. "They were crafted to look like autumn leaves. Is there such a thing as the art of fashion in Adare? I had nothing to do with what happened that night."

"I didn't either," I say.

"Then swear it," he says.

"What?" I ask.

"Swear a vow on it," he says. "Whatever kind of vow you swear here."

I take a breath and say, "I promise you, here, in the most sacred of places to me, that I did not enchant our families."

Gael's nod is so slight I wouldn't be able to see it if we weren't this close.

I keep my eyes on him. "Your turn."

His stare doesn't leave my face. "I vow with every loyalty I have to my home and to my princesa, I didn't curse anyone."

I think I believe him, yet there's no relief in any of this. We both know it. He just speaks it before I do.

"If you didn't do it, no one knows who did," he says. "And they're not waking up. And your home and my home will just go on destroying each other. Forever."

Even though that's exactly what I was thinking, I say, "We can't let that happen."

"'We'?" He straightens up, more on his guard. "There's a 'we' now?"

"Well, you don't want to let it happen, and I certainly don't want it to either. So, yes, 'we.'"

He turns away, and I'm sure I've lost him. But he's studying the outside wall of the chapel, the stone carvings of Saint Marinos.

"Our bodies will be as our hearts," he says.

"And we will be called awake," I say.

"Incorruptible," we say together.

Gael looks at me.

"Saint Marinos was declared a girl at birth, but he was just like us," I say.

"I don't belong here," Gael says.

"Believe me," I say. "At some point or another, nearly all of us think that."

The bells peal, and we watch monks process out of the chapel, followed by postulants. Dove-gray robes followed by robes the color of ripened wheat, or sand, or egg custard flecked with vanilla and nutmeg like Brother Béla makes. They all have their hoods up and their arms crossed into their sleeves.

From this distance, you have to look closely to see the differences between them: their choice of shoes, whether they have a knot cord trailing from a pocket or a delicate chain, how they carry themselves when their eyes are downcast to follow the monk or postulant in front of them.

"Have you met Brother Jeremiah yet?" I ask.

Gael looks at me with an expression that says, *And how would I know if I had?*

I laugh for the first time since Gael drew a blade in the courtyard. "He does everyone's tattoos, including some of his own. His hair is black and he wears it in a long tail, but the sides are shaved, around his ears."

"Oh," Gael says pointedly. "Right. We've met."

"He's a girl sometimes too," I say.

Gael blinks at me. "Really?"

"Yes," I say. "He uses different names. Talk with him. He'll tell you."

Gael's eyes go back to the carvings on the outside wall of the chapel.

"You grew up here," Gael says.

"In every possible way," I say.

"So when Jeremiah and Owain tried to tell me how to walk . . ."

"They were trying to do with you what we all do for each other, for anyone who comes here looking for help."

I think of the brothers who were here when I was, and who aren't anymore. The ones who left to build new lives.

"Who else knows?" Gael asks.

"About me?" I ask. "Well, the queen and the king, and Patrick, of course. And a few of the older advisors. But they're all in the forest. So, not counting them, besides Patrick, it's just Siobhán. And now you."

"That makes sense," Gael nods. "You and Siobhán are close, aren't you?"

The way he says *close* seems to carry extra weight.

"What do you mean?" I ask.

"You spend a lot of time together," he says. "I've seen the two of you talking a lot, in a way that looks . . . intimate."

"No, we're not"—I can't get the words out fast enough—"it's not like that. She's like a sister to me. She's an O'Loingsigh."

"So? Don't the McKennas and the O'Loingsighs marry each other all the time?"

I start laughing. Gael's not wrong. It's not just the ruling family. It's Fergus and Deirdre. And our cousins who went to live in the O'Loingsigh castle. At this point, our families are so interconnected we have to make sure we're not pairing up couples who are already distantly related.

That's when I realize Gael must not have put everything together.

It's strange to know that these two secrets about me can exist entirely separately. I always assumed that once people knew one, they'd know the other.

"Gael," I say, "Siobhán and I are related. We're cousins."

"But she's an O'Loingsigh," Gael says.

"Yes," I say. "And so am I."

"I thought you were a McKenna," Gael says.

"I am," I say.

"So you're a McKenna, like your mother, and an O'Loingsigh like . . ."

Gael stops before he finishes the sentence. Color drains from his face. His dark eyes widen, making them seem even darker against his now slightly paler skin. I see his knee heading for the ground.

I'm far slower than usual with the sling, but I still manage to catch his chest in my open hand before his knee gets anywhere near the grass.

"You cannot do that here," I say. "Or anywhere."

Gael nods. The way our scouts nod when I'm dressed as Patrick and give them a directive. Not good.

"I appreciate the gesture, but not only does no one kneel before anyone but God here, you could also destroy years of hard work by many people if you do that," I say. "Please. You cannot bow to me or treat me in any way as you would treat your princess or my brother. Ever."

Gael's breathing is faster than usual.

"Can't you just go back to quietly hating me?" I ask.

"That was quiet?" Gael asks.

"Good point," I say. "Nothing quiet about it. Exceedingly clear."

"Thank you," Gael says. "I was hurt for a minute. I put a great deal of dedication into hating you."

Gael is serious again when he asks, "So, Karlynn's eldest child is you."

"Yes," I admit.

"So you volunteered to go get . . . someone who doesn't exist."

"More or less," I say.

"And when anyone has been wondering where Karlynn's daughter is, where Patrick's sister is, they've been wondering about someone who doesn't exist," Gael says. "Who never existed."

I feel my mouth open slightly.

"Thank you for putting it like that," I say.

We look at each other for a moment.

"So your brother didn't kill or banish anyone," Gael says slowly.

"Far from it," I say. "Not much of a soldier either, to be honest. He really doesn't do well with killing."

"So I don't need to live in mortal fear of Bryna being near him," Gael says.

"I truly believe you don't," I say.

"And them falling in love with each other, that's not the disaster I thought it was."

"No," I say. "It could change everything. It could end the war."

"Then tell me what you want me to do."

"What?" I ask. I heard him, but I don't understand.

"Bryna wants to end this war," Gael says. "So do you. And you are the heir to a nation my princess wants allied to ours. In this, I follow your orders second only to hers."

"No, no, no," I say. I was afraid that's where this was going. "Listen to me. I am not a prince. Do you understand?"

I can't read Gael's expression, so I go on. "Even if I were, I wouldn't be yours. Please. I don't command you. I can't. So no oaths for loyalty. None of that. All right?"

Gael quickly gathers himself and starts walking back toward the central courtyard.

"Gael," I say, following him again.

"I'll stay to escort you back, or I'll leave in the morning, as you prefer," he says.

He turns toward the arched corridors.

"Gael," I say again, more urgently.

He looks back at me.

"Don't go back yet. Please," I blurt out. "Stay."

Gael nods as though I've issued an order. He keeps walking and I just watch him go.

CHAPTER FORTY-THREE

VALENCIA

I'm not sure what wakes me up after midnight, but there's a shivering energy around the monastery.

When I encounter Silas in the corridor, I'm pretty sure his presence explains it.

I stop.

He stops.

"I'm sorry," I say. "For drawing a knife in here."

I reach for one of the blades in my braided hair.

"Spare me the ceremonial gesture," Silas says. "However many you hand over, I know you'll be hiding more."

How does he know? I mean, he's not wrong. But how does he know?

"I wish someone had told you who we are," he says.

"I think they thought I knew," I say.

Silas considers a crack in a stone pillar. "Strange, isn't it?"

"What?" I ask.

"How you came here on Patrick McKenna's orders with such speed and yet have no horse," he says. "How does one manage such a feat of athleticism?"

My throat tightens.

"Centzontleh," he says. "That's what they call you in Eliana, isn't it?" He casts the appraising gray of his stare on me.

"How do you know that?" I ask.

"We have more in common than you think," he says.

He continues down the corridor, the hem of his robe sweeping after him.

"He's in the courtyard," Silas says without turning around. "In case you were wondering."

I find Cade exactly where Silas said, among the moon-silvered leaves and stone. He's moving in a way that might look like the slow blocking of a dance if I didn't know how Adare fighting works.

His sling is off. I hope the monks gave him permission for that.

I set my cane against the ground, anchoring my stance. "You're up late."

"If I stay in that bed another hour, I'll not only be a secret prince"— Cade turns, setting down the base of his staff—"I'll be a mad one."

I can tell from his smile that he's trying to make a joke, but it reminds me who I'm talking to.

"I'm sorry," I say. More stammer than say. "I shouldn't . . ." And so the stammering continues. I'm a picture of composure tonight.

He comes toward me, his staff in soft rhythm against the grass. "This isn't going to work."

"Altezo?" I say.

"That," Cade says. "Exactly that." He comes close enough that I can see the glint of dew on his robes. "If you act like I'm anything except Patrick's bastard half brother," he says—with a look that tells me he knows exactly what they call him around court—"if you change how you act around me, I'm finished. So we're settling this now."

"Settling what?" I ask.

202

He breathes out. "I need to get back into fighting shape. And I need a sparring partner."

He can't be serious.

I can't fight Karlynn's firstborn.

Well, I guess I already did, but *I* can't do it now that I know.

I can't fight the boy who should be ruling Adare.

"Don't make me command you," he says.

Before I can stop myself, I laugh.

"There you go," he says. "We're laughing."

He thinks I'm doing what he wants because he's loosened me up.

But I'm doing what he wants because unless Bryna is around, I follow his orders. Bryna wants to end this war, and Karlynn McKenna's firstborn is the most likely candidate in Adare to help her do it. He wants what she wants. That means I help him.

So here I am, on the damp grass in the courtyard, throwing my cane at Cade McKenna because he asked me to.

"And now we're fighting," he says. "This is good."

"How is this good?" I ask.

He blocks my next strike, his bastón stopping mine short. "You're halfway to not-so-quietly hating me again."

I'm still getting used to how Cade moves, his style of fighting. I've sparred with partners who had to take care with certain parts of their bodies. I've sparred with partners who use canes. But most had a style closer to what I learned, or I learned theirs as they taught me how to fight. Cade's style is as unmapped to me as the changing walls of the castle.

Cade comes at me. I block.

"Can I ask you something?" he says.

We disengage. I back up, nodding.

He doesn't come in again. "What should I call you?" he asks.

So I come in first. I can't have this conversation with him staring at me. "Don't overcomplicate this," I say. "When I look like the girl you know as Valencia, call me Valencia. When I look like the boy you know as Gael, call me Gael."

"I figured that much," he says. "I meant in my head."

He's wondering how to think about me in his head? I'm both touched and unnerved. Enough that he gets his staff close to my throat, stopping far before contact since we're just sparring.

"Are you talking about whether to think of me as *her* or *him*?" I ask.

"Sort of," he says. "Yes." He sounds adorably awkward about this.

"Both," I say. "Can I say both?"

"You can say anything you want," he says. "Especially here."

"Okay," I tell him. "Then when I look like the girl you know, call me Valencia, when I look like the boy you know, call me Gael, and in your head call me both. Simple enough, no?"

I mean it as a joke. Asking for all of me to be acknowledged like this seems like asking him for the moon and all the accompanying stars. But Cade just nods like I've cleared something up, and now that I've cleared it up, it's easy.

"How did you choose it?" Cade asks.

"My name?" I ask.

He nods.

"It's my father's middle name." I swing my cane toward his uninjured arm. "What about yours?"

"It's a family name." He catches my cane in the right place to knock me back. "I wanted a family name. But I didn't want to be another Karlynn."

"I figured that much," I say. "Karlynn's a woman's name, isn't it?"

"It's not," Cade says. "In Adare it can be a name for any gender. But it was a lot to live up to."

"So is choosing your own name," I say.

"True," he says. "I can tell you this, though. There's a lot unlucky about me being Karlynn's firstborn, but the tradition of heirs choosing their own name? One of the greatest strokes of luck I've ever had."

I adjust my grip on my cane, and my stance to take pressure off my back. "Do you know one of the greatest strokes of luck I've ever had?"

I move fast enough to get my cane behind his back, pulling him into me in a way I don't realize is going to be as intimate as it is until I'm doing it.

"Every time you've ever let your guard down," I say.

That did not sound nearly as flirtatious in my head as it did out loud.

Cade smiles. "Well played."

We disengage.

"My mother would love you," he says.

"Even though I've thrown knives at you?" I ask.

"That might work in your favor," he says. "I've made her fairly angry at times."

My heart flinches as I think of his mother, his father, Bryna's parents, my father, all those caught within the enchantment, as unreachable to us as the sky. We cannot draw them back, not with a hundred maps, not with the fastest horses, not with a thousand of our best soldiers. Yet all I want right now is to tell my father about this place, where there are other boys like me. My father, for all his lies told and blades wielded in the service of the crown, is a religious enough man that he never misses a mass unless his work demands it. Being here, among these sacred stones, feels like being given some celestial seal of approval to tell him.

"My father would love you," I say, and every word clenches tighter on my heart.

I don't know if I've ever seen this particular Cade smile, a rare one without suspicion or arrogance. It makes the water on the grass turn to points of silver.

This is how it goes over the next nights, getting the rhythm of fighting, slower, more gradual than the actual fights we've had. During the day, I'm alongside los monjes, learning their work. They show me how they make the kind of binding Cade and most of them wear, the seams of the lacings, the resin-strengthened cloth in brown, black, midnight blue, green. (Brother Jeremiah hands me one he thinks will work for me, saying, "If you're ever comfortable enough with us to let us fit you, we'll measure you. In the meantime, try this one.") They tell me how the abbey stays solvent by selling these to noblemen, how the profit means they can give them to those who otherwise might not be able to afford them.

That afternoon, Cade finds me outside in the orchard, running cord through reinforced eyelets. "You're a quick study."

"I wanted to help, so they showed me how." I finish with one of the cords. I change positions, easing the pressure on my back. "I may not be able to transcribe texts or absolve anyone's sins, but I can do this."

Cade hovers near me.

"Are you waiting for permission to speak?" I ask. "Because I'm fairly sure I'm meant to ask you for that."

He looks at my legs, crossed under me as I work. "Are you all right sitting like that?"

"Don't older-brother me," I say.

"What?" he says. "I know you by now. Neither your body nor your mind seems to do very well staying still. You're worse than I am."

"You can't complain about me now." I pick up the cords and lacers. "You had plenty of chances to kill me." I move to the shade of a tree, the branches low enough that Cade can sit if he wants to without going all the way down to the ground. I have enough contradictions in my own

206

body that it doesn't take much for me to square the contradictions of this boy, how he does things in fights that seem physically impossible but winces doing the things most people do without thinking.

"I couldn't have killed you even if I wanted to." He braces his hands behind him on one of the lower branches, half sitting, half leaning. "We vow here not to hurt each other. If we know about each other, if we know someone is like us, we are brothers."

"So that's why you saved my life." I spread my work back out on the ground. "The second time we met."

He looks at me. "The second time?"

I keep working, but say in a high, breath-filled voice, "Abandon your plan."

His face changes, his shock an echo of when he realized I was both Valencia and Gael. He already knew I was the fairy who brought him here. I'm rather proud that he didn't realize I was the fairy who tried to warn him off a battle.

"Sorry about that," I say, and I really try to mean it.

"Don't apologize to me," he says. "Apologize to the sídhe. Or simply wait and let them exact their price. They do not take kindly to being impersonated."

"You sound like Ondina." I glance at his bastón. "Is it true you named your staff or is that a rumor?"

"Faolan's my best friend," Cade says. "He listens no matter what I say."

I start another lacing. "Meaning he doesn't object no matter how stupid your ideas?"

"And acts as a sounding board for my best, I'll have you know," he says. "Don't you get thrown off by having so many different canes? I've seen you with at least three."

"No," I say. "Why?"

"Well, calluses, for one," he says.

He's not wrong. Each time I use a new cane, I have to get used to the places it wears against my hands.

"These help." I show him the scars on my palms. "Plus I'm just used to it," I say. "Different canes for different situations. What I'll be doing, what I'm wearing."

"Do you also have several best friends you choose from depending on who goes with your outfit?" he asks.

I glance at his again. I've seen it grow offshoots like a branch and then contract again. I've seen it latch on to a holster on his back like it could feel it. I've seen the owl on top come to life and then go still again.

My curiosity is getting to me.

"How does yours"—how do I put this?—"do what yours does?"

"The short answer?" he says. "It's made from the tree you climbed. You know, the one you jumped on me from."

I stop mid-lacing. "You're allowed to do that? Use the wood for something else?"

"If you're my mother, you are," he says. "And she had the help of a very meticulous O'Loingsigh metalsmith."

It takes a while of us staying there, quiet, nothing but our breathing and the wind sweeping through the orchard. But Cade tells me about the weeks after the battle that took his knee out. How he tried getting up, tried doing things like he used to, got frustrated enough to want to break the walls around him apart. That's when his mother shoved Faolan in his hand and told him, *This is your life now. This is your body now. Become acquainted.*

I tell him about the court physician talking to my father about the state of my back, the bones I came into the world with and everything that came with them.

"So when I first met you," Cade says, "when you impersonated a fairy"—he feigns a glare at me about that—"you didn't use your cane."

"No," I say.

He cringes. "That sounds unpleasant."

"Have you ever heard of a fairy using one?" I ask.

He looks pained, as though he knows exactly what I mean. Storybooks either don't speak kindly of people like us, or they don't speak of us at all.

The more hours I spend here, the more I learn about this place I never knew existed. Los monjes tell me about Saint Genoveva's, a convent of nuns equivalent to this abbey. ("Girls who were called boys at birth?" I ask. "Yes," Brother Paul says. "And ones who are like you, whose hearts don't quite fit into one word.")

Cade shows me the stained-glass windows turning the sunlight green and blue. The panels depict Saint Marinos accused of getting a local lord's daughter pregnant and being made to face the sea monsters. ("Ironic, isn't it?" Owain says. "He couldn't exonerate himself without revealing something none of us want to reveal. But the sea monsters, they saw the truth in his heart.") As I follow the windows, the sea monsters bow before Saint Marinos, their reverence proving his innocence. And the center of me lights with the hope of knowing a place like this exists.

My body eases up in a way it hasn't since Ondina told me we were going to Adare. I don't stand or sit longer than I can. I don't hold my posture rigid in a dama's bearing. I get up during compline if I need to, closing my eyes and listening, pacing at the back of the chapel as quietly as I can. I wait for someone to glare at me, but no one does. Some of the monks seem to know what I'm doing—the ones who use canes, the ones who have old battle injuries. They give brief nods of recognition, as though encouraging me to do what I have to for my body.

As Cade gets stronger, I go less easy on him. When I get my cane behind his right ankle, it knocks him off-balance. I catch him, one arm around his lower back so he doesn't actually fall. I don't want him falling, especially on his arm.

"Don't forget your center of gravity," I say.

He breathes hard enough that I wonder how much I surprised him. But he gets his bearings, standing upright again.

"I know you have to keep your stance high when you're being Patrick," I say. "But when you're fighting, let it go back to its natural place."

His eyes keep going to the ground between us. Did I knock him off-kilter that badly? Maybe I still need to be gentler.

When my hand ends up on top of his, he asks me about the veins of scarring on my palms. "Did you get those from throwing?"

"More like from learning how to throw." An idea brightens at the back of my brain. "Do you want to learn how to hold one?"

"I'm not really used to handling anything that delicate," he says.

"You stole how many of them from me and you don't even want to know how to use them?" I ask.

"Stole them?" He laughs. "You threw them at me."

I touch my braid, adjusted, per the monks' advice, to look more masculine. "Do you want to start with learning to pull one out?" I ask.

"Try pulling a knife out of your hair?" He says it as though I've just offered him a pair of my chonies as a trophy to show fellow soldiers.

I take his hand and direct his fingers to one of the seams of my braid.

I don't realize how close this is going to get us, and how much different it's going to feel than grappling, until we're looking at each other.

I guide his fingers, helping him ease a knife out of my braid.

The blossoms in the orchard sugar the air, the sky is blue enough to look like a sea above us, and the sun brings out the faintest tint of copper in Cade's hair. But none of that makes me wonder how I feel about this boy. What makes me wonder is this sensation of both our hands on the same knife.

Then, with the same grip on my hand Silas used, he gets me to drop my knife.

"You're leaving your pressure points open again," he says.

"I know." I shake out my hand. "However you came by your reflexes, I want to learn."

A sad pallor crosses Cade's face. "No, you don't."

I realize how stupid what I just said was.

His reflexes kept him alive in battle, and now they probably keep him up at night. The fights that sharpened them probably haunt his nightmares.

Cade takes hold of my shoulder, pinching another point between his fingers. I drop my cane.

"You're still doing it." He hands my cane back to me.

I swear under my breath before remembering where I am.

I try going back at him. I've barely shoved my cane toward him when he's behind me, Faolan against my shoulders.

Even through his robe and his lacings, I can feel how hard he's breathing, the rhythm of his chest against my back.

"Do you know what happened there?" he asks. I know he's trying to sound in command, but his voices hitches.

"I let you get behind me?" I ask.

"No," he says, his voice level again. "You went in angry."

I tap the end of my cane twice on the ground, conceding the point.

He lets go. "You can't go into a fight angry. It doesn't make you stronger. It makes you sloppy. Sometimes waiting an extra moment is the thing that saves you."

With my next step, I lose my footing on the damp grass.

Cade throws a hand under my back, catching my weight. I set a hand against his chest, a reflex.

"Don't forget your center of gravity," he says.

His arm stays under me. My hand stays on his chest, the cloth of his gray robe between my palm and the firm plate of the lacings underneath.

His expression changes. He looks serious, almost worried.

He looks as worried as I probably should be. This boy is not like me. He's the eldest prince of Adare. I cannot think of kissing him, and this thought—of course—makes me think about it more.

"Uh," Cade stammers. "I'm sorry." He returns me to standing.

"No," I say. "I'm sorry."

When we're fighting, when we're moving against each other, he's the boy I've known this whole time. But as soon as we stop, I remember who he is. Karlynn's eldest son. Her oldest child.

I add, as quick as any nervous habit, "Su Altezo."

"Please don't start that again," he says. "It's still Cade."

I make myself say, "Good night, Cade."

"Good night," he says, followed by a mix of letters that sounds like Gael and the first syllable of Valencia at the same time.

Horror casts over his face.

"Sorry," he says. "I think I started to say both your names."

"Don't be," I say. "It sounded like Val. I like it."

"Really?" he asks.

Val. The single syllable holds both Valencia and Gael. I can taste the shape of it in my mouth. Sometimes I'm Valencia and sometimes I'm Gael and the name Val reconciles those two names in my one heart.

"It feels like all of me at once," I say.

Cade smiles like I've just drawn the moon closer.

CHAPTER FORTY-FOUR

CADE

I need to go to bed. The back of my head leans heavily against the stone corridor, and I still can't seem to catch my breath, even though we stopped sparring long ago.

This feeling makes all the other times I leaned my head against these corridor walls seem mild, a mere hint of the real thing. Even Isabel, who broke my heart when she told me I could never try to find her in her village. Or Dominus, who nearly coaxed me into doing things with him I knew I couldn't do. I remember trying to think through ways I could let him have me without him learning too much about me.

Problem is, Val already knows everything. Everything about who I am, who I was born to be, how I became Cade. And Val still wants me. I can tell. I've been able to feel it the whole time, and it makes me kick myself for not figuring out sooner that Gael and Valencia were the same person.

And worse, I still want him. Her. Val. Gael. Valencia. Every form of that gorgeous and glorious being. She fascinates me. He challenges me. He pulled me in even when she was pushing me away.

I start to wonder what's so wrong with this. Why can't I have Val?

Why can't he have me? She already knows everything, and I trust him to keep it all a secret. Why shouldn't we do what it seems we both want to do? Could I let Val see me? All of me? And if I did, who would it hurt?

Another part of my mind, one that's probably located closer to my brain and farther from my belt, tells me that even if I can't think of answers to those questions now, there most likely are answers.

I start walking toward the abbey's ofrenda. I pass some of the nooks with sculptures of Saint Marinos or reliefs of sea monsters frolicking above little fountains.

The closer I get to the ofrenda, the stronger the scent of flowers becomes. Palm branches come into view. The embroidered hand-kerchiefs. Dolls made from maize, beaded slippers, varnished fans. Although some of them now represent monks long passed, many were left here by those living now, but living new lives.

My old stuffed owl is on a shelf between a sun-faded portrait and a jeweled necklace. My mother told me about when she first put that owl in my cradle next to me, and about the first time she saw me rest one of my tiny hands on it. I held it every night as I slept for years after that. I looked into its eyes thinking about how I knew I was a boy, and how sad it was, because it was a mistake. I wasn't allowed to be a boy. I had to grow up to be a queen like my mother, like generations of queens before her, not a king.

I think about what Val might bring here, leave here, if he was going to take this path. I can't miss this chance. I need to tell Val how I feel.

When I knock on Val's door, I hear him tell me to come in.

When I go in, I see Val's feet against the wall, his hair spread out over the floor. For a moment, everything seems upside down to me, as if he's the one who's right-side up and I'm the one walking on the ceiling somehow.

"It's for my back," Val says. "It helps balance out the pressure from standing and sitting."

"Oh," I say.

Val pushes off the wall and throws his legs back toward the floor, flipping over and righting himself.

"I just came to . . ." I'm talking to Val's back. His arms are out from his body as though he's steadying himself.

"Say good night," I finish.

Val turns to me, settled except for his hair, which looks like the wind has gone through it.

"Well, good night," I say.

"Good night, Cade," Val says.

I'm such a chicken.

CHAPTER FORTY-FIVE

VAL

I'm not exactly sure what I'm looking at, but it has a lot in common with the altares and ofrendas we build in Eliana, especially in the fall. Except it's spring, and alongside the orange and gold and rich brown of marigolds there's the white of calla lilies, crisantemos, roses. In between the flowers and branches are pieces of jewelry and clothing, each carefully placed.

The rhythm of Faolan against the ground announces Cade even before he says, "You really do find your way into everywhere, don't you?"

When I turn around, I remember why I'm having so much trouble looking at him lately. It's not just who he is. It's how he looks at me, like he's looking at all of me. Gael, the equal balancing weight to Valencia, the unknown part of me that weaves together with the part everyone else knows.

"What is this place?" I ask.

"It's where we leave the pieces of us we need to let go of." Cade picks up a toy owl that's been so well-loved the stuffing has gone lopsided. Cade sets it in my palm, and the owl lists to one side in a way that lets me imagine a small Cade playing with it.

"But there's nothing girl-specific about this, is there?" I ask. "It's an owl."

"Correct," Cade says. "But he held a lot of the expectations about me being a queen like my mother. And he seems to like it here." Cade sets him back down among the ribbons and flowers and then startles, looking past me.

I check behind me, ready to pull a knife from my hair.

A fox with a red-orange coat, fur rippling with embers of light, tilts his head at Cade.

I look between them, Cade backing toward the altar while light shimmers over the fox's brush.

"Don't be scared," I say, though I'm not quite sure which of them I'm talking to.

The light goes through the true black at the tips of the fox's ears and tail. Just as Cade settles in the presence of this one, another appears, with white fur thick like a layer of snow. Then another with a coat as deep as well-made ink. The light that flickers across the tips of their fur tilts greener, like the winter lights I've heard about but that we don't usually see in Eliana.

"They like you," I say.

"They're huge," Cade says.

"They also wouldn't show up just to eat you," I say.

Cade reaches out a hand, trying to get them used to his scent.

"Probably," I say.

"Probably?" Cade looks at me, but he has enough instinct with animals not to move his hand suddenly.

When a fox nudges her head against Cade's hand, Cade cautiously strokes her fur.

"You look alarmed," Cade says to me. "Which makes me alarmed. Should I be alarmed?"

"I don't think so?" I say.

"You don't think so?" He gives a nervous laugh. "Thank you, I feel exceedingly better."

"No, I mean"—I watch a gray fox, the light at the tips of his fur turning him silver, make a curious survey of Faolan—"I've just never seen them take like this to anyone—" I cut the sentence off before I say *from Adare*, or *like you*.

"Do they just follow you around?" Cade asks.

"Sort of," I say.

"Why?" he asks.

"You wouldn't believe me if I told you," I say.

A wing of green flashes above us, deeper than the luminescent green crossing the foxes' fur. I look up and think I see a quetzal's silhouette against the moon. But before I can get a good look, the shape vanishes into the night.

At another flutter of wings, Cade and the foxes startle back. Not a quetzal this time. The stuffed owl shivers to life, cloth coat turning to feathers, embroidered eyes turning to the polished obsidian of owl's eyes. The owl flies off into the dark, a second silhouette alongside what might be a quetzal.

The foxes bound off into the night, light rippling over their fur in washes of green and gold. They follow the owl like he's a star leading them.

Cade and I stare at each other for the space of a breath, and we know what we have to do.

CHAPTER FORTY-SIX

CADE

"Am I really seeing this?" I ask.

When I don't hear an answer, I look around. It's as if Val just disappeared. It reminds me of traveling and training with Nessa, and not in a good way.

I go back to staring at the floating gardens that seem to have sprung up out of nowhere, with Elianan jardineros tending the beds and trees. Islands of greenery dot a brilliant blue-green lake that looks made from the river running through the castle. Without the motion of the river's current, the color of the water has cleared and settled. Looking through it toward the lakebed is like holding up a piece of polished aquamarine to the sunlight.

Some of the islands grow vegetables, the vines of yellow squashes trailing into the water while tomato and bean plants flower tall toward the center. Some have fruit trees with blossoms already appearing. Some are just flowers, giant ones with yellow petals opening themselves for the sun and shorter ruffled ones, their pink and orange and white petals falling into the water when the wind flutters over them.

"It is . . . beautiful," I admit, out loud.

Val has appeared, wearing a dress I've never seen before, dark blue, embroidered with flowers. Her hair is smoothly wound into twists and pinned in place, likely with more knives woven in than I can possibly guess. Her eyes look larger, and I notice she's lined them so they stand out against her rouged cheeks and deep red lips. Considering she only disappeared for a few minutes, I have no idea how all this happened. It takes longer for me to get into my lacings in the morning.

"How did you . . ." I don't finish the question; I just look Val over from head to foot a few times.

"A lifetime of practice," she says before turning her gaze to the gardens.

Fergus's sisters must have added a few touches: floating candles in the stone fountains that have come up from the ground among the hedge roses, lichen-covered rocks on the flowered islands, even some climbing vines to connect the new gardens with the castle walls. I'm surprised that last one got past Nessa. It's a clear security risk.

Then I think maybe they had nothing to do with it.

Maybe it was Patrick.

It had better be Patrick.

I march into the castle, Val still at my side. I'm gripping Faolan more tightly than usual and the owl begins to squawk, warning me that I am angry and need to calm down before I do something I'm likely to regret.

CHAPTER FORTY-SEVEN

VAL

The moment I walk into the tent I share with Ondina, I know some-thing's off. I can't tell what. Maybe the scent in here has changed, so slightly I can't place it, but enough to know someone's been in here. Or something's been moved, and I can't figure out what.

My hands scramble for the knots in the wooden bedframe. When I pull them aside, I sink to the rug in relief. The pieces are still there, winking at me from the dark hollows.

Nothing stolen. Not even what I stole.

I'm too tense. I'm starting to see things that aren't there. If I keep this up, I'll grab on to anything. A woman smiling at me. A guard nodding as I pass.

So I slow my breathing. I need to think clearly.

I pretend I'm thinking clearly as I change from Gael to Valencia. From my shirt and trousers into an indigo dress embroidered with the sky-blue and pink of borraja flowers. From my hair pulled back to being loose, with just enough pinned into twists to hold my knives.

I pretend I'm thinking clearly as I put away the deep berry red of my poison stain, and instead paint my lips with ordinary color. I pretend

I'm doing this as a sign that I'm not among enemies quite as much as I thought. I am most certainly not leaving my lips free of poison because I'm thinking about kissing someone. And if I am, it's definitely not Cade McKenna, the last boy in two kingdoms I can allow myself to want.

CHAPTER FORTY-EIGHT

CADE

"Should I disarm?" Val asks.

I watch as her hands reach for her hair, but stop her.

"No need," I say. "But kind of you to offer."

I take a deep breath, bracing myself for whatever is going on in the audience room, then burst in as always.

There's a cacophony of voices, as usual, but one rises above the din. It's Lowell, discussing his plan to oversee the maintenance of Adare's roads. All of them.

Patrick just nods along as Lowell is speaking, as if all this was decided before Lowell opened his pretty face.

I stop Lowell mid-sentence. If I wait till he's finished, we could be here all day.

"We have an urgent message for Prince Patrick," I say in my most commanding voice.

Val shoots me a look that says, *"We"? What do you mean "we"?*

Patrick takes one look at my face and clears the room, but not before thanking Lowell for his dedicated service. Lowell bows deeply, closing his eyes, before turning and exiting, the edges of his green-and-gold brocade tartan brushing various people and pieces of furniture. He doesn't shoot me a look or make some kind of remark. Maybe he doesn't feel he needs to, which is worse.

As soon as the door closes and it's just the three of us, I can help myself no longer.

"Brother, have you truly lost your wits?" I ask. "All the roads? To Lowell? How do you think that will go?"

"The rumors about the thefts are just that, rumors," he says. "I've been assured that any robbers are simply rogues, not anyone Lowell condones. In fact, he just explained his plan to apprehend them."

"I'm sure he did," I say. "You know how important those roads were to our mother. You know how much time she put into ensuring they would be safe. How can you let Lowell undermine years of her work?"

"You've had plenty of opportunities to step in, and you've chosen not to," Patrick says. "You have no desire to rule, and neither do I. Lowell does. You were planning to step aside anyway. Well, so will I. And Lowell can rule. He'll have what he wants, and so will we."

Patrick looks at me as if he's solved all our problems.

I've seen Patrick do so many things I never imagined he would. No whisper of this ever even crossed my mind.

"No," I say. "Not him. Almost anyone would be better than him."

"Why?" Patrick asks. "He was willing to do what you wouldn't. He was willing to actually help me. To teach me what I needed to learn. He didn't just tell me to do better. He has patience with me that you've never had."

His words stop me.

All my life, I've wanted to be like my mother. I still do. But right now all I can think of is her suppressing a sigh when Patrick faltered with a sword grip, when he secretly read plays while he was meant to be studying military history, when she tried to explain the bloodstained dance that was every battle plan and he winced away.

And then there was our father. His patience. His willingness to explain anything a hundred times. His faith that Patrick could and would understand the next time, or the time after. Whether it was the intricacies of ceremonies I rarely paid attention to, or the modulation of his tone and posture while meeting with leaders, our father taught Patrick the way our mother never could and I still can't. And because of it, I'm losing him, and the very ground of our home, to Lowell.

Out of the corner of my eye, I see Val backing toward the door. When I turn to look at her, she says, "I really should be going. No one knows I've returned."

"Stay," I say. "Please."

"What is this anyway?" Patrick asks, his narrowed eyes alternating between Val and me.

"I want some assurance you're not about to run this nation into the ground," I say.

"If you think you can do better, you're welcome to try," Patrick says. "Let the next in line take a turn. But you'd rather do as you please, I'm sure."

Any fondness I had for him drains away.

"Do as I please?" I repeat. "You really think that's what I've been doing? What are you doing? Letting your advisors make all your decisions for you? Letting one of them take over your throne and God knows what else because you find your responsibilities too difficult?"

His eyes flash a flinty gray, reflecting the shields on the walls. "You mean like you did?"

Heat rises from my chest to my face. "If you're serious about an alliance with Eliana, a marriage with Bryna," I say, "do not do this. Do you want to marry her? Do you want the war to end?"

"Of course," he says. "But Bryna cannot run this nation, and someone has to."

I stare at Patrick for a moment, probably the way our mother used to stare at us when she was trying to figure out what we were hiding from her.

"You want to move to Eliana when you marry, don't you?" I ask.

Patrick nods.

"Well, if you're going to let someone live your life for you," I say, "you could do worse than her."

I hear a slight metallic pinging and turn to see Val with a knife trained on each of us, as if she can't quite determine whether her monarch has just been insulted.

"Sorry," Val says, concealing both knives again. "Reflex."

"Go and get your princess," I say to Val.

Val hesitates.

"My brother won't listen to me," I say. "Maybe he'll listen to her."

Val opens the door—slowly, as if giving me as long as possible to change my mind. When I don't, she leaves, closing the door behind her.

As soon as Val is gone, Patrick's eyes bore into me. "You've gone too far this time," he says, his voice rising.

"And you haven't?" I match the volume of his voice, but without breathing the way I need to, pressing my voice thinner and rougher.

Patrick just seethes, so I go on.

"And where are the rest of the leaders?" I ask.

"They wouldn't wait," Patrick says. "They've left orders for you to bring our sister to them or to send word once she's here. How did you expect me to keep them here? And why? We both knew there wouldn't be anyone coming back with you."

"So they left angry," I say. "You let leaders who supported our mother's work leave angry."

"Lowell tried to keep them here, but they couldn't stay indefinitely," Patrick says. "They have their own responsibilities at home."

"Lowell," I say. "Because you can't do anything without him."

"Seriously, Cade?" Patrick asks. "You're in no position to challenge me."

"I came here ready to tell you I supported your union with Bryna," I say. "That I would stand by your side and help you build peace. Quell any uncertainty and rumors. But this. This is too much. Losing you to Eliana. Dropping your birthright and mine into Lowell's lap."

"So have you changed your mind?" Patrick asks. "Do you want to rule Adare?"

All my attention is going toward breathing to settle my blood.

Before I can answer, Patrick says, "Fine timing you have. I am closer than we've ever been to securing a treaty. Weeks from a wedding, months at the most. And now, now is when you decide to take over."

Patrick stares at me.

"No, Cade," he says, low and quiet. "You had your chance. Many chances, in fact. I've gone this far, and I intend to finish what I started."

"I cannot let you," I say. "I will not let you. Not after this."

I go to the wall to the left, my footsteps firm even though my hands are shaking. I steady them and pull down a longsword, the kind Patrick likes best. I hold it by the guard, the hilt facing toward him, and toss it. He catches it.

He says nothing, but sets his jaw and narrows his eyes, accepting my challenge.

I take down a broadsword my mother particularly liked, tucking Faolan into my left hand, despite the sling still around my arm. I've fought more challenging opponents with worse injuries.

Patrick's left hand begins to quiver as he raises it behind his head. I smile.

He closes his fingers like my mother taught him, pressing his thumb against his forefinger.

Faolan's different grips let me hold the one that's most like a walking stick while leaning the side of my hand on the one I use like a cane.

I let Patrick make the first move, like I've always done with him.

He goes for my left shoulder.

I bring my sword down with a decisive block, the kind that can knock a lighter sword like his out of grip.

But he holds fast, and sweeps for my right leg.

I lean my left hip back against Faolan and lift my sword and my right foot up for a moment. When my foot comes back down, there's a reverberation through the room, and my sword clangs against Patrick's.

My eyes blink against the crash and when they open again, the walls of the audience room are gone. Patrick and I are still on the floor of the room, but only part of it. The high-backed audience seat remains, on its platform behind Patrick, but all the other furniture has disappeared.

It's as if the castle has been reduced to its skeleton around us, as if we can see through some of the walls, the ones that don't bear weight.

For a moment, Patrick looks as shocked as I feel. Then he says, "I take it this was convenient for you? Is that why you did it?"

"It wasn't intentional," I say. "It just happened."

"So it can be unintentional for you, but when it's unintentional for me, I'm not trying hard enough, right?" Patrick says. "You tell me to focus, don't you? To clear my mind and calm my heart?"

His voice and face are taunting, mimicking me. He knows how much I hate that.

"It could have been Lowell," I say, my eyes boring into him. "Did you even know? How much of your power you've already given him? And mine?"

Patrick's chest rises and falls quickly, but I can't read his expression. He takes a swing for my head.

I block and direct the rebound off his sword toward the middle of his back.

He's far more agile than I am and does a full turn over his left shoulder, his sword arm arcing back toward my upper chest.

He must be practicing with Siobhán. I've never seen him this good.

I turn too, but only halfway, pulling both Faolan and my sword arm in toward my body. Using the point where Faolan's sturdy edge meets the floor, I propel myself backward.

My shoulder blades hit Patrick square in the chest. I jam my right elbow into the upper part of his stomach.

He grunts and flies backward, but hangs on to his sword.

A wall catches him, and as I turn I realize we're in the great hall. I have no idea how we got here. What feels like the entire Adare court and half the Elianan contingent are watching us.

My brother pulls his knees in toward his chest as he hits the wall so he can spring back off it.

I check my grip on my sword, blocking my body as I face Patrick. I wrap my left leg around Faolan, locking my bad knee into one position. I slide into a deep lunge, pressing my grip on Faolan into my left side just above my hip joint.

When Patrick lands, steady on both feet, sword still in hand, his face is inches from the tip of my blade.

Patrick smiles. "You don't scare me anymore," he whispers.

"I've always been able to scare you," I say. "It was always so easy."

I hear my own tone and feel my face twisting into an expression I haven't worn since we were children. Patrick and I fought all the time then, and I always won. I was bigger, stronger, ruthless. He could just be himself. He could just be a boy. And I hated him for it.

Our swords meet again. We both cry out as we attack, but I still hear an occasional gasp from our audience.

"You've undermined faith in my rule, in one of the most embarrassing ways possible," Patrick says.

I know he must be referring to the sea monster. What I don't know is how he found out. Or how I thought he wouldn't.

Patrick's blade flashes. I grip Faolan in my left hand as I dodge, but my fingers are going numb. I nearly lose my grip on him and stumble slightly.

As I recover my stance, I feel a sting on my forearm. I look down and see a thin red slash, a drop of blood at the end. It's a tiny wound by my standards, but it's the first time Patrick has drawn blood from me in years.

I lunge forward again, crashing my sword into his.

"You know I'm better," Patrick taunts. "You know I could beat you now."

"You don't have a chance," I say. "You never have, and you never will."

CHAPTER FORTY-NINE

VAL

When I find Bryna in the gardens, it's clear that neither she nor anyone she's with knows what's going on inside the castle. Adare children and their mothers are teaching Bryna one of the more complicated dances, to the sound of musicians playing flutes from Eliana and whistles from Adare. Even Ondina seems to be having a good time, laughing as Nessa twirls her around.

Bryna tumbles out of a set, laughing, when she sees me.

"You're back!" She sounds as delighted as when a maracayá purrs at her.

My compliments to Ondina. However she covered for me was good enough that Bryna doesn't even seem worried.

"Have you come to join us?" Bryna asks.

Then she sees my face. "What is it?"

I glance at the assembly. It all looks thrown together out on the grass, spontaneous. I might as well be barging into a scene of her petting deer and rabbits, or weaving flowers into children's hair.

"Words, Valencia," Bryna says.

I hesitate. Maybe I'm raising an alarm for no reason. Are Cade and

Patrick trying to kill each other, or is this simply how the McKennas have heated conversations?

But the look on my face must be enough, because she comes with me.

CHAPTER FIFTY

CADE

As we're staring at each other, eyes and swords locked, hilt to hilt, something shiny zings between our blades and faces.

We both turn to see a heavily bejeweled dagger vibrating in the wall opposite us. Everyone is silent, including us, and all that can be heard is the blade itself.

Patrick and I look around, moving only our heads, our sword arms still pressing into our blades.

I see Val and narrow my eyes, but she lifts her shoulders and shakes her head as if to say, *What? I didn't do it.*

Then I see where Patrick is looking.

Bryna is standing in the middle of the hall, eyes stormy. Her open hand rests against her thigh. Her breath is fast, shifting the embroidery on her dress.

"I came here to broker a peace," she says. "After years of war. A peace with people who killed my brothers. My cousins. My blood."

She wraps her right hand into a fist and holds it against the core of her body, right in front of the filigree cross she often wears.

"If I could have known of this," she says as she walks toward us, "of your infighting, your destruction of your own families, brothers fighting brothers, and over what?"

When she is nearly even with us, Patrick and I break apart, the tips of both our swords hitting the floor in front of us.

Bryna pulls her dagger from the wall, slipping it back into its sheath, which is somewhere in the rippling amber of her curls. When the dagger is back in place, I recognize the hilt. It masquerades well as a hair adornment.

As she passes between Patrick and me again, she turns to him and says, "Perhaps my coming here was nothing more than a waste of time."

Patrick's eyes take on the warmer brown they have when he feels hopeless. He watches as the princess moves closer to Val.

"Shall we get some air?" Bryna asks Val. "I don't care for the atmosphere in here."

As Bryna proceeds out the main doors, Patrick's eyes are stuck to the floor a few feet in front of him.

I notice the sling that was holding my left arm has crept up higher than my elbow in back. Rather than reposition it, I just pull it off over my head.

As I'm walking away, I hear Patrick say to Val, "Let him go. Trust me, you don't want to be around him right now."

I'm sure he's right.

As I pass Fergus, I press both the sling and the hilt of the broadsword I borrowed into his chest, point toward the floor below us. He takes them and nods. I don't explain anything to him. He doesn't ask that of me. He never has.

I'm making my way out of the castle when a rich voice with a marked Elianan lilt behind me makes me pause.

"You are a fine swordsman," the nobleman says. "Your brother is lucky to have our princess spare him from your blade."

"I wouldn't have hurt him," I say.

"I only joke," he says with a light laugh. "However, I do think it was rather uncharitable to stop you—to you and to us all."

One of the others speaks now, his voice as deep as his eyes. "We are of the opinion that you would have been the victor had the duel reached its natural conclusion."

The third continues. "And we therefore believe you to be deserving of a victor's prize."

He hands a flat metal box with intricate patterns on the lid to the first nobleman who spoke.

The first one takes it and presents it to me, saying, "The finest sword an Elianan warrior ever carries."

He opens the box as he speaks, revealing a short, thick sword studded with obsidian blades. They ring the blade like teeth.

He places the box in my hands. I stare at the sword lying on the burgundy satin within the box.

I'm back outside the gates of the castle years ago, staring at the hilt of a sword just like this one jutting out of my knee.

I can't take my eyes off the hilt of this sword either. By the time I look up, the noblemen are gone. I close the box and set it down on a sideboard.

I get out the main gates as quickly as I can. The ground ahead of me sways, and people seem to be walking at an angle. I go far enough into the hedge roses that I'll be alone.

I lean my chest against the back of a stone bench and gasp for air. My blood rushes, alternating between the sensations of boiling water and an icy river under my skin.

I press the heels of my hands into the back of the bench, swallowing against the pressure from my stomach.

I'm back to when it happened. The day we nearly lost the war. The Elianans surprised us and attacked from multiple directions at once. One flank burst from the forest and rained arrows on our castle defenses, which were sorely unprepared. When a messenger rode up to tell me what was happening at the castle, I rode back from the battlefields as swiftly as I could. When I got there, the Elianans were practically at our doorstep. The castle was roiling, trying to defend itself. Spiked vines burst from the windows and roofs; torrents of water broke from the ground to form rivulets that were either freezing cold or burning hot depending on how much ground they'd had to push through to come to the surface.

I rode in swinging my broadsword just the way my mother taught me, leaning in to strike down any Elianans within reach of my blade. The next thing I knew, my horse was gone and I was fighting on the ground, blade to armor, something my mother always warned me not to do. *Never let them take you to the ground.*

I didn't feel the knife until the man holding it twisted it and pulled it out. He was on the ground, already dying from his own injuries. I remember seeing blood coming from his nose and mouth, the lines of blood in his eyes as he smiled, knowing he had wounded the prince of Adare. I saw the knife in his hand, the main blade covered in my blood, and the little bits of the tiny blades around it, like the teeth of a broken comb. I knew the other pieces were in my knee. I felt their splinters the moment I tried to take a step. My leg was covered in blood.

I remember Fergus's face as I limped toward him. He caught me and pulled me toward the castle, calling out for Siobhán the whole way. He got me inside and into Siobhán's arms. I'd never seen her face go ashen like that. Not even when she was sick when we were children, or when she'd attended to her first kitchen injuries while in training.

When I woke up, I was in the bed I'm used to, in the chambers I share with Patrick, hidden away in our tree tower. I'd never felt closer to death, and I'd never seen Patrick look more alive. He told me how he'd had to pretend to be me, something he'd never done before. He told me how he mussed his hair and put on a scowl along with my armor. How he yelled like he'd heard me yell during maneuvers.

But once I was out of bed, once Faolan was made for me and I could get around more easily, it was as if that had never happened. As if Patrick had forgotten that he led an army, turned around a battle we were losing, and defended a castle, exactly when and how he needed to. That he had done that part of ruling, not just the endless negotiations and tense conversations.

Faolan's owl has hopped from his perch and is nuzzling my cheek and neck. I reach up and ruffle the feathers at the back of his head. He coos and trills.

As I breathe deeply, I catch the piney scent of the hedges, not unlike Lowell's favorite rosemary. I look closely to see if he's turned them. He hasn't. But I'm not waiting until he does.

When I knock on the door to Lowell's chambers, there's no answer. I find the room empty. So there's no one to stop me from going through drawers and papers, opening wardrobes and trunks.

A bolt of beautifully textured fabric sits in one of the closets. It's not unlike Lowell to spend what he's stolen on the showiest things he can buy, but this isn't his usual fashion. The colors are more Eliana than Adare, deep oranges and golds with a sheen of purple and blue when the light hits it.

I barely touch it, but my fingers sting and come away red and blistered. Like Valencia's skin from the poisoned dress.

I tear through his chambers, not caring to put anything back, not caring if he knows I've been here. I look for anything that could complete the picture forming in my mind.

At the back of a drawer, I find a ring in an ornate box. The center stone is green like a quetzal, with some of the metalwork clearly designed to resemble feathers. Around the center stone are the glimmering seedlings I'm used to seeing in the tree room. I know they're Lowell's. I all but know this ring is meant for Bryna. And that nothing short of a proposal would warrant using his own stones from our family's tree.

I can't do what I want to do to Lowell right now. I can't even take the bolt of fabric, not without the risk of poisoning anyone who brushes past me. And I need it to stay here. I need Patrick to see it here.

But I put the ring in my pocket.

I need to find Patrick, and show him this ring. For once, he might hear me, and Nessa, and everyone else who's been trying to warn him this whole time.

CHAPTER FIFTY-ONE

VAL

Whenever a man looks serious while holding a ring, I worry. Especially after all the cortesanos' sons with their ridiculous proposals, their recitations of stolen love poetry, their jewels so heavy Bryna would need to train her hands to hold them up. But this time it isn't a cortesano's son, it's Cade, and he doesn't look infatuated, he looks pissed off. Even worse than when he was fighting Patrick.

He's staring at me from across the courtyard like I should know why. I don't, but he's succeeded in getting my attention, because I can see the ring from where I stand. I could probably see that ring from the moon.

The weight of my cane pushes the green smell of the ground into the air. The embroidered satin of my dress sweeps the grass, the pink deer and turquoise rabbits looking as though they're leaping across the dark fabric.

As I get closer to Cade, I can see the ring better. The fire trees flash their light off an enormous green jewel, and amber catches in the round gems framing the center stone. From the design of the metalwork, I'm pretty sure it's supposed to be for Bryna; the scrolling mimics her best necklace. But I can tell it's wrong for her. And Cade is staring at it like he's suspicious of it.

Is this another task that falls to Cade? Help Patrick court the visiting princess? Evaluate his jewelry selections?

"If I may be of assistance," I say, closing the space between us, "that's really not her taste."

Not even the breath of a laugh from Cade.

He just stares, his expression blank except for fear.

"Cade?" I touch his arm.

He keeps gazing into that center stone. "I have to kill him."

Now I hold on to his arm. "No," I say. "You don't."

They cannot do this. Patrick and Cade cannot be at war when we're all trying to end one.

"This is all my fault." Cade's eyes scan the ground.

"No, it's not." I come closer, enough to feel the heat off his body.

"This is all because I can't rule," he says.

"You could." I look around to make sure there's no one close enough to hear us. "Adare has had kings before."

"Rarely," he says. "And they all had anatomy I don't, at least as far as anyone knows."

"And why is such anatomy necessary?" I ask. "Did they use their bichos as scepters?"

Cade actually laughs, and it's a sound beautiful enough to coat a meadow in the silver of spring frost. But it doesn't last.

"Adare may let people like us live in peace," he says. "But I've never heard of one ruling."

I hear the box the ring is in snap closed. Cade tucks it into a pocket somewhere under his tartan. I close more of the space between us, as though the tree branches might eavesdrop.

"You asked me what I would do if I could do anything," I say. "Now I'm asking you. Would you rule, as you, if you could?"

"I can't let myself think about something I can't have," he says.

I'm beginning to know the feeling.

Basta, Val. This is not about you right now.

"So you'd rule as you," I say.

"It doesn't matter," he says. "I ruined everything by being a boy. That's why there never could really be a me. I have to be whatever Adare needs."

"What do you need?" I ask.

Cade flinches. "I need this war to be over. I need to stop killing people."

The brown of his eyes is tinted gold from the fire trees. The look he has, etched with every battle he's ever fought, makes me not notice that I'm lifting my hand to his face until I'm doing it. My fingers brush his hair out of his eyes.

"It should never have gotten this far," he says. "But I couldn't fix it." He laughs in a tired way, like he's making himself find something funny. "Because I never wanted to be a prince nearly as badly as I didn't want to be a princess."

"You're not," I say. "You never were. Do you know what you are?" How do I say this in a way that sounds encouraging without making it obvious that I've thought about kissing him? "You're a prince I would swear an oath for."

There. That was halfway decent, right? That sounded like I'm wishing the best for him but not thinking about how the muscle between his shoulder blades feels, doesn't it? I want him to know that what I think of him, what I think he could do for Adare, has nothing to do with me.

"Maybe your own people deserve more credit than you're giving them," I say.

"Oh, because your home is so understanding of people like us?" Cade asks.

Like us. He just included me in that. I didn't think it was possible

241

for corners of my heart to tear into pieces in the same moment others knit together.

But I know he's right. This is something Adare has in common with Eliana. If you want to live as the gender that's true to who you are, and that gender isn't the one set on you at your birth, you move somewhere else. The understanding is that you will start a new life. You will not speak of who you were once assumed to be, and in return, those you live among will not ask rude questions.

It's a bitter option. And even that Cade didn't have.

My fingers brush his temple. "You're exactly who you're supposed to be."

His lips part like he's about to say something, and then thinks better of it.

I want to tell him he can't look at me that way, that who he is can't look at who I am that way. It knocks me so off-balance that for a moment I think the cobalt of bluebells across the grass is water, that we've wandered toward the sea or into the night sky.

Later, I will consider it extremely important to figure out if Karlynn's heir kissed me first or I kissed him first, because me kissing him first is so much worse. But right now I really don't care. I care that he smells like the green salt marshes near the sea. I care about how the chill of the evening on his lips makes me think of the bright blue of Adare lakes, the brilliant turquoise shrugged off mountain glaciers, the cold salt of the sea. I care more about this boy in my arms than about who he is and who I'm not.

But I feel him going slack in my arms, even as his lips are still on mine.

CHAPTER FIFTY-TWO

CADE

I hear Val saying my name over and over, but it gets quieter and quieter. I feel my arms fall, and then I don't feel my hands at all.

I hear Faolan's owl screeching wildly, and the flapping of his wings as he swoops low toward my face.

My vision swims until all I see is darkness.

CHAPTER FIFTY-THREE

VAL

I say his name, but Cade doesn't come back to me. I feel the warmth
of his breath on my hands and the warmth of his blood in his body.
He's still here.

But he doesn't come back to me.

CHAPTER FIFTY-FOUR

CADE

"No, not like that," I hear Siobhán say. "More gently. Here, let me."

"That might be the first time you've ever asked anyone to be gentle." Patrick's voice this time.

I can feel their hands on me, but it's as if every part of me weighs a thousand stone. Lifting an eyelid feels impossible, as does parting my lips to speak.

I can feel the weight of different clothes on me. The formality of a dress shirt and tartan.

"I know you have great concern for your brother, but this is simply not appropriate." Lowell.

"Don't you dare," I hear Patrick saying. "This is a symbol of the love I have for my brother, and the love Siobhán and Deirdre have for him. The love my father has for him. The king."

Patrick lands heavily on the last two words.

That explains the dress clothes and why they feel so unfamiliar. I'm glad I heard Patrick, and not just because he knocked Lowell down a peg. Without his words, I would have panicked when I awoke in the color that symbolizes our father's lineage. Wearing

O'Loingsigh blue could unravel every secret I've held so close for so long.

"I only mean that it might suggest that you consider him your equal," Lowell says. "Which could cause undue confusion."

"Haven't we heard enough out of you?" Siobhán asks.

The distinctive sound of the way Lowell's feet shift when he bows to Patrick comes to my ears, followed by his even footsteps, loud at first, then quieter.

Siobhán's footsteps are next, fast and sure as they fade.

I feel Patrick take my hand in both of his. I hear him say that my spirit has gotten lost, and I realize he's praying, asking that I'll find the way back. When he prays, he sounds like our father.

I hear him sniffle and imagine him wiping his cheek with the back of his hand the way he did as a child. The way he still does sometimes.

"I didn't hear you come in," he says.

"My apologies," Val says. "I'm used to moving quietly."

I hear Val coming closer. Then I feel my staff next to me, resting along my right side. The back of the owl's head settles into the hollow of my shoulder.

"He'll be ready now," Val says. "When he wakes."

I feel Val tuck something into my shirt.

When it touches me, a jolt runs through me, almost enough to pull me into fully waking, but not quite.

"I think this might be yours," Val says, to me, not Patrick.

She's still speaking to me, but her voice grows fainter. Not because she's leaving the room, but because I am.

The weight of the stone presses into my chest. It feels as heavy as the entire tree Faolan came from.

Even though my eyes are closed, I see a burst of light, and it leaves me floating like a leaf on a river.

CHAPTER FIFTY-FIVE

VAL

Bryna summons me.

Via Ondina.

Like she would with someone she barely knows.

So I stand just inside the tent, waiting for her to address me.

Bryna's gown is so silver it looks made of poured metal or spun from gray clouds. It throws a contrast with the warmth of her brown skin and the red undertones in her dark hair, but her expression is all steel.

This isn't the Bryna I know, who kneels alongside the granjeras in the floating gardens, encouraging new vegetable seedlings. This isn't the Bryna I waded alongside into the waterways, who loved the horror on her suitors' faces.

This is my future queen. She will wear gowns of black and violet adorned with gold thread and crystal. She will look like the night sky. She will throw out shards of light so keen they make her enemies step back.

"Strange," she says, looking into her mirror, and not at me, "how Patrick's brother fell ill and you didn't."

She meets my eyes in the mirror, and the accusation lands.

"Whatever you're thinking," I say.

She stops me. "Don't insult my intelligence. You think I don't know how often you wear poison on your lips?"

"But I wasn't wearing it," I say. "It was ordinary color. That's not a mistake I'd make."

Is it?

Did I?

Could I have been that distracted?

"You've had it in for all of them." Bryna pushes away from the carved wood of her dressing table. "And you especially seem to have had it in for Cade."

"No," I say, a protest against her words and everything running through my head.

I knew what I was doing. Even if I knew I should know better, I chose it. I wanted the chance that I could kiss Cade or Cade could kiss me. I chose to leave the poison aside.

At least that's what I thought I did. That's what I meant to do.

"And this was, what, your idea of an elegant way to take care of at least one McKenna brother?" Bryna asks. Her words sound bitter as ash.

"No," I say.

If I put on the wrong lip color, I am too careless to be worthy of the word *centzontleh* or my father's name. If I got something so simple so wrong, I can't trust myself with anything.

And my father should never have trusted me with anything.

I wanted my father back so he could know me as I am. But Bryna needs him back to do the work I can't do. Whatever he tried to teach me about being thorough and careful, I didn't learn. He believed in me, and everything in me on which he set that belief has proved as flimsy as kindling.

"You've been fighting Cade," Bryna says. "This whole time."

"Yes," I say.

"And still you want me to believe you didn't do this?" she asks.

"Yes," I say.

"Why?" she asks. "How?"

"Because I love him."

It slips out and falls between us, heavy and fast as a dropped blade. Her face brightens into shock.

I can't lie to my best friend. So there's nothing for me to do except open my hands and throw myself at the mercy of my future queen. "I love him."

Bryna's expression softens, and I can tell she wants to say something comforting. I can tell she wants to say all sorts of encouraging things. That he'll wake up. That I could have told her earlier. That there was nothing wrong with this, that on the contrary, it could be a signal to the rest of the cortesanos if one of Bryna's ladies is with a McKenna. And a hundred other things I do not want to hear because none of them matter because I cannot love this boy. But I can't tell Bryna why, not without telling her who Cade really is.

CHAPTER FIFTY-SIX

CADE

I know exactly where I am, and yet where I am is impossible, for so many reasons. I am in that most disputed stretch of land between Adare and Eliana. I am in the middle of a stand of trees. And yet I know I am not really here—I am still lying fully dressed on a bed somewhere in the castle.

When I step, my foot feels light, but the sound reverberates as if I'm in the least tapestried corridor of the castle. It's a hollow, bouncing sound of leaves crushing over and over, even though I've taken only one step.

Faolan is with me, but he is still, unmoving, just like everything around me. Except the air itself. It looks like ripples of water, but with more colors. Greens, blues, purples, reds, golds—all flowing one into the next, over and over. All the streaks of color seem to form and re-form, slightly different every time. When I try to reach out to touch one, my finger leaves an imprint, still and green for a moment, and then all those colors ripple out from it in circles, as if I'd tossed a pebble into a lake.

I'm on the other side of the barrier. The spell. I'm in it.

The moment this dawns on me, I hear the voice I've wanted to hear for so long it nearly tears my heart open.

"Cade," she says. "I knew it."

"Mother Queen."

I hold Faolan in my left hand and bend low, my right hand on my chest.

"Oh, child, get up," she says. "I have missed you far too much for formalities."

She holds me close for a long time. I bend my head low, resting it on her shoulder. Her McKenna tartan looks exactly as it did when she rode out that day. The day she never came back. I can feel it against my cheek, just as I can feel her hands and arms around me, the heavy cuffs and armbands pressing into my back.

What's strange is that there is no scent. None. It didn't occur to me before, but I can't smell the trees or the undergrowth. I can't smell the fresh dirt my feet turn up. And I cannot smell my mother's scent. One I would recognize anywhere. I can't smell it on the woven green-and-brown cloth of her tartan or on her intricately braided white hair.

"Mother," I ask, ending our embrace. "Can you smell things here?"

"Eerie, isn't it?" she says. "I would say you get used to it, but I haven't."

She looks at me more closely. Sees how much more of my hair has gone gray early just like hers did, the wear on my body from the battles she missed.

"Has it been so long?" she says. "The light is always the same in here." She gives a wave of her hand that causes wide and sweeping color shifts in the air around her. "Tell me how you got in here, boy. And tell me how we get out."

She's holding my shoulders, the sides of them, like she always did when I did well in a training exercise, or my lessons, or a battle. My stomach drops to know I'm about to disappoint her.

"I tried before," I say. "Many times. Everyone has. We've all tried everything. Us, the Elianans. We even brought in experts from ally nations. No one could get any of you out or any of us in."

"Then what happened?" she asks. "How are you here?"

CHAPTER FIFTY-SEVEN

VAL

I didn't realize until now. The stones flashing different colors, those are Cade's. Their color has gone cooler, but they still flash between colors like winter stars, and the glow hasn't dulled. I know for sure when I bring one close to him and it brightens.

Bryna touches Cade's shoulder like he's exactly what he'll probably be to her: her brother by marriage.

She holds my hand tight, so my thoughts can't wade too deep into the murk of all my mistakes.

Ondina puts drops of agua bendita on Cade's forehead. Bryna slips hierbas into his hands and pockets, the leaves soaking his clothes in their green scent. The curanderas throws cleansing salt on the fire that turns it deep blue.

I carry the globe of glass and light in one of my pockets, as though magic drawn from the monastery's earth might call him back.

"Talk to him," Bryna tells me. "Do you remember Ondina's primo? We all told him stories, and he woke from that fever."

"This isn't a fever," I say.

Bryna pauses at the threshold. "If it might work, do you really want to chance it?"

As her gown sweeps after her, the deep brown and green make me remember the grounds at the monastery. And a question Cade asked me.

Do they just follow you around?

And my answer. *You wouldn't believe me if I told you.*

On the off chance Bryna's right, I tell him.

I tell him how, in Eliana, we're used to foxes everywhere from woods to desert to hills. But generations ago, luminous foxes appeared, larger than anyone thought possible, some as big as horses. Everyone hid in their houses, fearing the foxes' size, the gleaming threat of their teeth, the light bristling over the tips of their fur.

But my father's family came out at midnight to watch them scavenging brambles and curling up under their tree-sized tails. Our family stared, enchanted, admiring. And when the fox kits admired our shoes—from our boots to our beaded slippers—we let them have them to chew on, to play with, to collect in their earths. In return they invited us onto their backs, taking us where we needed to go or where they knew we needed to go even if we didn't.

I hear footsteps. That's all the warning I get before Lowell is in the doorway.

"My apologies for interrupting," he says. I catch him glancing up and down the corridor.

"What's wrong?" I ask. "Not enough witnesses to your generous act of visiting Patrick's brother?"

Lowell looks more embarrassed for me than shocked, as though I've just made a scene during mass.

"I know why you're here," I say. "I know this is all to impress Patrick. Everything you do is to impress Patrick so he'll lay down his cloak to soften your way to the throne."

I try not to look at Cade, because I don't want Lowell looking at Cade. And I don't need to look at Cade to remember his face when he found out Patrick was handing everything over to Lowell. In that moment, I saw more fear in him than any time I've fought him or fought alongside him.

Now Lowell doesn't need Cade to abdicate. He just needs Cade to stay in his cursed sleep, and for Patrick to hand him the throne.

"You're not going to rule." I keep my voice as flat as a sheet of frost. "I don't care what I have to do. You are not taking the throne."

"I assure you," Lowell says, "I mean nothing but to be of help in any way I can."

"Straight from the horse's ass," I say.

Lowell's smile slips.

"Isn't that how the saying goes?" I blink at him, as though I've simply gotten the phrasing of an Adare dicho wrong. Nothing could be more innocent.

A shard of sunlight brightens the sword at Lowell's hip, illuminating the hilt. The metal shows none of the gleam of wear. Everything about Lowell, from his perfectly arranged clothes to his evenly trimmed nails, tells me he's no threat with a blade. I could fight him, and win. His hands have fewer calluses than Bryna's.

But I can't fight Lowell with my hands. And my aim with knives won't help me here. Fighting him will mean dealing in the manners and secrets of the Adare court. Our battles from here forward will be fought with smiles and charming words.

The floor under my feet buckles, hard and fast as a tide crashing in. I stumble, trying to get my balance. The next square of stone cracks and shudders, and the next. The floor crumbles and rises, and doesn't stop until Lowell McKenna has a short sword to my throat.

CHAPTER FIFTY-EIGHT

CADE

"No," my mother says simply.

Before I can respond, I feel disturbingly familiar hands on me. Hands that I am disturbingly certain helped pull me from my mother's womb.

"He feels fine," she says.

"Are you sure?" the queen asks, as if I am not there.

This would be less unsettling if I could see Siobhán's mother, but I can't yet. She's still behind me.

She comes around to face me. I didn't see her the morning she set out, but she looks exactly the same as when I last saw her. Rionach's eyes are clearer than Siobhán's, especially with the tired cast Siobhán's have taken on lately.

"Sorry to trouble you," my mother tells her, following it with a slight bow.

I've never quite understood the strange mix of formality and endearment between them. But, then again, I do not yet have any sisters by marriage. Mine or my brother's.

Rionach disappears to who knows where, and I know better than to ask.

Instead, I say exactly the thing I shouldn't. "He's going to marry her."

And, as usual, my mother knows what I'm saying without any context.

"A thiarna Íosa," she whispers, as if I don't know her thinly veiled prayers when I hear them. As if I didn't learn to pray that way myself from her.

She touches her right temple with the fingers of her left hand the way she does when she's trying to gather herself. I can't bear to go on, to tell her about Patrick's plan to leave Adare for Eliana. Or about Lowell. Not yet.

"It's a bad idea, isn't it?" I ask instead. "There's a reason you all got stuck here, right? Does it have something to do with that?"

"No," she says. "I always thought they'd make a good match. I just . . . we just . . . It's not what was discussed."

Of course it wasn't. Because I was supposed to be like her. Because I was supposed to be a girl.

"Mam," I say. "I'm sorry."

It's all I can get out.

"Don't," she says, her arms around me again. "Don't you dare be sorry for who you are."

VAL

"If you move," Lowell whispers at me, "you'll dye your own dress red."

I've gotten my arm between my neck and his short sword. But now the blade presses into my forearm.

A reddened patch on the heel of his hand draws my eye. Without moving my head, I shift my gaze toward it.

It's blotchy, uneven. Though his skin is lighter than mine, I match it to the burns a poisoned dress left on my body.

My next breath spins in my chest. Without thinking as much as I should, I voice the one question I can't stop myself from saying out loud.

"Did you poison Cade?" I ask.

"No," Lowell says, so levelly he might be telling the truth.

"Just me," I say, careful.

"Just you," he says.

Before this moment, I had no respect for Lowell McKenna. Him admitting what he's done gives me the smallest amount.

"The question is"—he tightens his grip on me—"do you know why?"

He lands on the words in a way that's emphatic but not as menacing as I'd expect, as though he truly wants me to understand.

"Because I was inconvenient to you," I say. Again, not a question. "Because you knew I'd get in the way of you getting everything you wanted."

"It was for Patrick." He chokes up on his grip on the blade so I can't see as much of his hand. "All of this was for Patrick and for Adare."

He even sounds like he believes it.

"Patrick needs me," Lowell says. "And whether he needs me on the throne or doing things he's unwilling to do, that will be up to him. But he does need me. This family, our home, needs me. And the last thing my cousin needs is a spy in our own house." He's talking low to me now, as though there's anyone around to hear. "But there was no way to prove it. I couldn't even try without risking irreparable offense to your princess. Does she even know what you are?"

I almost say no, a reflex. But the faster I say it, the more likely he'll know I'm trying to protect her.

"She doesn't know the half of it, does she?" Lowell asks. "I bet you helped that assassin boy."

There's no triumph in how well I've done at keeping Valencia and Gael apart. Whether Lowell knows it or not, both are me. Right now, there is a blade too close for either Valencia or Gael to do anything.

When the castle trembles, I know it might be the only chance I get.

I reach for the knives in my hair.

Lowell pins my arm. "This is what will happen next. Either you'll be arrested for attempting to kill the prince's half brother. That's the choice that gives you a slight chance of keeping your life, if your princess pleads on your behalf. Or you continue to fight, in which case I'll have to kill you for attempting to finish off the prince's half brother. For all we know, maybe you were even in league with the assassin boy."

My thoughts knock into one another.

He doesn't know I'm Gael. But for once, that doesn't help me.

I have to get to a knife, either one in my hair or the dagger in my boot.

And if I get this wrong, Cade dies.

My hands want to try everything at once, grab for every blade, and hope this will all add up to something.

Then I remember Cade's voice in a monastery courtyard.

Sometimes waiting an extra moment is the thing that saves you.

I didn't wait before, when I said everything I said to Lowell.

It got me here.

Now I pause, so I can decide what to do next.

A tone builds in the room, a sound halfway between a note and the charge of a storm in the air.

I hear two words in two voices. One, my own voice, an echo of what I said to Cade before I threw a knife over his shoulder. The second, a queen I've never met, but the calm and power of that voice tells me exactly who she is.

Stay still, I say.

Stay still, Karlynn McKenna says.

And for the first time in my life, I truly do it.

My hair falls down my back, a curtain between me and Lowell.

I see the flash of blades that just came out of my hair. Lowell yells, letting me go. He grabs at the wounds slashed through his sleeve and into his arm.

He picks up his short sword, cutting his glare at me as though I sent knives into him by spite and brujería.

I reach for my dagger. He lunges at me.

Then I hear the bright noise of a blade being drawn. Not one of mine. A sword.

A stone flashing different colors—a stone I saw growing from a tree—falls to the floor.

That's the first moment I realize who pulled the knives from my hair, the boy I taught to pull them from my hair, and who's now wielding a sword against Lowell McKenna.

CHAPTER SIXTY

CADE

The guards burst in, swords pointed at Val and me. Add Lowell's blade to that, and we're staring down a lot of metal. One of the guards moves faster, and both Val and I defend ourselves. My sword flashes against the guard's, and Val throws a knife aimed at his head. The knife misses, but my sword keeps him busy long enough for Val to prepare another. That one hits, in the guard's shoulder. He drops his sword and slumps forward, clearing the way for the other guard and Lowell. Val takes on the guard, evading his sword and throwing more of her knives.

Lowell circles me, taking his time, short sword in one hand, dagger in the other. The surprise that I'm awake and fighting registered in his eyes, but he already has it in check.

"You didn't want this," he says. "Patrick couldn't bring himself to lead us. You certainly couldn't."

I'm not moving like I need to. Lying still has left me slower to respond than a fight like this requires. The only way I'm hiding it is how different our fighting styles are. Lowell's is as precise as Patrick's. Even on a good day, mine is less polished, more unpredictable.

Lowell engages my sword, each move individual, calculated. It's like fighting my instructor from years ago.

My peripheral senses tell me Val is gaining on her opponent. There's blood on the guard's clothes, and his moves seem more erratic.

I keep my focus on Lowell, countering his more traditional moves with my rougher ones. His restrained parries meet my expansive lunges. His precise blocks meet my broader thrusts. Sensation comes back into my hands and feet more sharply. Unevenly, but enough to let me knock Lowell's dagger from his hand.

I'm still trying to get myself to move the way I'm used to moving. The more suddenly and forcefully I try to move my body, the more it lags and twinges.

Then I feel my sword being lifted from my grip. It falls away as Lowell's sword snaps it up, giving my cousin both his sword and my own to use against me.

CHAPTER SIXTY-ONE

VAL

Never throw your last or best weapon. Even if it lands, you've left yourself few remaining moves.

Another rule of my father's that I just broke. But right now, holding anything back isn't an option either Cade or I have.

My last knife slows Lowell, but it's not enough to stop him. Now I'm unarmed, Cade's unarmed and worn down, and Lowell's about to kill him.

I draw the glass globe from my pocket. If I can break it, I'll have pieces to throw and jagged edges to slash with.

As hard as I can, I slam it into the floor. Instead of breaking, it lodges into the stone. The stones making up the floor break into pieces, and the pieces rumble and ripple like water. I stay on my hands and knees, trying to keep my center.

Lowell trips on the moving stone, falling toward me.

His eyes land on me, the leading edge of his blade a line of silver.

A shiver of heat crosses my collarbone. My blood lights up like embers.

I scramble for one of my knives, one that missed and fell, but they're so small that I can't find them in the cracks between stones.

The glint of Lowell's sword is now close enough that I can feel the chill off the metal.

Then he stops, the shine of metal and blood gleaming in his chest.

CHAPTER SIXTY-TWO

CADE

"I thought you were gone," Val breathes, looking me up and down.

"I think I was," I admit between gasps.

I realize Val is holding me up. Faolan's staff is on the ground and the owl is on her head. At least he was on her head a moment ago. Now the owl is gone, and I wonder if I'm seeing things. I still don't feel entirely in the room, or in my body. If Val wasn't holding on to me, I worry I might swoon in a most un-princely fashion.

Having just killed my own cousin doesn't help. Each of my heart's beats feels heavy enough to pull me into the cracked floor.

The owl's hoot fills the room, and his wings fill the doorway.

Patrick is next to us, touching my shoulder and Val's, looking around.

I take in Patrick as he takes in the scene.

"¿Qué está pasando aquí?" I hear Bryna's voice before I see her.

"Fair question." I nod at her.

Nessa and Fergus burst in, weapons at the ready. Fergus's lip is bleeding and Nessa's braid has come partially undone.

Bryna is staring at Patrick and Val. At the same time. Like one of the tapestries on the walls in the Elianan palace. The ones with the cats and birds whose eyes follow you around the room.

Both Patrick and Val seem completely frozen in her stare.

I hold on to Val's arms under her elbows.

"I am Cade McKenna," I tell Bryna. "I was born to Queen Karlynn. And King Niall. I'm Karlynn's eldest."

My head drops. My eyes don't know where is safe to look.

The room is very quiet. All I hear is a lot of people doing a lot of breathing.

My eyes slowly make their way up from the hem of Val's flame-orange dress to those moonless-night-sky eyes. Her smile reassures me that I haven't just done something catastrophically stupid.

My eyes meet Bryna's next. She keeps looking between Patrick and Val and me.

Nessa's dark eyes pull me in next. "I knew it," she whispers.

Those three words draw everyone's attention, including Fergus's.

"Well, maybe not all of it," Nessa says. "But some of it."

What happens next finds me the most nervous I have ever been walking into a room. My heart will not stop trying to hammer itself through my lacings. I want to fidget with my sash, but I don't have enough fingers. One set is wrapped around Faolan, as usual, and the other set is altogether too close to my brother.

He insisted on walking next to me and is keeping a very close eye on my movements, lest I faint. Or bolt. Fergus is in front of us, then Bryna and Val, shoulder to shoulder. Well, more like shoulder to jawline, really, but same idea. Nessa and Siobhán follow at a respectful distance.

Before I know it, we're up on that ridiculous platform I don't understand. Well, I understood it till now. It made it easy for guards like me to see royals like Patrick from anywhere in the room. But from this perspective, it just feels cruel.

I look down and see Siobhán first. She's still by Nessa, up at the front. One hand is suspiciously tucked in one of her pockets, and from how tense her arm is, I'm guessing she's preparing for the worst. Just in case.

Nessa looks ready to fight too. Ondina is very close by, and not-so-subtly nodding to Bryna and Val. No idea what that means.

My eyes move to Fergus, who is with his family, littlest child up on his shoulders. Deirdre holds two of the others by the hands, but looks straight at me. She's almost as frightening to stare down as Faolan's owl when he's stock-still.

But as I watch, she smiles at me. And nods.

I look around some more. And see more nodding.

I clear my throat. No small feat at the moment.

"My name is Cade McKenna," I begin, just as I did before. "I was born to Queen Karlynn."

Everyone already knows this. And I know they know this. So I get to the point.

"And King Niall," I say. "I am Queen Karlynn's oldest child. I am her heir."

There are a few gasps, but also what sounds like some sighs of relief. Deirdre's already crying. She's such a custard out of uniform.

No one's trying to kill me yet. So far so good.

"My cousin and former advisor Lowell McKenna is dead," I say. "We shall mourn him in proper form. Despite his treachery."

That last bit gets some real gasps. I'm not sure whether it's because people didn't know it or because I said it out loud.

"My cousin organized a plot to overthrow my brother, who was trained to rule in my place by our parents," I say.

Silence. Complete silence. I go on. Might as well finish the job now that I've started.

"If any of you doubt any of this, my younger brother, Patrick, and others here will vouch for me," I say. "And if that's not enough for you, don't worry. It wouldn't be enough for me either."

I lean heavily on my right leg and bend it slightly. I put my chin to my chest to make it look like I'm bowing lower, like I've done for years now.

I take a deep breath and lift Faolan up off the floor, keeping my left leg firmly behind me, holding my braced knee straight.

When Faolan comes back down, there's a loud crack, even though all I did was set him firmly down where he was before. Strong but contained, just like my mother taught me when I was a child.

The owl circles back to me with one of my stones in his talons. He drops it in my hand. I close my fingers around it, letting its light burst through my fingers.

I set it against my chest, like I watched my mother do with hers. But instead of raising it to my head, I keep my hand where it is and slowly let go.

From the gasps in the crowd, I can tell it worked. The stone is stuck to my sash. My O'Loingsigh blue sash.

I slowly raise myself back up to standing. This thing had better stay stuck till I can get off this stupid platform. That's when I realize there is no platform anymore. I stand face-to-face, eye to eye, with everyone watching. Which is exactly what I didn't know I'd always needed. I know exactly where I stand.

A rumbling outside gets everyone's attention. Patrick, Bryna, Val, and I all look at one another with identical expressions of *Now what?*

I run out in time to meet three of the largest sea monsters I've ever faced, rearing out of the river. Their long bodies are deep green, with fins along their backs and the sides and tops of their heads. The fins are darker green and blue, and their amber eyes gleam as brightly as their teeth.

I bow in deference to them, hoping to hide whatever fear they might find on my face. I hear running footsteps behind me and turn to see the whole court gathering.

The sea monsters crest farther out of the water and bow low. My heart stops hammering and I bow again, relieved to have done enough for them to make their approval clear.

CHAPTER SIXTY-THREE

VAL

Ondina is perhaps the least frightening person I know. But when I wake up to her standing over my bed, I startle enough to fall out of it.

I get free of the blanket I've taken down with me. "How long have I been asleep?" I hear the roar of the fire trees. When the wind stirs the tent flaps, slices of dark sky show.

Then I remember.

Cade told everyone who he was. And everyone looked at him with the same awed respect they might show his mother.

The joy of that barely rises through me before wilting under Ondina's stare.

"¿Qué tienes?" I scramble to my feet.

Ondina is nearly as pale as the ribbon tying back her hair. It's worse against the deep blue of her dress, usually a perfect shade for her when her own color hasn't drained.

"Why do you look like this?" I ask.

"They've embraced Cade as Karlynn's heir," she says.

I splash water onto my face from the jofaina. "That's a good thing."

"They betrothed them," Ondina says.

I pat a cloth against my face. I have a lot to answer for, starting with all my misplaced venom toward the McKenna brothers. But before I begin this long-overdue conversation with Ondina, she goes on.

"Los consejeros," she says. "Their advisors and ours. They betrothed Bryna and Cade."

I let the cloth fall away from my face. "What?"

"Bryna's our heir." Ondina's voice trembles. "And Cade is Karlynn's. Cade is Karlynn's eldest son."

"They can't do that to them," I say. "Bryna wants to be with Patrick."

"Who isn't Karlynn's eldest son," she says. "Cade is. Do you think this is the first time that's ever happened, that a princess has to marry the brother of the man she actually loves? Do you think her parents, her abuelos, do you think any of them were love matches? You know how this works."

"Where is this coming from?" I ask. "You've been against this from the beginning."

"I was against her being with Patrick," she says. "Especially because we had every reason to think he had banished or killed his sister. But he doesn't have a sister. He has a brother who could change everything for us. Do you know what this could mean for anyone after him? Anyone like him? Anyone like us?"

She's pinned me with it.

Eldest child with eldest child.

Heir with heir.

"Every leader from the villages who's sent word," Ondina says, "they're for this. They have faith in Cade. They believe he can carry on the best of what his mother was doing and leave aside the war."

I flinch at remembering Cade's words. *I need to stop killing people.* He needs this to end. And Bryna needs to stop losing cousins and friends.

This is the surest way to do it. And Cade could change everything for anyone like Cade. Like me. Like everyone at the monastery.

My heart gives.

I give.

"Where are you going?" Ondina asks when I get up.

"I need to be with Bryna," I say.

"You think you'll make this better for her right now?" Ondina asks.

"She's my best friend," I say.

"So leave your best friend be to let go of the life she thought she'd have," Ondina says. "She does not need you rushing in there cursing her unhappiness or your own. Tomorrow, you will stand next to her, and you will be the friend to her that she depends on, because she is marrying the brother of the man she truly loves. And I know you love the man she's marrying, but you are not going to have to pretend to love someone else for the sake of Eliana. She is."

Ondina isn't yelling. Or lecturing. She's pleading.

"Please," Ondina says. "She does not need this. She is going through everything you're going through, only she has to smile and look magnanimous as she does it."

I can hear her love for Bryna, sharp in her voice, as though the jagged pieces of her own heart are going to cut through the front of her dress.

So I nod. And I mean it.

I've never been good at staying still. I did it the moment Cade woke up, and it saved me, just like he said it could. But right now I'm still because my body doesn't know what to do next. I sit on the edge of my bed after Ondina leaves. My feet brace against the ground the way I've learned to, taking the strain off my back. But it's more habit than hearing my body. I barely feel my body. An ache hums at the base of my spine, but like everything else, it feels far from me. I barely pick up the scent of flower water in the air. The embroidery I've run my hands over so many times hardly registers against my fingertips.

As the velvet of the night sky deepens, I stay still. Not because my body doesn't know what to do. Because it's realized, along with the rest of me, that the only thing I can do is nothing.

When I hear Cade's voice, it sounds as distant as the river.

"Tell me I don't have to do this," he says.

I stand up, ready to show my reverence to Karlynn's heir like everyone else.

But the boy in front of me isn't the one who stood in front of everyone. His shirt's gone slack with sweat, and he looks worse than when he woke up. He holds his jaw tight. I might not be able to tell the difference from how he usually holds it if it wasn't for the cracks in his voice.

"Tell me this one part of my life can be mine," he says.

I imagine a hard shell around my heart, like the outer layer of a tree's bark.

I'm not naturally good at comforting. The first time a boy broke Bryna's heart—a visiting dignitario's son who said he preferred girls who didn't look so proud—she wanted me to sit with her as she cried and stared out her window. I kept fidgeting because I wanted to go find the guaje and throw a knife at him. Not to hurt him, not seriously. Maybe to cut a corner off that jacket he walked around in as though el palacio was his to rule.

But if I want to serve Bryna as the princess she is, if I want to serve Cade as the prince he is, I have to help this boy in front of me stay upright.

"This is good," I tell him. "They accept you as the man you are."

It's a dry, unconvincing mimic of Ondina's words. The words are true, but I don't sound half as encouraging as I mean to.

"Then tell me you don't want me," Cade says. "Tell me you don't feel anything for me." He steps closer. "Tell me you don't love me."

"We can't do this," I whisper.

"Please," he says. Not whispering. "Please. Tell me I'm wrong about what I think I'm seeing when you look at me. Because if you don't love me, then at least I'm only wrecking three lives, not four."

The light from the fire trees falls through the cloth and onto him. It tints his lips. It adds copper to the brown of his hair and his eyes.

"Please," he says. "Tell me."

With my next breath, I prove myself unworthy of the word *dama*, or *centzontleh*, or any other title I have ever been called.

I hold this boy who has carried a kingdom on his worn-out back and broken-down knee.

I kiss this boy who smells like metal and resin and blood.

I take the weight of him, flesh, bone, muscle, a heart that's had to get harder and heavier to take on everything it's been expected to hold. I let him come apart in my arms.

I say his name, over and over, learning its taste in my mouth, the shape of the letters on my tongue. Soon it won't be mine to say. I will call him by his title.

So I say his name now. I call him Cade while I still can.

CHAPTER SIXTY-FOUR

CADE

At first, I can still feel Val's hands on me. On my chest, my back. Every scar on my arms. Even my knee.

I can feel how we planted our mouths against each other's shoulders. I can feel how we were cautious with each other's bodies. How I kept an arm under Val's back, how Val looked out for my knee, how we shifted positions to take pressure off joints or to keep muscles from knotting.

Even when we were hesitant or awkward, even when we were asking each other if this felt good or if that hurt, we fell into how completely we knew each other's bodies.

Val held me as close as when he'd taken me down to the ground. But this time there was no shadow of him blocking or guarding against me the way he had in every fight.

I didn't have to teach Val my weak points. She already knew them. She'd found them before, and she was as careful with me now as she'd been ruthless with me then.

But even as my face presses against the mattress, before I even lift my head, I know Val is gone.

CHAPTER SIXTY-FIVE

VAL

Entre la espada y la pared. My father used to say that all the time. Between the sword and the wall. A place you find yourself in which there is no way to win, no matter how well you've planned.

I never believed my father when he told me there were situations that were impossible to train for. I didn't want to.

I knew, even then, that things go wrong, that no plan ever holds up when it meets daylight. But I didn't want to believe that there were scenarios so unsolvable that no instinct would click into place. No training would pull at you, giving you a sense of what to do next.

That, however, was exactly what my father was trying to tell me. Some situations defy preparation.

Like the boy you love telling you that he wants you, days after telling you that he needs to stop fighting, after you've seen the ways that war has broken him down.

If I leave him, I break his heart. If I love him, I leave him in the world of his nightmares. If he doesn't marry Bryna, then this war goes on, and every time he dreams he'll wonder when someone's going to drag him to his feet, shove armor onto his wounded body, and make him fight as his own brother.

Each of these facts becomes a knot in my body. They work so far into me that they feel as though they've always been there, as deep as knots in wood.

Cade wants to love me.

Cade needs the fighting to stop.

He can't have both. But he's not thinking clearly enough to realize that.

So I have to realize it for him.

CHAPTER SIXTY-SIX

CADE

It's all I can do to tear myself away from this tree, this room. I've spent so much time in here since I saw my mother. I've tried to talk to her and hoped she can somehow hear me. I've prayed. I've tried to will myself back to the forest. I've slept in here, hoping to dream my way back in. But I've just woken up sore and stiff from whatever strange position I've taken on the hard floor. It's a habit that has me needing, and taking, more of Siobhán's advice and remedies lately.

I've been trying to fall into something of a normal rhythm with my body, and with the exercises I'm used to. But I haven't fully broken out of the stiffness I woke up with after being that still.

Something about my final fight with Lowell feels unfinished. Or something about his death, perhaps. And going back to where it happened might help me figure out what.

That room has been cleaned and neatened. All signs of the fight are gone. The blood is fading into the floor, as though the castle is turning it into color within the stones themselves.

As I'm walking around the bed, a bright glint catches my eye. I lower myself to the floor with Faolan's help and examine the shiny partial sphere wedged between stones. I would recognize it anywhere, the way it catches the light and sends it back out in different colors. It's the orb that topped my mother's staff.

But how did it get here? My mother would have taken her staff with her to the negotiations.

I pry it loose and examine its uneven edges, hoping this will tell me how it broke off. It doesn't.

My first thought is that I should ask Val, but then I remember.

Maybe it's time I spoke with the princess directly.

I make my way to the great hall, but stop when I see Patrick on the stairs. He leans his elbow against one of them, his loose shirt billowing around him. A girl I've never seen before sits next to him, laughing.

Patrick sets down the goblet he'd been holding and tucks a stray dark curl behind the girl's ear. She blushes and bats her eyelashes at him.

What on earth is in that goblet? Or was in that goblet, more likely.

I need some air.

Tonight's festivities have expanded into the floating gardens. Lights follow the vines from the islands of vibrant green and red to the hedge roses, lilacs, and daffodils I've watched bloom every year.

Bryna leans on one of our stone overlooks, one I've loved for a long time. Her curls tumble down the deep blue and purple of her dress.

At first, she seems to be taking in the gardens. But then I notice how far away her guards and even the nearby ladies are standing from her. She is as alone as she likely ever is.

I look back into the great hall and manage to catch Deirdre's eye first. I meet her at the threshold.

"You've been missing quite the party," she says.

"I can tell," I say. "Is there any left of what you all have been drinking?"

"Plenty," she says. "I'll get you some."

Her words blur together slightly.

"Get me two, will you?" I call after her, following quite a few steps behind.

I've been with her after enough battles to know that even when she's had a bit too much to drink, her speed and reflexes don't suffer.

She hands me two full goblets, and I leave her to the dancing, watching for just a moment as she collides with her husband. Fergus catches her and pulls her into a low, gentle dip, kissing her deeply.

Whatever everyone's drinking must be magic. I haven't seen Fergus this effusive with Deirdre in public since their last anniversary party.

I say a prayer as I walk toward the overlook.

"Princesa," I say when I'm close enough not to have to speak at full voice, but far enough to be respectful.

She turns.

I extend one of the goblets with a slight bow.

She takes it with a nod.

"Salud," I say to her.

"Sláinte," she says to me, her accent impeccable.

I take a sip from mine.

The princess drains hers and sets it down on the ledge.

When her expression doesn't change, I say, "I'm impressed. You'll fit in well in any company here."

I'm trying to lighten the mood, but she keeps staring out over the gardens. I begin to wonder if she saw Patrick on the stairs.

"Did something give you need of taking a drink down in one?" I ask.

She barely turns her head. "It pains me that my parents will not see my wedding."

The thought of that had not yet occurred to me. Now it hits me harder having come from someone else.

"We don't have to do this," I say slowly, and quietly enough that her attendants won't hear us.

"The contract betrothed me to the eldest marriageable son," she says. "That would be you."

"Are you angry with me?" I ask. "For lying about my age?"

Her fingers grip the edge of the overlook. "Am I angry with you? Yes. For lying about your age? No. Not at all. I understand why you had to do what you did."

"Then why are you angry with me?" I ask.

She turns to me fully, her face catching the firelight.

"Because you are questioning what we must do," she says. "I would never have expected that of you."

I stare at her, somewhere between honored and insulted.

"No, I do not love you," she says. "You do not love me. Irrelevant. This is what is best for our nations. For our people. If we are to rule together, you will find it is not wise to cross me."

Like my mother, instead of raising her voice, she chooses to deepen it when she wants to make a point.

"I was born to be a queen," she says. "You were born to be a king. Start acting like it."

She strides away, each step decisive, as if she goes toward an important destination instead of away from me.

Her entourage follows, knowing how critical the next few moments are in determining the course of their evenings.

Ondina moves most slowly, catching my eye as she passes. Her expression is sympathetic, as if she remembers exactly what it felt like the first time she was on the receiving end of Bryna's wrath. I look back at her, with the best approximation of appreciation that I can muster.

She takes a few running steps to close the gap between the other ladies' slippered feet and her own.

I know better than to follow.

CHAPTER SIXTY-SEVEN

VAL

I finish lacing the cords on a binding garment, this one deep blue. I start the next one, the damp from the courtyard grass soaking through my robe to my knees.

Silas stands over me.

I hold up my hands. "No knives." I go back to pulling cords through eyelets. "At least none that you'll find."

"Notice I didn't ask." Silas watches me work. "You've gotten quick."

As though I mean to prove his point, I lace up the final seam and move on to the next.

"So what did I do wrong this time?" I ask.

"Why do you assume you did something wrong?" Silas asks.

I work at a stubborn eyelet. "Because you're talking to me."

"I don't just talk to people when they've erred, you know."

He pauses, surveying the pale robe I'm wearing. I'm not completely sure why they handed me this one, except that it has something to do with vows, time at the monastery, the angle of sun through the stained-glass windows or something, I don't know. What I do know is that it has nothing to do with age. There are monjes years younger than I am who wear the same dark gray robes Cade wore when he was here.

"Does this mean you'll be staying with us for a while?" Silas asks.

"Are you throwing me out?" I ask.

"By the heart of Saint Marinos," he says. "Do you spend your life anticipating bad news?"

I finish another seam. "I've gotten to like it here," I say. "And to like my brothers. Now that I know why they're giving me so much advice on my voice and walk." I untangle the next lace. "And I'm glad to know there are no vows of silence. It would make the voice-practicing a lot harder."

"Yes, thought did go into that." Silas sits on the edge of the fountain.

"Oh good," I say. "You're staying."

"You're awful at veiling your sarcasm," he says.

"You're awful at sensing when I'm not trying to."

He laughs, which at first makes me want to glare, but he has an unexpectedly catching laugh, so soon I'm joining him.

"Have you realized yet?" he asks.

"Realized what?"

He crosses his arms. "What a mistake you've made."

With sudden panic, I check the binding garment in front of me.

"Not the lacings." Silas sounds impatient, as though I've ruined whatever little sermon he had planned.

"Can we skip to the end where you tell me what I did wrong?" I ask. "And also where you tell me I was right, because I knew you were here to critique me chopping onions or ringing bells or lighting candles." I am now rage-lacing the garment in front of me. "Adelante. Let's hear it."

But when I look up, Silas's face has softened.

"You love him," he says.

"Is that a question?" I ask.

"Are you giving an answer?" Silas asks.

I pull the cord through the next eyelet. "No."

"No," Silas repeats, as though confirming.

"Because it makes no difference," I say.

"It makes no difference," Silas says.

"This discussion has begun to circle." I stack the laced garments together.

"You can't just hide here," Silas says.

"Why not?" I gather up the garments to bring to el jefe of lacings (Brother Peter, who inspects my work with a hand glass). "You just said I was getting good at this."

"Because you will never forgive yourself if you let the boy you love marry someone he doesn't love and who doesn't love him," Silas says.

"He is the prince of Adare," I say, and I don't realize I'm raising my voice until the stone arches throw it back at me.

But now I'm angry.

Angry enough to yell in a monastery.

"I can swear my loyalty," I say. "I can guard him. I can protect him. But I cannot love him."

Silas rises from the edge of the fountain. "Centzontleh."

That catches me enough to bring down my own yelling.

"Possessor of four hundred tongues," Silas says. "¿Verdad?"

I nod. "Four hundred voices." As soon as I say it, I feel like a failure, especially compared to my father. My father has been a hundred different men in his life, whoever he needed to be to go unnoticed into that court, or this guild hall, or that town. He has been scholars, builders, visiting dignitaries, craftsmen, living a hundred lives depending on what information the king and queen needed. He goes in, and he leaves, and everyone forgets he was even there. But I've left wreckage in my wake that will stay with people I care about. Even if I could make myself not care about Cade, I've abandoned my friends. I couldn't keep distance between my work and my heart any more than I could keep my lip color straight from my poison.

"My work," I tell Silas, "is to have any tongue or voice I need to."

Silas pauses long enough for his robe to go still around him. "Just be sure you don't forget the sound of your own."

He continues toward the corridor.

I shut my eyes, holding the lacings in my arms.

Mierda, Brother Silas. I was all right. The scent of wildflowers in the orchard was growing stronger than the memory of Bryna's and Ondina's perfumes. I was getting in several breaths between each time I thought about the friends I left. The sound of the canes some of the monks here use was replacing the sound of Faolan against Adare stone. I was lacing up entire seams without thinking of the boy I can never have.

The boy I met when I was a fairy and he was Patrick.

The boy I met again when I was Gael and he was still Patrick.

The boy I met when he was himself and I was one version of myself, and then again when I was the other.

We are so used to being different people. It took us so many tries to recognize each other, to meet each other as who we truly are.

And he wanted every version he met of me. He wanted me as a boy and as a girl. He knew that each version of me was both all of me and only part of me.

I carry the lacings into the workshop.

"Vale." I set them down. "I'm ready."

"Ready for?" Peter asks.

"For whatever stupid way you wanted to dress me," I say.

"You won't be sorry." Owain lights up like he's just convinced me to hear the word of the Lord. "Every time I have to leave the abbey, I do it, and it works."

Jeremiah sorts the lacings. "Why the sudden willingness?"

"Because Brother Silas has talked me into a foolish, ill-advised, possibly-ruinous-for-everyone-involved idea," I say.

Now they all light up.

"Does that mean?" Jeremiah asks.

I sigh, nodding. "I'm going back."

CHAPTER SIXTY-EIGHT

CADE

I run my hand along my shirt. It's soft with a gentle sheen, making it look closer to red in shadow and closer to aflame in sunlight. There are embroidered accents in panels down the front and along some of the edges, forming lacelike twines. This is what I'll wear to marry Bryna. This is what I'll wear to marry the woman my brother loves. Maybe if I think this enough times, I'll get used to it.

I open a drawer in my night table. I pull out the bulb from my mother's staff and hold it in my hand. I lift and lower my fingers under it, letting it move just enough to catch the light from different angles. I've done this a thousand times, day and night, hoping to hear my mother's voice again. But I never have.

I slip the bulb into a soft inner pocket of my jacket, likely meant for wedding rings or a spare knife.

I shine up Faolan's head and grips so he looks his best. Years ago, I saw a wedding where the groom used a cane. He'd been injured in battle and he and his bride had their ceremony here before moving away to the countryside. He had looked so polished and proper as he walked down the aisle. I hope I look that pulled together. I hope my doubts about this union don't show.

As I'm adjusting the fit of the jacket on my shoulders, I hear a knock at the door. It's faint, reluctant. When I open the door, I'm not surprised to see Ondina.

Even as she bows low, I can see how concerned she looks.

"What is it?" I ask.

"It's Bryna," she says. "No one knows where she is."

I think back on my last conversation with the princess. I made her angry. But earlier on, she spoke of how her family wouldn't see her wedding.

If I were her, I can imagine only one place I would go.

"I do," I say.

CHAPTER SIXTY-NINE

VAL

Ondina always thinks she's being exceptionally subtle as she cuts hierbas at the edge of the gardens. Sure, she always puts mejorana to good use. But really she's listening outside the tents, hoping someone forgets to lower their voice.

"Who are you trying to eavesdrop on?" I whisper.

She doesn't startle. I wonder if she noticed my shadow first.

Ondina draws me into the trees. "Chisme of all kinds about the wedding," she says. "But I can't make sense of any of it." Ondina surveys the outfit the monjes put me in, the loose shirt over the binding garment, the hem tucked into trousers that are tighter than I ever thought I could get away with as a boy. My hair is pulled back a little differently, showing the angles in my face.

"Better," she says.

"Really?" I ask.

"Much," she says. "The last time I saw you like this you looked like you were stealing clothes from an older primo. Now you look like a proper young man."

"I had help," I say.

"From whom?" she asks. "Where have you been? Do you know what? I shouldn't even be talking to you. You left without saying goodbye to anyone."

"I left a—"

"Your resignation to Bryna does not count as a goodbye."

"I know," I say. "I'm sorry. I owed you better. Especially after everything you've done for me."

That gets me the smallest smile. Which she immediately tries to hide.

"And why have you graced us with your presence?" she asks.

"Because we can't let this wedding happen," I say.

Ondina sighs. "I thought we were past this."

"A pack of arrogant sons acting like their fathers have the nerve to decide Bryna's marrying a man she barely knows?" I say. "That's what you want for her?" I glance toward our tents. "Where's Bryna?"

"Dressing in some royal bridal chamber in the castle," Ondina says. "Walls of Adare stone for her. Our tents and fire trees aren't good enough for her anymore, I suppose." She sighs. "Vamos. I'll take you to her."

Ondina leads me toward the castle. "But I make clear at this moment," she says, "I want no part in this conversation. If she decides to go through with it, she's going to remember this as the horrible moment you tried to talk her out of it. I'm not even coming in the door."

We're both checking that there's no one in this section of the gardens when she says, "We're going to need a shortcut." I follow her to where the castle walls disappear into the earth.

"Aren't you full of surprises?" I ask as she kneels and pulls aside sheets of moss.

Ondina brushes dirt away, revealing a lock and the handle of a cellar door. "You think you're the only one with a pretty enough smile to win a few secrets?" She slips both the lock and its key into her dress.

We climb down into what looks like an old dungeon, one that's been long ignored. Which makes sense considering Adare doesn't much bother with capture. They either kill you or decide you're not worth the trouble and leave you be. I've never heard of them taking anyone prisoner except me.

The earth is practically taking the space back. Green moss stripes the walls. There's even a small offshoot of the river that flows through the castle. It bubbles through a rend in the stone floor.

"You go through here?" I ask. "Alone?"

Ondina smiles. "I don't need your chivalry."

I crouch to check the depth of the stream. "Anywhere there's enough water for a duck there's enough for those little sea monsters."

"I'm careful," Ondina says. "The question is, are you?"

She's not going to be happy until she gives me a full lecture about coming back as Gael, so we might as well get this over with.

"Fine." I turn toward her. "Tell me how reckless I've been. I can take it."

She grabs me by the shoulders. This is it. She's going to let fly everything she's wanted to say. How much she's had to cover for me. How often she's had to do the work of two damas whenever I've disappeared. How she's had to ask just the right questions, so she knew enough about what I was doing but not more than she wanted to.

And I'll let her. She deserves to say it, and for me to hear it.

But then Ondina shoves me toward one of the stone cells, hard enough that I lose my footing. I try to get it back but my cane slips on the mineral-slick floor.

Ondina throws the rusted grate closed. She slips the lock from her pocket and through the rusted holding.

"What are you doing?" I ask.

Ondina casts her eyes at the wet floor, looking genuinely sad. "I can't let you stop this wedding."

"Ondina," I say, my breath torn raw.

"He will ruin us," she says.

"With everything you know about him?" I ask. "You still think that?"

"Not Cade," she says. "Patrick."

"Patrick," I say. "But he didn't kill his sister. Or banish her. He never had a sister."

Ondina shakes her head, slow and sad. "It doesn't matter. If she marries Patrick, things will be awful for people like you and me and Cade and Nessa. He made Cade pretend to be him. He literally made him fight his battles for him. And he wouldn't even listen to Nessa. He let his cousin use her as a prop, all for his own standing."

My mouth is empty of any words. She's wrong. And she's not wrong. This was an arrangement Cade wanted or at least thought he wanted. But then Patrick got far too comfortable with it. And Nessa. My thoughts halt on Nessa.

That was what Ondina wanted to tell me, then didn't, because I didn't leave any space for her to.

She's in love with Nessa.

Now that I know to look for it, it's so obvious. Nessa giving Ondina as much attention as if she was Ondina's personal guard. Ondina's clear joy at how dashing Nessa was during dances on the hillsides.

"To Patrick, that's all we are," Ondina says. "We're there to be whatever he needs in the moment. And if he rules with Bryna, he'll push her that way."

"She'd never let that happen," I say. "She loves you and she loves me."

"She's from a traditional family in a traditional court in a traditional land," Ondina says. "Traditional meaning we need to shut up and be discreet about who we are and who we love and how we live. And if Bryna is with Patrick, it will get worse."

"That's not true," I say. "She would stand up for us."

"Then why haven't you told her what you want to tell her?" Ondina asks.

Any words I'm grasping at slip off my tongue.

In that quiet, something clicks into place, like the latching of the lock.

"The poison," I say.

"No." Ondina sounds truly startled. "I would never. That could have killed you."

"Not the dress," I say. "My lip color."

Ondina's face falls into a heartbroken expression.

"What did you do?" I ask.

"I never would have done that if I'd known what I know now," Ondina says. "I thought Cade was just another murderous McKenna brother. And you were falling for him."

"What did you do, Ondina?" I ask.

"The moment he told us who he was, I knew he could change everything," she says.

"What did you do?" I'm yelling now, my words echoing off the water and the wet stone.

Light glances off the tears in her eyes, and I know what's she's going to say before she says it.

"I added some of your poison," she says. "To your plain lip color."

I reel back from the words.

"I've never regretted anything I've done more." She lifts her head. "And after their wedding, I'll confess it. Bryna and Cade can deal with me as they wish to. I'll accept it."

Her eyes are still tear-glossed, but she looks unafraid. Ready.

I thought I knew Ondina. She's the girl who climbs the palace trellises to drape cloths, shielding the birds nesting in the eaves from storms. The girl who believes in los cuentos de hadas, the rumors of fairies in the woods.

But all this is just one piece of her.

There's so much else I've missed.

She holds out a handful of my knives through the metal of the door. By instinct, I take them.

"If Bryna marries a McKenna, it has to be Cade," Ondina says. "For all our sakes. But even if she marries Cade, even if she forgets she ever loved Patrick, Patrick will still be powerful. We'll still have to worry about him. So there's only one way this can end." She hands me a dagger. "Do you understand what I'm saying?"

"I don't know," I say. "I don't know you right now."

"Yes, you do," she says. "I'm you when you came here. You were willing to do anything to protect her and us. And you're going to have to be willing to do anything again. So make sure you win."

"What are you talking about?" I ask.

"You're going to win," Ondina says. "I know you will. And you're going to tell the story this way: He attacked you. He drew first. You had to defend yourself. Even Bryna with all that love and polvo de hadas in her eyes can't ignore that."

Ondina steps away from the door. I try to calm my heartbeat. I have to think. But it's still loud in my ears when she comes back and slips the key into the lock.

"Our men found him near our camp," Ondina says.

Patrick McKenna steps out from her shadow.

"This is the boy who tried to kill your brother," she says.

"Thank you." Patrick gives her a gentlemanly bow. "I won't forget this."

When Ondina leaves, she takes the lock with her.

She knows only one of us is leaving these walls alive.

She's counting on it being me.

Considering the look in Patrick McKenna's eyes and the way he's holding his sword, she's being wildly optimistic.

CHAPTER SEVENTY

CADE

I see her as I approach, her wedding dress with its combination of the deep mossy McKenna green and the O'Loingsigh blue that echoes the sea. She sparkles as she moves, the crystals on her gown catching the light from the enchantment and throwing it back at the forest.

There's a small trunk on the ground next to her. Did she plan to leave and just stop here on the way?

I wish I knew what to say to her. I wish I knew what I would need to hear if I were her.

As I get closer, I feel a tingling in my chest. There's a soft, low humming sound along with the sense of vibration. I ease my horse to a stop and pull the orb out of my pocket. The colors are shifting through it. The humming gets louder, and I can feel the vibration against my hand.

I dismount, with Faolan's help.

"It's because of me," I say.

She looks at me, tears at the edges of her eyes.

"You think if you refuse to marry me, it will tell everyone that you do not acknowledge me as my mother's son," I say.

"You are her son," she says. "You are her eldest son. And the contract was between your parents' eldest son and my parents' eldest daughter. It seems that of Patrick, you, and me, I am the only one who actually read the contract and the only one who didn't know you were eighteen, not sixteen."

"You think if you don't marry me, it will send the message that you don't see me as a man," I say.

"You are a man," she says. "You are Adare's firstborn prince. It's done, Cade. You must stop fighting it."

"You are a future queen," I say. "You can fight anything you want, can't you? If I'm a future king, why can't I fight a marriage neither of us wants?"

"It is our duty to marry," she says. "To unite our nations. You know that as well as I do. And because you are about to become mi marido, it is my duty to be honest with you."

I see her breathing deeply, putting great effort into maintaining what's left of her composure.

"I have to tell you something," she says. "And please know that whatever measure in which you hate me is nothing compared to how much I hate myself."

She stares at the wavering wall between us and the part of the forest where our relatives and friends are trapped.

"This is my fault." She skims her fingers along the wall, making the color currents pool around them.

"This curse," she says. "It's mine."

CHAPTER SEVENTY-ONE

VAL

Patrick McKenna throws a sword at me. At least I think it's supposed to be a sword. It's as thin as one of Bryna's finest hair ornaments, and I swear it's almost as long as I am tall, and I don't even like swords. What am I supposed to do with this?

So I decline this rather unsubtle offer of a weapon. I step out of the way, and the sword clatters to the floor, just short of the water trickling over the stone.

"I know it's not the most chivalrous thing to call a duel and then choose the weapons myself." Patrick gets the tip of his sword under the fallen one. "But then you weren't exactly chivalrous toward my brother, were you?" He flicks the fallen sword up.

By instinct, I open my hand to catch the hilt. Mierda.

Spend all your anger on something and it might be worthless by the time you get it.

It's not something my father said as often as a lot of the other things he said, but right now, how could I not remember it? I finally get a chance to take down Patrick McKenna, and I don't want to anymore.

"If you'll just let me explain," I say.

"Oh, I don't think I need anything explained to me." Patrick jumps the hilt of his sword in his hand, like he's itching to fight me. "You stole from a sacred room. You tried to kill my brother."

"I wasn't exactly trying to kill him," I say. "That seems like a bit of an exaggeration."

Patrick's grip steadies on the hilt. "Bryna banished you but somehow you wormed your way out of that too, which I consider an insult to her. One I intend to repay."

My left palm grows damp against my cane, my right against the grip of this extremely awkward weapon. This thing looks more ceremonial than practical.

"That part's really a funny story," I say.

Patrick takes his stance, sword poised. "My brother may be the better fighter, but I think you'll find he's been far more merciful with you than I intend to be."

The ground shifts. The rocks roil beneath us, as though agreeing with Patrick's anger.

Perfect. Even the castle is on his side.

Patrick jabs his sword toward me.

I dodge out of the way, grounding my stance with my cane. "This is all a big misunderstanding."

The ground shifts again. Patrick takes the moment of me being off-balance to thrust his sword at me. This time I stumble out of the way. But the ground has shifted so much that the stream off the castle river is now right next to me. Which I don't realize until I'm falling into it.

Forget the sword. I throw it, forcing Patrick back enough that I get mostly out of the water and onto the stone. But I stay low. The next time Patrick advances, I swing my cane at his legs.

This accomplishes nothing. Except provoking Patrick into leaping on me and shoving my head underwater.

He starts yelling at me, probably about his brother's life and Bryna's honor. I let him go on with his speech as I shut my eyes, preserving my breath, trying to think of how I can get out of this.

A trilling, like a bird's chirp heard through rain, ripples within the water.

A slight weight clings to my head, like a drift of algae and moss tangling in my hair.

Patrick pulls me up from underwater. I inhale hard.

The trilling turns crisp, and my fear along with it.

This time, I know the animal on my head is not an axolotl. Not some blue-green salamander.

This time, I know that the chirping, trilling creature on my head is a small sea monster. And I know it's no less poisonous than the enormous, full-grown ones in Adare's widest rivers and on the monastery's stained-glass windows.

Patrick lets me go.

"Why do they like me so much?" My voice is frayed and pinched and I sound like a coward, but I don't care. If Patrick doesn't kill me this instant, the not-an-axolotl climbing on my head will.

"Yes." Patrick stares. "Why do they?"

"I don't know," I say, wincing. "This might have been a mistake." I pull back the shoulder of my shirt just enough to show him my Saint Marinos tattoo.

Patrick stares at the inked rivulets beneath my collarbone. Thanks to Brother's Jeremiah's steady hand, a trio of oak leaves, turning the gold and deep orange of autumn, seem to be floating on the water.

I hope with everything in me that Patrick has gone speechless from

Jeremiah's artistry, rather than gaming out exactly how he plans to kill me.

I wanted this on me, this sign that there were others like me, and that they welcomed me among them. No one warned me that sea monsters might have a certain affinity for those who revere Saint Marinos.

A potentially deadly affinity, if I make any sudden movements. I know it. Patrick must know it. It's really the perfect time for him to finish me off.

The sea monster climbs down my hair and onto my shoulder, and every muscle in my back tenses.

"If you value your life"—Patrick lowers his sword—"start talking."

I take a slow breath, the kind that's always an effort for me, like doing anything slowly.

I tell him everything.

CHAPTER SEVENTY-TWO

CADE

"Your mother asked me to meet her in the forest," Bryna says. "She got one of the quetzals to carry her message. I have no idea how. She asked me to come alone and tell no one. I was afraid, but I went anyway. I found her near where we are now. She had her staff with her. I had never seen it up close."

As soon as Bryna mentions any details about it, I remember them vividly. Its silver boughs, the crystal inlays, the perfect sphere of stone at the top that shone in a whole range of colors at once. The branches of silver wrapped around it to protect it. The way its unsettled magic coursed through it, changing its colors unpredictably. How it could brighten almost blindingly in my mother's hand without warning.

"She told me to come close to her," Bryna says. "As I bowed, she touched each of my shoulders with the staff. When I rose, she handed it to me. She said, 'I have no daughter. This staff is yours now.' I thought it meant she had disowned her daughter, or that her daughter had rejected a future ruling Adare.

"I didn't know what to do with the staff. Your mother said that one day she would teach me how to use it, but that for now, I needed to hide it somewhere no one else could find it. The last thing she said to me before she left me with it was 'I'm giving this to you so you will remember something very important. One day, you will have a chance to end this war. Take it.'

"I did as she told me. I brought the staff home and hid it. Later, when I heard negotiations were beginning again, and that they would take place in the forest, I tried to convince my parents I should be there. That we all should be there. Our generation. Their negotiations would affect the rest of our lives. And we were not permitted to attend, let alone participate?"

Bryna turns to me and holds one hand open. I can imagine her reaching for something just out of her grasp. Reaching for a place here.

"When they insisted I stay, I was so angry," she says. "I heard this humming, and I thought it was my own rage. But then I realized it was the staff. It was humming, glowing. It felt nervous, tense, frantic. It was as if it was trying to tell me that something was wrong.

"So I snuck out, with the staff. By the time I got to the border with the forest, I could hear the arguing. I just wanted it to stop. I wanted them to do what they said they were going to do, what they insisted on doing without me and without you and Patrick or anyone our age, all of us who were going to have to live with what they did, or what they didn't do. I just wanted to get their attention. I just wanted them to stop arguing. That's why I did it."

"Did what?" I ask.

"I thought that moment was what your mother meant, about ending the war," Bryna says. "I thought I had to do something right then. So I raised the staff above my head and drove it into the ground. I thought they'd see the light catching on it, or that the humming would get loud enough for them to hear it. But the moment I did it, I knew it was wrong. I was too angry. And it shattered. All the pieces flew

304

everywhere, some of them far, like the wind was pulling them away. Then it was gone.

"When I looked up, I saw all those colors, the way they moved but wouldn't yield. I tried everything I could think of to break through it. To destroy it. But nothing worked. Nothing anyone did worked. And it's my fault."

Bryna's voice echoes in my ears.

"Your mother was right," Bryna says. "I have the chance to end this war. You and I both do. Together. And we must take it."

When I just stand there, she goes on.

"Valencia and I have been trying to find the pieces ever since," she says. "The quetzals have been helping. They can feel when a piece is surfacing. That's how you met Valencia. She was going after one of them."

"Does Val know?" I ask.

"No," Bryna says. "All I told her was that we needed to find all the lost pieces of a relic from Adare, and that they held a power we barely understood."

I think back to what Bryna said when I asked her if she knew of any plot to curse our families. She didn't technically lie. There was no plot. It just happened.

Bryna opens the trunk on the ground in front of her. She shows me the pieces she and Val have desperately been trying to knit back together.

The lining of the trunk is midnight velvet, soft and deep. The pieces glow gently, casting light on the lining, making it paler blue.

I reach into the pocket of my jacket and pull out the globe. It's glowing like the rest of the pieces, humming quietly like it was as I approached.

Bryna's doesn't try to hide her shock. She makes no effort to be a royal right now. She is just herself.

I owe it to her and to myself to do the same. To just be myself. To stop blaming myself for not being a future queen. I'm just not. I wasn't meant to be. It doesn't do any good to keep pushing myself down whenever I try to stand up. All I can do is be who I am.

I extend my hand.

She takes a few steps back, as though she's afraid of doing more damage.

"My mother gave this to you for a reason," I say. "Take it."

I take a step toward her, and she cautiously takes one toward me. She opens her hand and holds it out. I touch my fingers to hers and let the nearly complete sphere roll into her hand from mine.

I look into her eyes. I see her in a way I never have before. She is my sister. She is meant to be my sister. And I am meant to be her brother.

I think that might be true even if she weren't in love with my brother. Bryna and I would still share this bond, this solid ground we stand on together as if we had been born siblings.

Our fingers are still touching, and the sphere rests on both sets of them, hers and mine. It hums higher and louder. It shivers until panes of light burst in all directions. Each pane is a range of colors, blues and greens, reds and golds, all pressed together.

The power of it moves across both of us like wind, blowing through our hair. Bryna looks like the queen she was born to be. And I feel more like myself than I ever have.

CHAPTER SEVENTY-THREE

VAL

"What do you mean you don't know where they are?" Patrick asks.

Patrick has pulled me, along with Eamon and Deirdre, into a stone alcove, out of view of the court gossiping about the upcoming wedding.

Or gossiping about the apparently missing bride and groom.

"They're not in the castle," Deirdre says.

"Or on the grounds," Eamon says. "And the leaders from the villages are starting to ask questions."

Deirdre says something that sounds like an older word from Adare's language, and though I don't know the translation, I gather from the tone it's a word no dama would repeat.

"We asked the musicians for just enough volume for atmosphere," Eamon says. "But we could ask them to play too loudly to permit conversation."

"A temporary remedy," Deirdre says. "But better than none at all."

Patrick leans his head back like he's gathering himself. For a flash, it makes him look exactly like Cade.

Deirdre and Eamon eye me with nearly as much suspicion as Patrick just did.

"Yes, it's me," I say, holding Eamon's gaze, then Deirdre's.

Deirdre thinks she's being subtle as her hand moves toward the hilt of her sword.

"He's on our side, and he'll explain everything later," Patrick tells Deirdre and Eamon. "Right now we need to find Bryna and my brother."

I hear him conferring with Eamon and Deirdre, trying to list off where they might have gone.

But all I see is the flash of green landing on a wall lantern, a familiar quetzal who's always happy to tell me what to do.

CHAPTER SEVENTY-FOUR

CADE

The pieces float toward us, spinning into place.

Light envelops them, as if it's welding them together, seams of light along each of the cracks.

The bottom of the staff begins to feel tremendously heavy. Despite our combined strength, Bryna and I cannot hold it. It falls to the ground, anchoring itself below the surface.

As the bottom grows heavier, the top seems to float. The panes of light blur into deep green and blue, and the colors arc through the branches and leaves and out over the land.

CHAPTER SEVENTY-FIVE

VAL

I know what Bryna's wedding dress looks like, even if I didn't stay to help her into it. The blue like snow at dusk. The flashes of leaf green. The cloth shimmers under the trees' shadows.

I breathe in, taking in all the air I can to call out to Bryna.

But then there's a burst of light as bright as if all the stars fell at once and then turned to liquid. The force that comes with it is the strongest gale I've ever felt, and it spools the air from my lungs.

Patrick and I brace, staring into light that looks exactly like I saw the first time I came here.

Patrick calls his brother's name and Bryna's.

The air around Bryna and Cade fills with tiny glittering points, like the way I've heard snow looks when the air is so cold it turns fine and sparkling as crushed crystals.

When the force coming at us eases, Patrick and I rush forward, blinking into the sparkling air, looking for his brother and my best friend.

They're here, both of them, upright as though they just stood against nothing stronger than the wind off the sea.

Patrick stops, halted by the sight of Bryna in her wedding gown. It glitters even more now, like the tiny points of light have stuck to it.

She looks back at him, stunned either by him being here or by the way he looks like he was just in a fight.

Faolan glints with the same points of light as Bryna's dress, like the wood and the metal owl is set with that dusting of fine snow.

Cade looks surprised to see Patrick and shocked to see me.

A blush of heat spreads under my lacings, both because Cade is wearing more distinctly Elianan clothing than I've ever seen on him and because he's never seen me dressed quite like I am right now.

"What are you doing here?" Cade and Bryna ask Patrick and me, in near unison.

Their identical questions turn to identical stares, toward the enchanted space in the woods. The translucent wall between us and everyone we miss spills toward the ground. Its colors fall like sheets of water.

The first sets of eyes I see are amber, brown, gold, marked by the vertical pupils of foxes. The points of light on their fur echo the falling colors.

Then I see a set of human eyes, brown irises against the familiar brown of a familiar face. Luminous foxes gather around him as though greeting him.

Joy rises in me only until dread grabs at it and weighs it down.

My father is here, and awake.

And I'm dressed like this. I'm not even going to get the chance to tell him; he's just going to see it.

Any thought I have of fleeing crumbles when one of the foxes leaps toward me, and my father's attention follows her.

My father comes toward me, the lines on his face and the pattern on his coat clearer with each step.

I freeze, feeling every thread of the boys' shirt and men's trousers on my body.

My father looks at me, and at my clothes.

A glimmer of surprise crosses his face, and I don't know if it's surprise at seeing me like this or seeing me at all.

Then he smiles at me with something I can't quite place. Recognition. Pride. Whatever it is, I'm his son and his daughter, and I know it.

CHAPTER SEVENTY-SIX

CADE

The forest is waking as much as its inhabitants are. The trees shake in the wind as if stretching after a long sleep. Groggy animals stagger about in the shrubbery.

Bryna runs to her mother and father, who are leaning on each other. They both wear indigo and cobalt rather than the crimsons, burgundies, and oranges they are known for. The king is clearly the source of both Bryna's stature and her deep red hair. The queen is slight and shorter than Val. The king's arms wrap around her protectively.

I see my father, walking tall and graceful despite the confused expression on his face. When Patrick catches his eye, it's as if he melts. He must be surprised that Patrick looks so much a man, and a bit like he's been fighting.

My mother emerges, looking as powerful and self-possessed as ever, exactly like she did in my dream. She surveys the scene and meets my eyes.

"Are you really here?" I ask.

She wraps her arms around me, her armbands digging into me.

I close my eyes and take a deep breath. I can smell the dried meadow dew on her tartan, the herbs she braids into her hair, the oil she rubs into her skin to protect it from the elements.

She's really here. She's really back.

"I am so proud of you," she says, holding me by my shoulders and looking at me up and down.

"I knew you could do it." She looks over at Bryna. "Both of you together."

She remembers our conversation while I was asleep. She sees me as I really am.

"Faolan looks good this way, does he not?" she asks.

Now that I look at him, he sparkles as much as Bryna's dress. He was complicated already, glazed wood around metal, the owl's eyes glowing deeply. But now, he glimmers as if covered in snowflakes. The light catches reflective points all along the length of the staff and dusts the owl's wings.

"He really does," I say.

I see my mother's eyes lock onto Gael.

Gael looks terrified, which is a normal and reasonable reaction to my mother.

He bows deeply and stays in that position.

"Will you rise already?" she asks.

Gael looks at his father, who gives an encouraging nod.

"You," my mother says. "I know you. You threw a knife at my son."

I have no idea how she knows about that. It makes me wonder what else she knows.

"Several," Gael says.

I hear scattered laughter.

I take this moment to interrupt.

"Mother," I begin. "This is . . ."

I wish I had thought through what to say next.

"Val," he says. "My name is Val."

As my mother and Val officially meet, I catch the sparkle of Bryna's dress out of the corner of my eye.

She and Patrick hold hands, gazing into each other's eyes, as if they've been apart for ages.

I turn and face all the advisors and courtiers emerging from the forest. I clear my throat and tap Faolan against the ground.

"People of Eliana and Adare," I begin.

I look at Bryna and then back at our parents.

"Your children have been ruling," I say. "Your children have led both your nations. If we can do that, we can decide our own fates. The princess and I will lead our nations together, but not through marriage."

Bryna beams at me, a smile of not only joy and relief but pride.

"We inherited this war." She looks from me to everyone watching. "Now we end it."

Her gaze is both calm and a challenge, daring anyone to object.

"Well," my mother says. "You're all dressed for a wedding." She eyes Patrick and Bryna. "Why don't we have one?"

She gestures to gather everyone. "Shall we?"

CHAPTER SEVENTY-SEVEN

VAL

I hope Bryna trained for this. Traditional royal Elianan wedding bouquets are gardens in themselves, and she has to carry it in the seemingly effortless manner of a princesa. The queen's damas have just sent me to double its size, so I'm kneeling in the floating gardens that have come up from Adare ground.

Ondina kneels alongside me. "I'm sorry."

"For sending me to my possible death?" I cut another stem. "Already forgotten."

"I couldn't imagine you losing." Ondina's skirt settles, the fabric cut into layers like the red leaves of cuetlaxochitl. If she danced or twirled, she'd look like a flower in the form of a girl, but I doubt she's in the mood to do either. "Those swords he was carrying? They looked like children's toys. I even handed you more knives. I couldn't have tilted the fight more in your favor."

"Except I didn't want to hurt him," I say. "Not anymore. We have got to talk about this. There's so much you don't know."

"It doesn't matter anymore," Ondina says.

I pause at the stalks of sword lilies. "Why?"

"Because it doesn't." She cuts one of the stalks, more cleanly than I've been managing. "I'm resigned."

"To what?" I ask.

"My death by sea monster," Ondina says. "Or whatever Patrick and Bryna decide."

"I didn't tell either of them anything," I say.

Ondina stares at me, the delicate shadows of ahuejote branches crossing her face. "You didn't?"

I shake my head. "As far as Patrick knows, my disguise was so good you didn't know Gael and I were the same person. You thought Gael was a boy assassin, an enemy. As for Bryna, I hope you decide to tell her what you told me. What you've been afraid of. She'll listen. And if you want me there with you when you do, I will be."

"But why didn't you tell them?" she asks.

I tilt my head. "How many secrets have you kept for me?"

"I could have gotten you killed," she says.

"We've been friends since we were children," I say. "What's a brush with death compared to that?"

Ondina looks like she doesn't want to smile but can't help it.

"I brought reinforcements." She hands me an armful of hawthorn branches, flowering deep and pale pink, and dark purple lilacs. The violet sea holly and tiny blossoms of sea aster. Trees and flowers that grow thick in Adare meadows and salt marshes, but that we rarely see in Eliana. It's as much of a blessing on Bryna and Patrick's wedding as Ondina probably has in her.

Ondina lifts her gaze to the leaves of flame, the marvel of these lamps the ingenieros made to look like trees. They've even tinted the metal and oils with different elements so precisely that the flames turn bright red like cuetlaxochitl petals, then blue like the dusk sky, then green as quetzals in flight.

317

"What do you think?" I gather the stems and branches together. "Enough to be seen from the moon?"

"And farther." Ondina fastens it with ribbon.

We bring it in to Bryna, who, every bit la princesa, doesn't flinch at the span of the maíz and squash blossoms, the delicate purple and orange of bean blossoms, the sunflowers alongside Adare roses and flowering branches.

Bryna rises from her dressing table. The deep violet of the tent's interior ripples around her, strands of copper thread flashing bright as her hair.

Only then do I remember my clothes, the ones I've been wearing since the monastery.

I look down. "I'll go change."

Bryna catches my free hand. "Change or don't change. Change in the middle of the celebration and come back in something else. I don't care. Just be here."

My heart unclenches. She may not know everything about who I am. But I know I can tell her. When I'm ready.

We fix Bryna's hair, smooth out her dress.

"Espera." Ondina dashes out of the tent and comes back with handfuls of fruit blossoms.

She tucks them into Bryna's hair, their perfume tumbling onto her shoulders.

"There," Ondina says. "Now you're ready."

Bryna takes the extras from Ondina's hands and slips some into Ondina's hair, then mine.

"In my court, boys wear flowers in their hair." She adds a last bloom to my braid.

We go out into the night, where the pools and fountains reflect back the stars and the glint of Bryna's dress. The floating gardens have grown trees like the ones filling our palace gardens. The pitaya grow starbursts of pink-red and yellow fruit like ornaments at the ends of bowing branches. Blooms float on the water that's turned more vivid blue, like the bright silt of Adare's glacier lakes.

With each step, Bryna's dress catches the color and light from the fire trees, and she glitters like the sky above us.

I have to keep shifting my grip on my cane to stand for the length of the ceremony. But I try to worry a little less than I usually do about whether anyone sees me doing it. Especially now that Adare has a prince who needs his own bastón.

I watch my best friend with the McKenna boy she loves, neither of them caring how much they're smiling, neither of them trying to look regal. I can picture her now as both queen and the Bryna I know. I can picture her addressing embajadores in that gown she packed into her trunk when I was trying to talk her out of all this, all those layers of filmy gold like spun light. She will strike speechless men who underestimate her, and she'll still be flashing secret looks to Ondina and me.

The air hums with the approving purr of the jaguares, the ocelotls, the maracayás and jaguarundis. I wonder if the foxes will show up later. They're talented at raiding the floating gardens, so they don't need my help for that. But they might come for shoes.

After the ceremony, the floating gardens are all music, the dark sugar of wine, the cacao and orange of xocolatl. The fire trees spill gold and purple into everyone's cups, and when Patrick spins Bryna during a dance, her dress throws off a dusting of light.

I turn to Ondina, but she's not where she was a minute ago. If I look for Nessa, I'll probably find her, but I leave them be.

I spot my father. He's been alongside Bryna's parents, but right now he's with a group of cortesanos from both Eliana and Adare.

Karlynn McKenna is easy to find, her silver hair as pale as Deirdre's is white-blond. She's saying something to Bryna, holding my best friend's hands as though blessing her. Bryna carries herself like a princesa, unintimidated by her new mother-in-law.

Everyone is distracted. This is the best chance I'll have.

I'm fast moving between the tents. Fast with my hands finding the trick spots in familiar wood. Less fast when I'm sneaking through the slate walls of a castle that changes every time I think I've gotten my bearings.

I try to find my way by the tapestries, marking the scenes of rivers and woods. But the next row of panels stops me.

There's more to them now. Embroidered quetzals alongside embroidered owls, maracayás and ocelotls alongside sea monsters. At first I think they must be to commemorate the wedding, but they appeared so quickly no one could have added them. It's as though our ascendientes flew or leapt into them, as though they can rest now.

My fingers carefully trace the new shapes, almost touching the dense needlework, but not quite. Those wings, those eyes, those fins, seem so alive I expect them to move. I watch them so carefully that I don't hear the footsteps until they're close behind me.

I turn around. By instinct, my hands change their grip on my cane. One palm overhand, one underhand, ready to fight.

"Really?" Cade backs up. "We're doing that again? Now?"

My nerves settle.

"I don't know what happens in Adare," I say. "But back home, there's nothing like a brawl to liven up a party."

He laughs. "In that, I assure you, our homes are alike."

My heartbeat evens. "What are you doing here?"

"Me?" he asks. "What are you doing in here?"

I reach into the pockets of my capa. "What do you think?" I unfold the cloths, showing him the stolen pieces. They look like jewels of frost perched on tiny needles of ice.

"Ah," he says.

But he doesn't take them.

He starts down the corridor.

When I don't follow, he pauses. "Shall we?"

"They're your family's," I say. "Shouldn't you do this?"

"You stole them," he says. "Unless you want an enchanted tree to bear you ill will, I suggest you do it yourself."

I go with him.

Light catches on the stones pinned to his jacket. The color no longer blinks. It's settled between deep blue and deep green. They declare him prince of Adare. But the clothes he's wearing, the nearly violet shade of blue, the brown-red that gleams like copper, the trousers our men love but that he doesn't love because they're almost shiny, they're all Eliana. Just like the ice-blue brocade Ondina's now wearing and the deep green velvet I'll put on later tonight are all Adare. We're all declaring loyalties we never thought could live alongside one another.

"You wear our colors well," I say.

He eyes my outfit in return. "Did the monks finally get to you?"

"How did you guess?" I ask.

He leads me into the room where I fought him, when I was the boy I once pretended not to be. The tree opens over us, the leaves pulling the starlight down from the cracks in the ceiling.

I unfold the corners of the cloths. The pieces float away, as though they're light as the fluff off a dandelion. The ice and frost coating them glints blue and silver and then vanishes. The tiny round stones turn back to violet and blue, back to deep amber or summer-leaf green. They drift up toward the boughs and join the branches again, the stems glowing like embers as they touch and seal back to the wood.

The tree shifts above us, swaying in the night breeze. At least that's what I think it's doing until I realize we're in the center of the castle.

The tree isn't swaying.

It's growing.

Branches spread and twist, sending out filaments of new wood and green. Leaves unfurl, filling out the new branches. Tiny shells of green open, revealing buds as shining wet as drops of sap.

"Whose are those?" I ask.

With a breath out, Cade smiles. "Whose do you think?"

I look closer. The leaves hold buds that look like amber with fire caught inside, the color of Bryna's hair when the sun hits it.

My smile, my breath out, matches Cade's.

Cade looks at me. "Why did you come back?"

"Because I have a bad habit of telling my best friend when I think she's making a mistake," I say.

That instinct I had in the corridor, ready to fight, still echoes in me. So I use it to give myself enough nerve to say what I say next.

"And also because I thought you might be in love with me," I say.

"Thought I might?" Cade asks. "Was I really that subtle about it?"

Two memories bloom in me at once.

The first, in a forest:

I had a feeling you'd be a problem.
A feeling? Just a feeling? I'm hurt.
You're a problem. Are you happy?

The second, at a monastery:

Can't you just go back to quietly hating me?
That was quiet?
Good point. Nothing quiet about it. Exceedingly clear.

Before I come up with a response as perfect as I want it to be, something that will tell him I know what he's calling back to, he starts talking again.

"You know, I've put a great deal of determination into trying not to be in love with you," he says.

I take a step closer to him, my cane nearly crossing Faolan. "And how did you fare?"

He laughs. "Not well."

I last through a blink or two of his dark, beautiful gaze, and then I kiss him. I kiss him, and his fingers brush the blossoms woven into my braid. He kisses me, the clean cold of the night on his lips. We stand beneath this enchanted tree, and I kiss this boy who looks like the stars are catching in his hair.

CHAPTER SEVENTY-EIGHT

CADE

I n the days after my brother's wedding to Bryna, I find out so many
things I didn't know.

Ondina tells me about mixing Val's poison and lip color. She only
half seems to believe me when I tell her I don't want her blood for it,
and even that takes me convincing her. I understand everything she's
been afraid of. I've been that afraid.

I find out Nessa has fallen in love with Ondina. Nessa tells me this
with the ceremony of relaying an official message. That's how I know
it's serious, the formality she layers over her feelings.

I find out Val fought Patrick—real Patrick, not me as Patrick—
which is something they're both already joking about. But my brain is
too full to ask about it, so I don't, not yet.

And one night, I see a figure out along the rock ridges. There's
only a slight breeze in the evening air, but the figure looks surrounded
by a whirlpool of blazing autumn leaves. Or flames. The cloak. The
enchantress. Val.

When she sees me, she lowers the hood of the cape. Her hair is loose, the wind streaming through it. Its deep brown is rich against the cape's gold, orange, and amber leaves.

I expect her to make a joke or a point about the fashions of Eliana. But her face is serious.

"Do you feel that?" Val asks.

I give my attention to the ground under us. But I'm still getting used to Faolan. The glittering pieces from my mother's staff have added weight, the balance different.

Whatever drew Val out here, it pulls Bryna too. Patrick comes with her, both of them followed by a quetzal and the flammulated owl. Patrick looks at me, as though asking if I know more than he does.

Later, we'll learn about the rocks moving through the earth. Some plain and pale and gray, like the ones that form our castle. Some pink and textured like Eliana's palace. We'll find the stones deep in the forest, forming walls. We'll see the gold of witch's butter mushrooms sprouting between them, sealing them together.

We don't know anything of that yet. But we can feel something stirring in the air. We hold it between us. The four of us face one another as we truly are, so we can go forward into everything that comes next.

ACKNOWLEDGMENTS

There are many people without whom we wouldn't have written *Venom & Vow* and without whom it wouldn't be the book you're reading now. Here, we name a few:

Kat Brzozowski, for the always-spectacular notes and for making everything from deep revision to title brainstorming more fun.

Emily Settle, for bringing your fantasy lover heart to this book.

Jean Feiwel, for making a beautiful literary home for books with intersectional identities.

L. Whitt and Mx. Morgan for the spectacular cover, Virginia Allyn for the stunning map, and Elizabeth Clark for the wonderful art direction at MacKids.

The teams at Feiwel & Friends and Macmillan Children's Publishing Group: Tatiana Merced-Zarou, Liz Szabla, Rich Deas, Erin Siu, Teresa Ferraiolo, Kim Waymer, Ilana Worrell, Dawn Ryan, Jessica White, Jon Yaged, Allison Verost, Jennifer Edwards, Molly Ellis, Melissa Zar, Nicole Schaefer, Carlee Maurier, Samantha Fabbricatore, Leigh Ann Higgins, Cynthia Lliguichuzhca, Allegra Green, Jo Kirby, Julia Gardiner, Lauren Scobell, Mariel Dawson, Alyssa Mauren, Dominique Jenkins, Meg Collins, Gabriella Salpeter, Ebony Lane, Kristin Dulaney, Jordan Winch, Kaitlin Loss, Rachel Diebel, Foyinsi Adegbonmire, Katy Robitzski, Amber Cortes, Amanda Barillas, Morgan Dubin, Rosanne

Lauer, Morgan Rath, Madison Furr, Mary Van Akin, Kelsey Marrujo, Holly West, Anna Roberto, Katie Quinn, Brittany Groves, Jesse Cole, Hana Tzou, Chantal Gersch, Amybeth Menendez, Kelly Markus; Lucy Del Priore, Kristen Luby, Cierra Bland, Elysse Villalobos, and Grace Tyler of Macmillan Children's School & Library; and the many more who turn stories into books and help readers find them.

Wallieke Sutton, and everyone who gets the mail where it's going.

The fellow writers who were there during the drafting and revision process: Lisa McMann and Matt McMann, and Cory McCarthy and A.R. Capetta, who mentored us about writing together. Nova Ren Suma, Emily X.R. Pan, Anica Mrose Rissi, Aisha Saeed, Emery Lord, Dahlia Adler, Rebecca Kim Wells, Elana K. Arnold, A. J. Sass, Alex Villasante, Katie Patterson, Mallory Lass, and Mary Chadd, who made and shared creative space with us as we were writing this book.

Ennis Rook Bashe, for your excitement for this story and for helping us make it even better.

William Alexander, for your cane mentorship, and discussions of everything from theater blocking to languages to Lorca.

Aiden Thomas, for your attention to Cade's and Val's identities and your enthusiasm for their stories and worlds.

Karen McCoy, what would we do without your technical knowledge and sharp sense of logic?

Taylor Martindale Kean, Stefanie Sanchez Von Borstel, and the Full Circle Literary team (with a particular nod to Taylor's fantasy trope jokes).

Michael Bourret, for your guidance and support, Mike Whatnall, Lauren Abramo, Nataly Gruender, Andrew Dugan, Gracie Freeman-Lifschutz, and the DGB team.

Readers: for going on this adventure with a transgender prince and bigender lady-in-waiting/boy assassin. Thank you.

THANK YOU FOR READING THIS FEIWEL & FRIENDS BOOK.
THE FRIENDS WHO MADE VENOM & VOW POSSIBLE ARE:

JEAN FEIWEL, PUBLISHER

LIZ SZABLA, VP, ASSOCIATE PUBLISHER

RICH DEAS, SENIOR CREATIVE DIRECTOR

HOLLY WEST, SENIOR EDITOR

ANNA ROBERTO, SENIOR EDITOR

KAT BRZOZOWSKI, SENIOR EDITOR

DAWN RYAN, EXECUTIVE MANAGING EDITOR

KIM WAYMER, SENIOR PRODUCTION MANAGER

EMILY SETTLE, EDITOR

RACHEL DIEBEL, ASSOCIATE EDITOR

FOYINSI ADEGBONMIRE, ASSOCIATE EDITOR

BRITTANY GROVES, ASSISTANT EDITOR

ILANA WORRELL, SENIOR PRODUCTION EDITOR

L. WHITT, DESIGNER

FOLLOW US ON FACEBOOK OR VISIT US ONLINE AT MACKIDS.COM.
OUR BOOKS ARE FRIENDS FOR LIFE.